TWO NAILS,

Alden M. Hayashi

Black Rose Writing | Texas

ISBN: 978-1-68433-801-6
PUBLISHED BY BLACK ROSE WRITING
www.blackrosewriting.com

Printed in the United States of America
Suggested Retail Price (SRP) $17.95

Two Nails, One Love is printed in Calluna

*As a planet-friendly publisher, Black Rose Writing does its best to eliminate unnecessary waste to reduce paper usage and energy costs, while never compromising the reading experience. As a result, the final word count vs. page count may not meet common expectations.

Cover art by Jana Brenning
Author photo by Gerard Flood

This book is dedicated to my mother: *Okage sama de*
(Because of you I am)

TWO NAILS, One Love

Deru kugi wa utareru
(The nail that sticks up gets hammered down)
– Old Japanese saying

PART I

The Present: New York City
(Autumn 2000)

CHAPTER ONE

I'm not the type to wallow in a bad situation. I'm more apt to pack my things and move on. Much of this comes from my mother, who never looks backward and is as averse to self-pity as anyone I've ever known. Whenever she suffers a major setback or disappointment, she shakes her head, mutters "shikata ga nai"—a Japanese saying that roughly translates to, "it can't be helped"—and then deals with the problem as best she can, or she pivots to plan B. Whining is not an option.

Her stoicism in the face of adversity is something that, as a kid growing up in Honolulu, often annoyed me to no end. I remember when her washing machine broke down one week after the warranty had expired. Instead of complaining, she swallowed her frustration, said "shikata ga nai," and called Sears. After the repairman—a stout Hawaiian-Chinese man with a sour disposition and no shortage of complaints about his life— finished the job and presented her with the bill, she thanked him as she rifled through the kitchen drawers, searching for her checkbook. But when she apologized for making him wait (her checkbook was in her purse, not a kitchen drawer), I was angry at her, and more so when she thanked him again, this time with added effusiveness, as she tipped him with a ten-dollar bill. I didn't understand why she didn't share my sense of resentment.

What I failed to realize then is that my mother carefully chooses her battles with pragmatic efficiency. It's a skill that's taken me years to develop. But even as I've learned to appreciate her deep wisdom, I've had trouble understanding something equally important—the inadvertent ways in which our greatest strengths can, at times, become our biggest weaknesses. Stoic determination in one situation becomes foolish

I

stubbornness in another. And that stubbornness has resulted in years of estrangement between a son, me, now living in New York City, and his mother, who has remained residing five thousand miles away in Honolulu.

·   ·   ·   ·   ·

Waiting for Mom's flight to arrive from Hawaii, I'm filled with remorse and apprehension. I haven't seen her since Dad's funeral, a little more than ten years ago. It was a time of unbearable pain for both of us, not just because of the overwhelming grief we felt but also because of the ugly fight we had. For the first time in my life, I shouted at her—a blitzkrieg of harsh, irretrievable words spoken in too much haste with too little regard for the consequences.

Today, as I wait at the airport in Newark, it saddens me that I can't be wholeheartedly eager to see her, to hear her voice again, to be with her. I'm still mad, even after all these years, angry at not just the things she said but also at her reluctance to recognize the sacrifices I've made in my own life in an attempt to fulfill her vision of what a dutiful Japanese American son should be.

I check the display board near the Continental counter and see that Mom's flight will be more than an hour late because of bad weather in the Midwest. That's just great. The extra time will only ratchet up my anxiety.

To calm my nerves, I walk through the terminal concourse in search of a place where I can have a cup of coffee. As I sit at a McDonald's my mind wanders into the past. In actuality, the blowout Mom and I had the day before Dad's funeral wasn't the worst of it. No less painful was the ensuing silence between us, a silence filled with recrimination and anger. Eventually, after almost a year, Mom sent me a birthday card with the shortest of notes: "I can't believe you're now 31. Happy birthday! Love, Mom."

That gesture opened a welcome period of détente, when obligatory greeting cards for birthdays, Mother's Days, Thanksgivings, Christmases, and New Year's Days went back and forth between two islands, Oahu and Manhattan, as she and I tried to maintain at least some level of contact, however minimal. I suppose we've both been fearful that any silence stretching too long might potentially lead to a permanent severing of our ties.

The truth, though, is that Dad's funeral wasn't the cause of our estrangement, merely the breaking point in our relationship. Even before he died, things between Mom and me were strained. Now, I realize it was essentially a battle of East versus West playing out on our intimate family stage—family harmony clashing with personal fulfillment.

From my earliest years, I was taught the importance of family. "Friends may come and go," my father often lectured me, "but your family will always be there." A seemingly comforting sentiment. But, if family is everything, it also means that the individuals within it are always secondary to the greater whole. And this, in turn, means that any individual's transgressions—my transgressions—would not only reflect badly on that person but bring down the family as well. "What would the neighbors think?" was a frequent admonishment in our home, where bringing shame through our doors was often considered a crime worse even than the original offense. This extended to any acts of individualism, however well-intentioned. It's a sentiment aptly captured by the old Japanese saying, "deru kugi wa utareru"—literally, "the nail that sticks up gets hammered down."

Along with lectures on the inherent dangers of Western individualism, I was also taught the beauty of Eastern group unity. In high school, when my parents and I traveled to Japan one spring, my father continually marveled at the spectacular beauty of the blossoming cherry trees. "Just look," Dad told me. "Each of those individual blossoms might not be anything special, but taken together, they're truly exquisite."

It wasn't until my late teens and early adulthood that I began to feel suffocated by these sentiments—and by my parents' expectations. For one thing, I'd fallen in love with playing the oboe, and my dreams of becoming a professional musician ran directly counter to my parents' assumption that I'd one day become a doctor, dentist, lawyer, or engineer. And, perhaps more importantly, I had become increasingly certain my attraction to other boys wasn't a passing phase but a permanent sexual orientation. I didn't actually know my parents' view of homosexuality, but I was certain of one thing: They would eventually want me to marry a woman, start a traditional family, and bestow them with grandchildren to sustain our family line. Both parts of the person I saw myself as—a musician and a gay man—clashed with the son my parents thought I should be, and I chafed under their preconceived constraints. To be fair, Dad at least appeared open to me forging my own path; Mom remained adamantly opposed.

As I think about all this while waiting in the airport, a long-submerged resentment toward my mother begins to simmer. Thankfully, my thoughts are interrupted when a businessman's rolling carry-on sideswipes my chair, nearly causing me to spill my coffee. The man scurries off without apologizing, as if I'm merely an inconvenient, inanimate obstacle in his way. What's wrong with people like that? I glance at my watch and see it will be another fifteen minutes before Mom's flight arrives.

I head over to her gate, weaving through a gauntlet of people, a mix of humanity. Some trudge along, exhausted from a long flight, while others rush to make a tight connection. I'm amazed at how well we all manage to make it to our different destinations, each person going at a different speed and yet maintaining just enough distance from one other to avoid a collision, the occasional close call notwithstanding. It's individualism within a larger group context.

When I arrive at the gate, I'm annoyed to learn Mom's flight will be another half hour late. Oddly, even the smallest part of me isn't relieved by this delay. I guess I've anticipated her arrival with enough anxiety already that I just want it to happen. To pass the time, I wander around the terminal concourse and eventually step into a bookstore to browse the different magazines. Nothing in particular piques my interest, so I try the book section and am amazed that "Who Moved My Cheese?" is still a major bestseller, commanding an entire cardboard display by itself. I seem to have the opposite problem. I'm fine with having my cheese moved; what I fear is my cheese staying stationary for years, leaving me to stagnate.

And yet, perhaps I gave up too quickly once my relationship with Mom broke down. I've avoided the hard work of trying to fix it, because it was so much easier to tell myself "shikata ga nai" and move on. But it's more than that. I'm so angry at her, not just for what she said before Dad's funeral but for how she's always tried to box in my life. I'm also bitterly disappointed in her, a woman who claims to love me and yet wants me to sacrifice my own life so I would fit into her mold. To be brutally honest, a part of me wants to punish her for that, so it's been only too easy to let our relationship wither like an overripe tangerine left unpicked, or a piece of cheese left to dry out.

It was my mother, to her credit, who refused to give up on our relationship. It was she who finally sent a note longer than a couple sentences, sharing with me her keen desire to visit Washington, D.C., to see the recently unveiled Japanese American Memorial to Patriotism During World War II. "Maybe, if it's not too much trouble, you could join me," she wrote. I hadn't heard about the memorial and was surprised Mom wanted to see it. I assumed that that was just an excuse, her way of paving the way to a rapprochement.

I took a few days to think through my response, and I wrote back to suggest she also come to Manhattan for a few days. "If you're traveling all the way to the East Coast from Hawaii," I wrote, "you really should see New York City. You can stay with me, and I'll show you around." I figured I'd encourage her to visit me so she could at least get a glimpse of the life I live, which must be somewhat of a mystery to her. And besides, it was my stubborn and uncharitable refusal to fly from New York to Hawaii to visit her that had finally led her, a woman in her mid sixties, to decide to make such a long journey by herself to see her only child.

As I look at my watch to check the time, a sliver of remorse nicks my heart. The watch, with its round face, gold trim, and black leather band, was a high-school graduation gift from my parents, a present I've always cherished. Over the years, I've replaced the battery, crystal face, and leather band countless times. I've also had to fix an interior wheel, a couple levers, and the crown. At this point, I wonder how much of the original watch is left. But does that even matter? It's like the ship of Theseus, the hypothetical wooden vessel that had all its parts replaced. Was it still fundamentally the same ship? Or did it become an entirely different boat?

I wonder the same thing about myself. Since moving away from Hawaii for college, I've grown up and matured, slowly shedding different parts of myself—not just my youthful exuberance, my innocent idealism, and my annoying arrogance but also fundamental things, like deru kugi wa utareru, which had been ingrained in me from my earliest years. Living away from my parents (and from Hawaii itself) has changed me in so many ways, some obvious and others much subtler. In the past, when I visited Mom and Dad, I quickly reverted to being the son I was while growing up in Honolulu. Staying in my old bedroom in their house left me powerless to resist the strong forces tugging me back into the past, and I regressed into the person I used to be. It was like muscle memory, but it wasn't a physical reaction. It was a cultural, emotional, and mental boomerang slicing through the years, returning me to an idyllic yet complicated childhood.

Now, though, the situation is completely reversed. Mom will be on my turf, so to speak, and it will be the first time that's ever happened. How will she handle things? Will she expect me to revert to the child I was growing up under her roof? Or will she finally want to get to know the man her son has become?

And what about me? How will I react to the change in playing field? Will I assert myself as the adult who has independently forged his own way through life? Or will I revert to the obedient son ruled by a constant, oppressive need to avoid disappointing his parents?

Amid all this uncertainty, I'm apprehensive. I've no idea how our week together will play out. Will we pretend we didn't fight so bitterly before Dad's funeral, that our relationship hadn't devolved to polite superficiality from years of mutual neglect? Or will we finally be able to talk through the painful differences keeping us a continent and half an ocean away from each other?

I check the display board, which now indicates Mom's flight has just landed. I rush over to the gate and, soon enough, passengers begin disembarking, some dressed casually in aloha shirts, a few even wearing fragrant but fading leis. It's easy to separate the East Coasters returning from a dream vacation in paradise and those from Hawaii looking forward to an exciting adventure in New York City.

Eventually, I spot Mom. She's so tiny, almost lost among the throng of other passengers. And I'm taken aback by how much older she looks. Her hair betrays more salt than pepper, and there's a certain fragility to her walk. I remember her being so sprightly, with quick, almost birdlike movements. Now she seems to have entered a new stage in life, no longer middle-aged but not quite elderly. As I stand watching her, my heart begins to race, and I have to suppress the fight-or-flight mechanism urging me to bolt for the exit. To calm myself, I inhale a gulp of air, slowly forcing it deep into my lungs, quelling the instinct to flee.

Finally, just as I'm about to call out to her, she sees me and waves, her face exhausted yet warily joyful. I rush to meet her and, before I can say anything, she clasps my hands. "Ken-chan," she says, using my private family name, "honto-ni, hisashi buri desu ne."

"I know, Mom, it's been much too long."

CHAPTER TWO

My full name, Ethan Kenichi Taniguchi, is a cumbersome reminder of my complicated background. In Hawaii, neither my first nor my last name gives anyone any trouble, but on the mainland, it always takes me forever to spell out "Taniguchi." Half the letters house the irritating potential for error: "T" becomes "P," "n" becomes "m," and "g" becomes "c." For the sake of clarity, I've learned to use the military alphabet for each letter: "T" as in "tango," "a" as in "alpha," "n" as in "November," and so on. Going through that tedious routine always annoys me, given that, when pronounced properly, Japanese names like mine are the simplest to spell because they're purely phonetic: no silent letters, no bizarre rules, no ambiguity. Really, using the English alphabet, there is only one way to spell "Taniguchi," yet so few people on the mainland are up to the task. That's why I now give my last name only when I need to—when dealing with a bank, for instance. For restaurant reservations, I just go with my first name, "Ethan."

On the other hand, in Japan, people puzzle over how to say and write my first name. When hearing it, they often think it's "Ito," a common Japanese surname, and then they're confused as to why I have two Japanese last names. Eventually I decided to just use "Kenichi" or "Ken" whenever I introduce myself to anyone from Japan.

My parents had their own subconscious rules for my name. In ordinary conversation I was always "Ethan." Whenever they scolded, they used "Kenichi," as if reminding me that good Japanese sons need to obey their parents without question. On softer, more affectionate occasions, I was "Ken-chan." It was the same whenever I was sick as a child: "Ken-chan, please eat this rice with tea. It will calm your stomach." As an adult, "Ken-chan" had been reserved for special moments, like reminiscing about a particularly joyful time. Those tender moments, though, had grown increasingly infrequent, if not nonexistent, especially since Dad's death.

Mom calling me "Ken-chan" at the airport has caught me off guard. I don't remember the last time she did that, and it certainly wasn't at Dad's funeral. The words we spoke that day were anything but tender, and she used my full name—Ethan Kenichi Taniguchi—enunciating each syllable with such clarity, seemingly emphasizing every ounce of her anger, as she berated me for being an ungrateful son. Today, as we sit side by side in a cab headed to New York City, that brutal fight in Hawaii now seems so incongruous, even as I try to push that memory back down below the surface. Were we really going at each other's throats with such raw savagery?

When we arrive at my apartment on the Upper West Side, Mom gets out of the cab and shivers from the brisk air. I quickly usher her into my brownstone building, where she slowly climbs the two flights of stairs up to my apartment. As I unlock and open the door, she begins to take off her shoes, struggling because there's nowhere nearby for her to sit. "Oh, don't worry about that," I tell her.

"You mean you wear your shoes inside your own home?" she says, her voice a mix of surprise and concern.

"Well, it's just that, whenever I have guests over, it's always too humbug to ask them to take their shoes off, so I just got used to wearing my shoes inside too."

"But how can you keep your home clean with people always dragging in dirt from the outside?" she asks, trying to contain her revulsion.

"Don't worry; people always wipe their shoes on the welcome mat and, anyway, I keep my place clean enough."

Mom looks at me skeptically, but thankfully refrains from saying anything more. She merely shakes her head and proceeds to take off her shoes. Out of respect for her I remove my shoes as well, grateful that, in anticipation of her arrival, I'd spent an entire day thoroughly cleaning my place, vacuuming and scrubbing the hardwood floors so they're spotless.

Once we're in my apartment, it takes me less than a minute to show her the cramped, one-bedroom space. Mom looks like she wants to say something but doesn't, as if she doesn't want to risk unintentionally offending me. Instead, she starts unpacking one of her two large suitcases, which is full of omiyage, or souvenir gifts, especially food items from Hawaii that she knows I love but can't easily get in New York City. There are cans of macadamia nuts, packages of Kona coffee, a Tupperware of kulolo (steamed taro), and a jar of alaea salt. A small cooler bag has several plastic containers of poke, each with a different type of marinated seafood. I open one of them and inhale the smell of raw tuna, chopped seaweed, soy sauce, and sesame oil, my mind instantly transported back to the warm sunshine and gentle trade winds of Hawaii.

"It's fresh," Mom tells me, "bought just yesterday."

"I can't believe you brought all this omiyage. How did you even manage to lug two big suitcases to the airport?"

"You know I couldn't come empty-handed," she says, chidingly. "And, anyway, it's been such a long time since you've had this food. Look, Aunty June got you some shortbread cookies from Liliha Bakery and she wanted me to give you this CD of the Kamehameha School chorus."

I'm so touched, not only by her bringing so much omiyage but also by her remembering all my favorite childhood foods like pipikaula, the Hawaiian-style beef jerky that I loved as a kid but have forgotten about over the years.

"Aunty June wanted me to bring you some piri mango and lychee too, but I told her we're not supposed to bring fresh fruits to the mainland," she says.

I thank her and hug her gently, careful of how slight and frail her body seems. She looks so exhausted from the long journey.

"Don't worry about your luggage, Mom. Why don't you take a nap, and we can unpack everything else later?"

·   ·   ·   ·   ·

As Mom sleeps, I can't help but think about our long estrangement. At first, it was easy to blame everything on my relationship with Lucas. Looking back, I can see clearly how things unfolded from my parents' perspective— how my emerging relationship with him threatened their long-held view of me as a respectful Japanese American son who would eventually get married and bestow them with grandchildren to perpetuate their family name. When I moved in with Lucas, I forever shattered that expectation. To be honest, though, my now ex-boyfriend was just an easy, convenient reason for why my relationship with Mom fell apart. The actual issues were far more complex and deep-rooted.

I realize something else. This trip represents a handful of firsts for my mother. It's the first time she's ever traveled alone, the first time she's traveled since Dad died, the first time she's been on the East Coast, and the first time she's seeing me in years. It's also the first time she and I are alone together in a crowded, bustling city so far away from our nostalgic, yet entangled past in Honolulu.

For my part, what I want most from this trip is for Mom and me to relate to each other as adults. With Dad, things were always so much easier. He taught me how to swim, play baseball, shave, and drive. No matter what, he was there for me when I needed him, never intrusive and always respectful of my privacy. But once I hit my twenties, he stopped being my father. I mean this in the best possible way, in that he stopped worrying about me and didn't feel the need to continually guide my decisions. His view was, "I did everything I could to raise my son right, and now I have to trust him to live his own life."

My relationship with Mom is a totally different story. She, too, has always been there for me. But at times what I needed most from her was more space than she was willing to allow. Throughout my school years, she had to know all the friends I spent time with, and she was quick to express her displeasure with anyone she thought might be a bad influence for whatever reason, however flimsy. She disliked my best friend in high school solely because he was a year older, constantly worrying when I hung out with him. Those unfounded anxieties never subsided, even as I got older and became more self-sufficient and independent, when she had far less reason to worry. Unlike with Dad, she never seemed to stop seeing me as a child who needed regular guidance and advice. It was a double-edged sword. Her constant worrying about me was, in its own way, like a warm security blanket, always reassuring me of her love and concern. And yet her anxieties fed my insecurities, making me doubt myself at crucial times. Her love tended to be smothering, especially as I began to come to terms with my sexuality and find my way through life as a young adult.

CHAPTER THREE

Mom sleeps much longer than I expect. What starts off as a short nap to refresh her body stretches to nearly four hours. And even when she makes her way out of my bedroom, she still looks a bit worn and disoriented, as if she's not quite sure whether or not she's dreaming.

"You must be hungry," I say to her. "We can order in some food."

"Please, no," she replies, her voice raspy from her nap. "Let's go out. I need to stretch my legs."

Outside, on West 89th Street, a brisk autumn breeze catches Mom off guard. "I didn't think it would be this chilly," she says, clutching her thin cotton jacket.

"This is nothing compared to winter," I tell her.

"After all these years, I still don't understand why you would want to be somewhere like New York City. Why not live back in Hawaii instead?"

To answer her, my explanation would take hours, so instead I let her comment disperse to the Hudson River on a gust of cool air. Before long, Mom says she's tiring, so we decide to have an early dinner at a small Japanese restaurant on Broadway, just a couple blocks from my apartment. As soon as we're seated there, we catch up on small talk from Hawaii: Aunt June got a promotion and is doing well, but she's thinking of retiring next year; Alyssa and Keola just celebrated the first birthday of their daughter with a big luau; cousin Debbie is studying tea ceremony; the new neighbors just chopped down the three papaya trees that had, for years, delivered such tasty, fulsome fruit.

Mom speaks to me pretty much in English, as she always has, but this time she sprinkles more and more Japanese words and phrases into the conversation, making it difficult at times to follow what she's saying.

Whenever she lapses into Japanese, I find myself frantically trying to keep up as I try to process her words. It feels like a delay switch has been flipped inside my brain. Before I can dig into my memory for what a particular word or phrase means, she's already moved on, saying something else that then takes me another few moments to comprehend.

I'm frustrated that I'm so out of practice. Mom and Dad often slipped between English and Japanese. They were completely bilingual, both born and raised in Hawaii, with parents who had emigrated from Japan. As infants, they spoke Japanese first, only later learning English from the neighborhood kids and then at school. Back in the early twentieth century, when Mom's father first arrived in Hawaii, he had only a rudimentary understanding of English, although he eventually became very proficient from studying the Honolulu Star-Bulletin every night, a second-hand Japanese/English dictionary at his side. Soon enough, he was conducting business in English as a merchant businessman in Honolulu.

I wish I'd worked harder to become bilingual. When I was a kid, my parents insisted I attend Japanese-language classes after my regular public school ended in the mid-afternoon. While all my friends had the rest of the day free to play Little League baseball, ride their bikes, or otherwise goof around in the neighborhood, I had to trudge over to a Japanese private school. I was resentful, not just because I missed out on all the afternoon hijinks with my friends but because I was being forced to learn a language in which I had little interest. The only time I enjoyed those classes was when the instructor read Japanese fables to us or taught us how to fold a new origami animal. Back then, I saw no purpose in learning the language of my ancestors. It's only now, much later in life, that I sorely regret not having applied myself then.

The waiter, a young Chinese American man, comes over to our table to take our order. After he leaves, I use the pause in our small talk to ask Mom how she's doing. She looks at me, as if unsure how to respond, and then abruptly turns her focus to our tray of condiments. "They really should use better-quality shoyu here," she says, referring to the brand of soy sauce. "Don't they have any Oriental customers who know the difference?"

I'm silenced not just by Mom's harsh tone—really, it's just a condiment—but by her use of "Oriental." The last thing I want to do is criticize her English, especially because everyone in Hawaii uses that word. But when I went to college in Los Angeles, I was firmly corrected by other Asian Americans. "We're not Oriental; we're Asian," they told me, shaking their heads as if I didn't know my own racial identity. I want to tell Mom she shouldn't use "Oriental" here on the mainland, but I figure it's a conversation better left for another time. When the food arrives, we eat in silence, like a bored husband and a disinterested wife who've been married for decades and have nothing left to say to each other. In actuality, Mom and I have much to talk about—if only we knew how.

As I pick up a large piece of shrimp tempura my grip on the chopsticks slips and the shrimp plops into the dashi, splashing the dark liquid onto my white cotton shirt. Mom's initial reaction of surprise quickly gives way to concern, then reproach. "Dame-da," she scolds, "So you've already forgotten how to use chopsticks!"

I use my napkin to try to rub out the stain with little success, and Mom says, "You're just spreading it. Don't you know? You have to dab it." She dips a corner of her napkin into the water in her glass and hands it to me.

"That's okay," I tell her, perhaps a bit too curtly. "It's an old shirt anyway."

She looks at me with such disappointment in her eyes. I'm not sure if that's because of my initial faux pas with the chopsticks or because I have brusquely brushed aside her help. Or maybe it's because I don't want to expend even a little effort to try to save my shirt. Or perhaps it's just all of the above.

After dinner, as we walk back to my apartment, I realize just how conflicted Mom and Dad must have been, always negotiating between two cultures. A part of them wanted their son to be as American as possible. They didn't want me to face the kind of discrimination they suffered growing up, especially during World War II. So, they spoke mainly English at home and taught me how to eat properly with a fork and knife. Yet another part of them wanted me to be proud of my heritage. Thus, they insisted I take Japanese-language classes and, whenever we ate Japanese or Chinese food, we always used chopsticks. Often, the two cultures would blend in odd ways. I grew up eating chili stew on top of white rice, grilled hamburgers marinated in teriyaki sauce, and potato salad mixed with mayonnaise and shoyu.

And it wasn't just odd combinations of food. Everything was a constant mix of East and West. I watched football, "The Fugitive," and "Gilligan's Island" on TV, but then Dad would take me to samurai movies at the Toyo Theater in downtown Honolulu. I listened to The Beatles and Mozart but also developed a deep fondness for enka (Japanese soul music) from the records Dad played at night as he drank his after-dinner sake. My comic book heroes included both Spider-Man and Astro Boy, and I had boyhood crushes on Paul Newman as well as Toshiro Mifune. Even today, I avoid staying on the thirteenth floor of any hotel as well as the fourth floor, because four in Japanese culture invites bad luck.

It seems like I've always straddled two cultures. Whenever I'm forced to choose, though, I tend to favor my American side—at least in theory, if not always in practice. This is especially true in my general outlook on life. I love the rugged individualism of the pioneers who settled the Western U.S., even though that mindset runs counter to the Japanese need for conformity, as captured so descriptively by the phrase "deru kugi wa utareru."

After hearing my parents repeat that proverb relentlessly in my youth it became the tender core of some of my most painful memories. One episode that remains lodged in my mind occurred when I was in the eighth grade. Our teacher, Mrs. Takemoto, was explaining to us that wars between countries are never a simple matter and that history books tend to be written through the eyes of the victorious. She gave the example of World War II. "For the United States," she said, "the war started when Japan bombed Pearl Harbor. But for Japan, the war had begun years earlier, when, starved of raw materials by the Western colonial powers, it invaded Manchuria and China." In retrospect, Mrs. Takemoto was trying to teach us about the value of taking into account different perspectives, but it was an important lesson that my young, smart-ass mind didn't yet have the capacity to appreciate.

"So, Japan had a right to bomb Pearl Harbor?" I asked, in front of the class.

"No, that's not what I'm saying at all," Mrs. Takemoto replied. "What I'm saying is that wars are always more complicated than you might think, and it's important to view things from all sides."

"But isn't there always a right side and a wrong side," I then asked, "or are you saying that all sides are the same?"

"What I'm saying, Ethan, is that no side will always be one-hundred percent right, nor one-hundred percent wrong."

"So, you're saying America is partially to blame for Japan attacking Pearl Harbor?"

The discussion went back and forth like that for a few minutes, until Mrs. Takemoto had had it. "That's enough, Ethan, let's move on."

I wasn't having it. "Mrs. Takemoto," I tried again, "you just told us that all sides should be heard, but now you don't want to hear the point I was trying to make." And for that remark, I had to stay after class to wipe down the chalkboard, dust the shelves, and clean the windows. I was also sent to the vice principal's office, where my parents were called in to discuss my impudent behavior.

Mom and Dad were livid. At home that evening, when I tried to explain what happened, they would hear none of it. "The teacher is always right," Dad yelled at me, as he pounded his fist on the wooden coffee table in our living room. The volume and intensity of his voice stunned me into silence, and I was afraid, for the first time in my life, that he might strike me. I really had no idea what he was going to do next. Then, looking straight into my eyes, his tone saturated with anger, he said, "Deru kugi wa utareru." As I struggled to hold back tears, I heard Mom add, "There is absolutely no room in this house for a son who wants to be a rebellious nail."

I ran to my bedroom, slamming the door behind me. I skipped dinner that night, instead huddled on my bed feeling betrayed by parents who wouldn't even consider listening to—never mind really sympathizing with—what I had to say. It wasn't just that they sided with a teacher over their own son, no questions asked; it was the realization that, as American as I may have wanted to be, I would forever be tethered to a culture far across an ocean. I cried myself to sleep that night, fearing the love of my parents would always be contingent on how well I obeyed their Japanese way of viewing the world.

Throughout those years, I think a huge part of me always wanted to be less Japanese and more American, if only to rebel against my parents' wishes. And yet, ironically, I never really realized—nor even suspected—

just how Japanese I truly am. Of course, even as a young child I knew our nuclear family of three was far from being typically American. I'd seen enough episodes of "The Brady Bunch" and "The Partridge Family" to know white families didn't eat raw fish and fermented soybeans, nor did they celebrate obon every summer in honor of their ancestors. But I still somehow thought of myself as a "banana": yellow on the exterior but white on the inside. As an adult, though, I began to realize how much my parents had shaped the way I view the world, either through nurture, nature, or, most likely, a combination of both.

In my childhood, I was always fascinated with boxes, tin cans, and other containers. Indeed, I often found them more intriguing than the things they were originally designed to hold. I also derived great pleasure in finding new uses for them. A purple cloth satchel for Crown Royal whiskey became a repository for my marbles, and an old wooden cigar box became the storage place for my prized baseball cards. It was particularly thrilling when I found a box or can in which some other item fit perfectly. I still remember a long, rectangular tin can of Japanese wafers that was just the right size to hold the small Hot Wheel cars I collected. It was the exact width to hold the cars snugly, but not too tightly, enabling me to put them in or take them out without any difficulty. Moreover, the length of the can was just right to fit nine cars in one row, parked side by side, and its height allowed exactly two rows of cars to be stacked, one on top of the other. That tin can, by itself, was one of my prized possessions. Whenever I went to a friend's house to race our Hot Wheels, I brought my can, and then proudly unpacked the cars one by one.

Later, when I was in high school and went to Japan for the first time, I was immediately struck by the Japanese's keen attention to detail, especially in packaging. A can of rice crackers had all the crackers individually wrapped to preserve the freshness of each one. And everything we bought, no matter how small or inexpensive, was wrapped for us. Done with a rectangular sheet of paper placed diagonally, the wrapping style not only conserves paper but requires just a single, short piece of tape strategically placed to complete the task. I also noticed that everything in Japan seems to have its proper place. On rainy days, stores place a rack near the front of the shop in which customers can leave their wet umbrellas before entering. The rack has numbered slots to keep the umbrellas organized and separate from one another, so people don't have to rummage through countless umbrellas to find theirs. As Dad remarked to me, "In Japan, they think of everything."

Also like many Japanese, I'm intensely fascinated with robots. Of course, virtually any child tends to find mechanical gadgets interesting, but Japanese boys have an almost near obsession with them, and I was no different. When I was eight years old, my Mom's parents, who were then living in a town near Hiroshima, sent me a battery-operated tin robot, about knee high in height. Powered by two D batteries, the robot had legs to walk, could swivel at its hips and move its arms, with various lights flashing in its eyes. When I think about it now, that robot could do only a handful of rudimentary things, but for me it was still an object of countless hours of fascination. During that time, money was very tight for my parents, and new batteries were a luxury, so I carefully rationed the amount of time I spent with my robot every day. And when the batteries started to wear down, I put them in the freezer overnight, just to eke out every last bit of juice from them.

Where does such sentiment come from—the pure joy of finding a container that can be reused to fit other items perfectly or the mindless pleasure of watching a mechanical toy with automated movements? How much of that is innate, baked into my psyche from generations of my Japanese forebears? Or did I, as a toddler, somehow pick up all this from my parents through some mysterious osmosis process?

· · · · ·

Back at my apartment, Mom heads straight for the sofa and eases her body into the plump pillows. I'm just about to brew some tea for us when, suddenly, she bounces up.

"I need to give you something from Dad," she says, as she heads for my bedroom.

"Why don't you get it later?" I ask her. "There's no rush. Why don't you sit and relax?" But I can already hear her rummaging through her luggage.

Just as I'm about to go to the bedroom to coax her to leave any unpacking for tomorrow, she heads back into the living room with something in her hand.

"This is for you," she says. "It's Dad's, and you should have it."

It's my father's prized possession, an antique gold Constantin Vacheron wristwatch. As Mom places the watch in my hands, I struggle to fight back a wave of emotion. My father was a simple, hardworking, blue-collar man who, aside from a taste for fine Japanese whiskeys, never allowed himself any extravagance. That watch was his one luxury item, the sole thing he bought as both an expensive treat that made him feel good about himself and a tangible reminder of how far he'd come in life. The son of poor Japanese immigrants who arrived in Hawaii with barely the clothes on their backs, my father was a man who had provided for his family, sent his son to college, and lived comfortably enough to take the occasional vacation in Las Vegas.

"Mom, I can't take this. That watch was Dad's, and you should keep it."

"What am I going to do with a man's watch?" she says. "And besides, I know he would have wanted you to have it. I also kept his nice aloha shirts that would fit you, and his ties. He had so many beautiful ties, a few made from silk. You can look through all those things the next time you're in Hawaii, but I wanted to bring you his watch now."

As I look at her, not knowing what to say, I remember just what that watch meant to Dad. Without fail, he would wind it every morning, even though he'd only wear it maybe a couple times a year, on very special occasions. I feel so honored to have his cherished possession, but my joy is overshadowed by a growing cloud of guilt. I really should've helped Mom go through Dad's things after the funeral. How horrible it must've been for her to undertake that painful process by herself.

"I even bet that it would fit your wrist without any adjustments," she says, as she takes my left wrist, slips it through the wristwatch band, and snaps the gold clasp. "See, I told you. It fits perfectly."

She's right; it does fit perfectly. And I'm touched beyond words.

"Ken-chan," she says, "now you can think of him every day when you wind it."

CHAPTER FOUR

The next morning, Mom is up early. From the pullout sofa in my small den, I hear her making coffee in the kitchen. Still half asleep, I try to soak in the weak autumn light that filters through the window, bringing a pleasant warmth to my face. I get up slowly and, moving into the living room, I see Mom looking at my homemade butsudan, the small altar I set up in honor of Dad, on the top shelf of my bookcase.

A five-by-seven photo of him sits in a koa wood frame. In the photo, he's about to climb a long flight of concrete steps. What's not in the photo, which I took on our family trip to Japan, is the Shinto shrine at the top of those stairs. Dad insisted on climbing the long, steep flight to pay his respects at the shrine where his paternal grandparents are interred. The photo frame is adorned with his juzu, the Buddhist black prayer beads draped on the side. To the right of the photo sits a Dodgers cap and on the left side a Red Sox cap—Dad's and my two favorite baseball teams. Every year we'd root for a Dodgers versus Red Sox World Series, because my father promised he'd finally make the trip to the East Coast to catch one of those games. Unfortunately, that matchup has never materialized in all the years I've lived in New York City.

"Mom, did you sleep okay?"

She turns around, startled. I hadn't realized she was deep in thought, looking at Dad's photo. She seems unhappy—something's definitely bothering her—but she quickly collects herself and tells me, perhaps a bit too emphatically, "I slept fine, but I'm so tiny so you should let me sleep on the sofa, and then you can sleep in your own bed."

"Don't be silly," I tell her. "The bedroom is yours. That way you can have your privacy and sleep in late if you like."

"I never sleep in late," she says, her voice curt. Then, as she moves to the living-room window to look outside, she asks me which way is east. Her question surprises me, but I tell her my apartment faces south, so east is to her left. She stands there, gazing outside, her right index finger intently tapping on the windowsill. "Then why do you have your bed set up that way?" she asks. "Don't you know it's bad luck to sleep with your head facing north?" Now Mom appears worried that she slept in my bed, which reminds me of just how superstitious she is. Once, on a family trip to the Big Island, she refused to stay at the Royal Kona Resort because the only rooms available were on the fourth floor. "The number four is 'shi' in Japanese, and 'shi' also means death," she explained. Unfortunately, all the other hotels in Kona were booked because of a convention, so we drove to Hilo, a trip that took us almost two hours.

My mother's myriad superstitions have always bugged me. I've never understood how such an intelligent woman could be controlled by so many irrational fears. Today, though, the last thing I want is to quarrel with her. So, to appease her, I make my way to the bedroom, where I rotate and push my bed against the closet so she can sleep tonight with her head pointed east instead of north. As she inspects the new arrangement, she tells me, "This is much better, and now maybe you won't have such bad luck." I'm not sure to what she refers: Dad's death, my breakup with Lucas, or maybe just the mere fact that I'm gay.

· · · · ·

Over a breakfast of sunny-side-up eggs, fried Spam, and toast we plan the day ahead. Because Mom's never been to New York City, we decide to visit many of the major tourist attractions first: the Empire State Building, Rockefeller Center, Times Square, and Central Park. But we decide against taking the ferry to see the Statue of Liberty just yet, because the weather forecast is for light showers.

Throughout the day, I can't help but notice how out of place Mom looks. I've seen her only in Hawaii, where she looks perfectly natural, and in Japan, where she also blends in, almost too well. But now, here on Manhattan, she's noticeably shorter among the crowd. She walks so much slower than everyone else, and she's dressed way too warmly. The thick overcoat and gloves she's wearing are more suitable for deep winter than mid-autumn, and yet for her they're all but necessary to make the adjustment from temperate Hawaii. Perhaps most striking is her relaxed, unhurried demeanor, which is such a contrast amid the rushed craziness that is life on the sidewalks of Manhattan. She's like a beautiful, rare orchid from the tropics that's been rudely transplanted to the cold, concrete jungle of New York City.

At the Empire State Building, we take the elevator to the observatory floor, where Mom and I stare out into the grid of skyscrapers that disappear into the horizon of low-hanging clouds, fog, and mist. "After all these years," she says, "I still have no idea why you choose to live somewhere like here." It's the second time she's said that and, as she turns to look at me, I realize her statement isn't rhetorical. She really wants an explanation. Unfortunately, I'm not sure how to walk through the door she's opened.

"What do you mean?" is all I can manage to say.

She stares at me, her eyes locked on mine, her brow furrowed, but she doesn't respond. Then she shifts her focus to the view, shakes her head, and sighs, and I'm surprised by how defensive I find myself becoming.

"Well, I know it's not Hawaii," I tell her, "but I like living here, and this is my home."

All of a sudden, it seems as if some sleeping serpent stirs inside my mother. She looks back and forth over the view, takes a deep breath, and then her words come tumbling out.

"How can you say that?" she says. "What kind of life do you have?" And then, waving her arm across the densely packed uptown in the distance, Mom adds, "Just look at this. How can you stand to live here? So cold and impersonal. All this concrete and steel. And so few Orientals, let alone any Japanese."

Her words slice through me. As she becomes angrier, she gradually switches from English to Japanese, perhaps subconsciously believing her intense, cutting words are best not understood by any eavesdroppers. But as she continues her tirade, barely keeping the volume of her voice within a normal conversational range, I notice a small group of Japanese tourists rounding the corner behind her. They divert my attention, and by the time I focus back on Mom I'm startled to hear her now talking about Dad.

"And what little respect you show your father," she tells me, unaware of the Japanese tourists behind her, who understand her every word. "You don't even have any offerings for him at your butsudan. Don't you know he would be hungry? What kind of son are you? Don't you see what's happened here? You are losing yourself!"

Right then she sees the Japanese tourists. She is instantly mortified, realizing these complete strangers have heard and understood her angry, deeply personal, all too intimate words. She rushes toward the elevator that will take us back down to the street, but there's a long line. We wait in silence, my head spinning.

●　　●　　●　　●　　●

Back at my apartment, Mom plops herself onto the sofa in the living room and stares at the wall. I head to the kitchen to steep some tea for us, wondering how to continue our earlier conversation, this time in a calmer, less emotionally charged way. When I bring the tea out to the living room, Mom rushes to my bedroom and returns with some large rice crackers.

"Here," she says. "We can put this with some tea for Dad."

She's referring to the Buddhist custom of making offerings to our deceased loved ones and ancestors. I grab a small plate for the rice crackers and the smallest glass I can find—a shot glass—for the tea.

"Don't you have a small Japanese teacup?" she asks.

"No, sorry. I always just use a coffee mug for ocha."

"Well," she says, "I guess this will have to do."

She makes the offering and uses Dad's juzu to pray for a few moments, and then I take a few moments to pray as well. Mom is calmer now, and I want to finish the argument from earlier but feel I need just the right approach.

"You know how much I loved Dad," I tell her, as I sit beside her on the sofa. Mom nods her head, and we both quietly drink our tea. After a minute or so, I continue, telling her I'm sorry she thinks it's disrespectful of me that I don't follow Buddhist customs in honor of Dad. "But Buddhism is your and Dad's religion, not mine," I try to explain.

She looks at me, her brown eyes softer, almost pleading, and I realize she too is struggling to find just the right words to reach through to me.

It's as if we need another language to communicate with each other, because neither English nor Japanese will do.

"I just wish," she finally tells me, "that you wouldn't forget our heritage, who you are."

There's so much I want to say at this moment. I want to ask her why her parents immigrated to Hawaii if they wanted their descendants to remain purely Japanese. I also want to point out that, in so many ways, she and Dad raised me to be as American as I turned out; otherwise, they'd have spoken only Japanese at home and we wouldn't have made a big deal when Thanksgiving and Christmas and the Fourth of July rolled around every year. But bringing up all this now would be viewed by her as terribly disrespectful, given the countless sacrifices she and Dad made to help me have a better life than they did. So I merely tell her, "I haven't forgotten who I am. It's just that we're in America now."

"Trust me," she says, "I already know that."

• • • • •

Later that afternoon, while Mom takes a nap in the bedroom, I lie on my den sofa, looking out the window. The trees on my street have already lost their leaves and a strong wind rustles through the bare branches, making a hollow sound.

Mom interrupts my thoughts when she enters the living room. I get off the sofa to see her looking not at Dad's small shrine but at a photo of Lucas and me that sits on a lower shelf in the same bookcase. Without turning toward me, she says, "I thought you and he weren't together anymore."

I find my mood immediately turning sour. "You know we broke up," I tell her, "but he will always be a huge part of my life, just as Dad will always be a huge part of yours."

She looks at me and wants to say something but swallows the words back. I'm afraid she'll chastise me for comparing my failed relationship with Lucas to her long marriage to Dad, and already I'm arming myself with the words I'll use to respond. Instead, after a long pause, she says, "The maneki-neko looks good there."

She's referring to the Japanese ceramic cat that's right next to the photo of Lucas and me. The white neko, with its red ears and raised right paw, was a gift from her to Lucas and me after I moved in with him. Initially, Mom didn't send anything to us, while Lucas's sisters and mother gave us beautiful housewarming gifts: a stoneware dish set for six, ultra-soft cotton sheets, and large fluffy towels. In fact, from the time Lucas and I first started dating, my mother barely acknowledged him. She would never bring him up in a conversation; it was always I who would have to insert him, saying, "Lucas has been working a lot of overtime recently," or, "Lucas and I are planning a trip to Boston next month," or, "Lucas's sister just had a baby." She never asked about him and never included his name on Christmas cards or gifts. Throughout my time with Lucas, this caused me no small amount of hurt and embarrassment.

Finally, I had it out with her. On a trip to Hawaii I took without Lucas, I couldn't bear her thoughtlessness in silence anymore. While driving her home from the supermarket, I questioned why she never asked about him, never included him in my life, even though he was so hugely important to me. Mom responded by insisting she frequently asked about Lucas. I was incredulous she would claim that, and her lies only angered me more. But she wouldn't budge an inch, and neither would I. Soon, we were almost yelling at each other in the car, and our harsh, angry words ended only when we arrived at home. Dad, who was gardening in the front yard, waved to us, his smile quickly dissolving into a wary look of concern as he immediately sensed something was wrong with the two people whom he loved most.

That evening, after the three of us had dinner and Mom turned in for the night, Dad and I stayed up watching an old samurai movie on TV. During a commercial break, he went to the kitchen and returned with two Sapporos. "You know," he told me, as he handed me my beer, "that's a part of your mom I've never liked."

I wasn't sure what he was talking about. Was he remembering some long-ago fight with her? Or maybe he was referring to some grievance that had quietly festered over the years. "What do you mean?" I asked.

"I scolded her," he said. "I told her, 'Why can't you just admit you're wrong and say you're sorry?'"

"Oh, so she told you about our fight."

Dad nodded. "We used to have so many arguments when we first got married. She just doesn't like to admit she's wrong, even when she knows she's made a mistake. Of course, I realize she's a proud woman, but still."

We sat in silence for a few minutes, both of us pretending to watch the samurai on TV, clashing their long slender katana with amazing agility. Every movement of their intense sword battle was choreographed with such balletic precision. It was such a contrast to Dad's and my conversation, each of us clumsily searching for just the right words to express only what needed to be said while being careful not to overstep that boundary.

"Thanks for trying to smooth things over," I said finally, as I turned to look at him, his gaze fixed on the TV.

"I don't mind anymore when she does that to me, refusing to admit when she's wrong," Dad continued, "but I really don't like when she does that to you."

"It's okay. She's Mom, so I really don't expect her to apologize to me."

"Yes, I know," he added, perhaps a bit too quickly, "but sometimes it would be nice."

Although we struggled for the exact words to tell each other how we felt, it was one of the best conversations Dad and I ever had. We were talking across a generation and yet connecting as if we were long-time buddies. I was so touched that night, but a pang of regret entered my mind. Why couldn't we have had more of these honest, candid exchanges before? When I was a kid, we'd sometimes be on a car ride, just the two of us, maybe with Dad having to do a number of errands, and we wouldn't say a word to each other the entire time. I'd just sit in the front seat, my eyes fixed on the road ahead, sometimes daydreaming but often uncomfortably wondering why we weren't talking. And he'd be driving, perhaps daydreaming too, but maybe also struggling with himself to try and think of something to talk about with his son, who seemed only interested in things—like classical music—that were foreign to him.

For the remainder of that trip to Hawaii, Mom and I barely spoke. And after I returned to New York City, our already infrequent phone calls became even less so. Months passed, and then one day I got a package in the mail. It was the maneki-neko. I called to thank her for the belated housewarming gift, but I kept that conversation brief, almost business-like.

·   ·   ·   ·   ·

Even after her nap Mom still seems a bit tired, so we decide to order some takeout Chinese food. Unfortunately, I forget that she's used to the Cantonese cuisine of Honolulu, so she finds the Kung Pao chicken and Mongolian beef a bit too spicy for her tastes. Thankfully, though, the dumplings and stir-fried noodles with vegetables are just right for her palate.

"What kind of Chinese food did you say this is?" she asks.

"I'm not sure, but I think some of the dishes are Szechuan and some are Mandarin."

"Interesting taste," she says. "Do the Chinese here look different?"

Her question gives me pause. "I don't know," I tell her. "I think the northern Chinese tend to be taller, but I've never really noticed a difference."

"Did you know Grandpa wouldn't allow Aunty June to date a nice Chinese boy who lived down the street from us?" As usual, when talking to me Mom refers to her father and sister from my perspective, the same way she refers to her husband as "Dad" or "your father." She continues, "Grandpa wouldn't even allow Aunty June to date any Okinawan boys. They had to be pure Japanese or else."

I don't want to think about what my grandfather, who died when I was in high school, would have thought of my relationship with Lucas, an Irish American from central New York. I don't even want to ask Mom what she thinks his reaction would have been.

Later that night, after Mom goes to bed, I'm restless and decide to go for a long walk. Outside, the slight chill and thin mist evoke a nostalgic ambience of melancholy in the city. As I stroll along Riverside Drive, a painful memory from a long-ago autumn bubbles up into my consciousness.

I was in my late twenties and had just moved to New York City to be with Lucas. Struggling to make it as a freelance musician, I took odd jobs here and there. Even though I had no experience as a waiter, an Italian restaurant just a few blocks from where we lived needed a part-time host, so I applied and got the job. One day, when the restaurant was nearly full, I tried to seat a couple at one of the tables near the restroom, but they told me they didn't want to sit there and, dissatisfied, left. My manager, who'd seen what happened, rushed over to me. He looked around the restaurant, spotted an Asian couple eating at a table near the front, and told me, "You should have seated them at one of the tables near the restroom." I explained to him that, when the Asian couple arrived, the restaurant was only half full, so I gave them the best available table. "Don't ever do that again," my manager snapped. "Always give any Asians one of the bad tables, because they won't complain."

To this day, it's painful for me to admit that, for months, I obeyed my manager's ugly, repugnant orders and always seated Asians near the restroom, even if other tables were available. I remember one Chinese American family in particular. As I ushered them toward the back of the restaurant, the father looked quizzically at the empty tables near the front. He was about to say something but then, after a long moment, decided not to make a fuss.

I really don't have any excuse for my disgraceful actions during that time. I knew what I was doing was wrong, and yet I still did it. The fact that I, myself, am Asian only makes my shame cut all the deeper. I shudder to think what Mom—who was incarcerated in a U.S. concentration camp for ethnic Japanese during World War II—would think of my actions. In my feeble defense, all I can say is that I was young and needed the money from that job.

Oddly, since that year, my first living in New York City, I've never once thought about my time at that Italian restaurant. Maybe I had subconsciously blocked it from my memory. Even so, when I was a kid and did something wrong, and then lied about it, Mom always admonished me with the cutting words, "You know what you did, and it's you who has to live with it." Yes, I know what I did years ago at that restaurant, and the shame and guilt will never leave me.

CHAPTER FIVE

The next morning the sun shines brilliantly through the windows of my apartment, and Mom and I quickly decide this is the day we'll take the ferry over to the Statue of Liberty. After waiting in a long line, we're on the ferry, invigorated by the fresh air and spectacular view of Manhattan. Standing outside on the top deck, watching the skyline slowly recede, Mom asks which of the skyscrapers is the Empire State Building. It's as if she's already moved beyond the harsh words she spoke there just yesterday, and I'm only too grateful to join her in that selective amnesia.

As the ferry passes Governors Island to the left and Ellis Island to the right, we soon see the Statue of Liberty clearly, just a short distance away. Mom and I stand silently as Lady Liberty slowly gets larger in our view, her pale-green robed body and outstretched arm lifting the torch of liberty to "pierce the darkness of ignorance and man's oppression," as President Grover Cleveland so eloquently put it decades ago.

Then, all of a sudden, Mom grabs my hand. I turn toward her and see tears beginning to well in her eyes. Soon, those tears are streaming down her face, which is now crumpled and overwrought with some powerful emotion. I'm more than startled; I'm shocked. I've never seen her so emotional in public. She didn't even cry at Dad's funeral, although Aunt June later told me that, for months after his death, Mom wept at night in the privacy of her own bedroom. Yesterday's scene at the Empire State Building was distressing enough; now, here she is on a ferry crowded with strangers, sobbing uncontrollably.

"What's wrong?" I ask in Japanese.

Mom clutches my wrist even tighter, her short fingernails digging into my flesh, and she shuts her eyes as she tries to collect herself. After a few minutes, she finally tells me, "I can't believe I'm seeing the Statue of Liberty again. But this time, it's getting bigger and bigger."

What? I have no idea what she's talking about. To my knowledge, she's never been to New York City before, so how could she have seen the Statue of Liberty in person? I begin to wonder if she's referring to some movie or TV show. Or if maybe she's really confused from jet lag.

Then Mom starts rambling, half in English and half in Japanese. It's something about her parents, Aunt June, Buenos Aires, a Peruvian schoolteacher, India, and the Philippines. Totally bewildered, I'm now frightened. "Mom, slow down," I say, as calmly as I can. "What are you trying to tell me?"

"Don't you understand," she pleads, her eyes begging me to grasp something far beyond my capacity to comprehend. "I never thought I would ever see the Statue of Liberty again, and here it is, getting bigger and bigger!"

I'm so confused. I have no idea how to respond, what words might bring some comfort to her rattled mind. But before she can explain anything, she suddenly realizes other passengers are staring at us, wondering what kind of drama is being played out between a mother and her son on such a beautiful autumn day. She closes her eyes as tightly as she can, takes a deep breath, and holds herself perfectly still. I can almost feel her summoning the strength from every fiber in her body as she fights to regain her composure. With her eyes still shut, she gradually releases her grasp on my wrist and reaches for a tissue from her purse to wipe the tears moistening her cheeks. Finally, when she opens her eyes, it's as if a switch has flipped, and we watch silently as the ferry docks at Liberty Island.

·　　·　　·　　·　　·

On the taxi back to my apartment, so many thoughts swirl in my head. Twice, Mom said she was seeing the Statue of Liberty "again." When was she in New York City before? And why was she going on about Buenos Aires and India? As the cab zigzags up 8th Avenue, the frightening thought crosses my mind that maybe Mom's mental faculties have seriously deteriorated since Dad's death. Living alone after being married for so long can't have been good for her. And now an overwhelming sense of guilt creeps into my being. Why didn't I check in with her by phone more often? Why didn't I visit her at least a few times?

Back at my apartment, Mom settles on the living-room sofa while I boil a kettle of water for some soothing tea. She stares out the window, looking so completely lost in her thoughts, her mind anywhere but in her son's cramped apartment on Manhattan. When the tea is done, I bring over a cup for her and she quickly snaps back to the present.

"I really don't know what got over me," she says, embarrassed and perplexed.

"You seem a lot better now," I tell her, "but I'm worried. You were saying so many kinds of crazy things, things I didn't understand."

Mom takes a healthy sip of the tea and looks directly at me, her large brown eyes heavy with the untold weight of decades of cooking meals, washing loads of laundry, and doing countless chores around the house. "You knew I was sent from Hawaii to Arkansas, right?" she asks, referring to the Jerome War Relocation Center, a World War II concentration camp for people of Japanese ancestry. "And you knew Dad and I met in Japan, even though we were both born in Hawaii, right?"

I nod my head.

She takes another sip of her tea. "But did you ever wonder why we were in Japan?"

I search through my memory, struggling to pull together important chunks of my family's history. It's as if someone just asked an ostensibly stupid question—like, why are manhole covers round?—that probes your fundamental understanding of something so familiar that might nevertheless become inexplicable when viewed from a different perspective.

"Well," I answer, "I knew Dad was in Japan for his grandmother's funeral."

"But what about me?" Mom asks. "Why was I in Japan?"

I'm bewildered and embarrassed, because her question exposes a huge gap in my knowledge. I guess I never really wondered why Mom was in Japan after the war. I suppose I just assumed she was visiting her parents there, even though she never told me that. But then it dawns on me—why were Grandpa and Grandma in Japan? Did they move there at some point after World War II had ended and they'd been released from the Arkansas camp?

Mom looks at me and says, "Please make more tea. I have so much to tell you. I wasn't going crazy on the ferry. You see, I had seen the Statue of Liberty before, but I was only a young child then. This was during the height of the war and, when our ship pulled out of the harbor headed for Japan, I watched the Statue of Liberty as it became smaller and smaller. I really thought I was saying goodbye to America forever."

PART II

The Past: Hawaii, Arkansas, Japan, Los Angeles, and New York City (1937 to 2000)

CHAPTER SIX

Before Japan attacked Pearl Harbor, Mom lived an idyllic childhood, growing up near Aala Park, on the outskirts of downtown Honolulu. As she often told me, Grandpa was a successful businessman who owned a small department store that sold a variety of goods, including the island territory's first electric refrigerators and washing machines. The store also sold the latest automobiles. Mom's older siblings—my Uncle Richard and Aunt June—would sometimes intentionally be late for school so Grandpa had to drive his son to McKinley High School and his daughter to Central Intermediate, instead of them having to walk or ride their bikes. For those short trips, Grandpa often took one of the new cars in order to combine two chores: his parental chauffeuring duties and a test drive of a vehicle. Usually, that car was a Chevy or a Ford, but sometimes it was a spanking new Cadillac. When Uncle Richard and Aunt June arrived at their schools, they'd be greeted with the unabashed envy of their classmates. "Just how many cars does your family own?" Aunt June's classmates asked her.

The children also had the best clothes, stylish Western dresses, shirts, and pants, but also exquisite Japanese silk kimonos, cotton yukatas, and happi coats. For Hinamatsuri (Girl's Day) and Tango no Sekku (Boy's Day), they received dozens of dolls, all ornately dressed in samurai gear, kimonos, and royal court clothing. The dolls, each displayed in individual rectangular glass cases delicately held together with slender joints of black lacquered wood, filled an entire shelf in the family's living room.

They also had, by far, the best kites in town. While the other neighborhood kids struggled with their simple two-dimensional diamond-shaped kites constructed of paper and flimsy balsa wood, Mom and her siblings had elaborate three-dimensional box kites, handmade in Japan.

The box kites soared high into the sky, even on days with the faintest of winds.

But it wasn't just their possessions that made the Minatoyas the subject of much admiration and envy. Uncle Richard was a star baseball player for his high-school team, the McKinley Tigers. Known for his preternatural versatility, he played every position on the team except catcher. As a pitcher, and at a very young age, he mastered a deceptive changeup and a wicked curve ball. Aunt June was a standout among her classmates as well. A talented violinist in the school orchestra at Central Intermediate, she also won several essay contests. For her part, Mom had just started school and had yet to begin leaving her own mark. But even at that young age she assumed she was special, her life always filled with joyous birthdays, wondrous surprises, and a long sequence of one cherished event after another. "Growing up in Honolulu, I really felt like a princess of privilege," she told me, on the rare occasions when she reminisced about the past. "It was like we lived in a fairy tale."

Those halcyon days were shattered on December 7, 1941.

On that fateful Sunday morning, Mom and Aunt June were walking to Chuo Gakuin, their Japanese-language school, when they noticed planes flying overhead. They paid little attention to the aircraft, thinking it was just a U.S. military exercise. When they got to the school auditorium, where the Sunday classes were held, their teacher passed them music books, as they always began their studies by singing the school song. They'd barely started singing when their voices were interrupted by a frightening, thundering crash nearby. Everyone rushed to the auditorium's large windows and saw smoke rising from the Ewa direction, the location of Pearl Harbor. Then, another shell exploded right in the schoolyard, shattering the windows with shrapnel, dirt, rocks, and debris. Mom's books and schoolbag went flying in the explosion, and some of her classmates were hit by the scattered desks, benches, and other loose objects. Their teacher tried her best to contain everyone's fear, but her voice trembled as she instructed the students, "Go outside and run home."

As they rushed home, Mom and Aunt June heard one explosion after another from the Ewa side of Honolulu. Through the rising black smoke, they saw a wave of small gray airplanes flying on the outskirts of the city, like a swarm of angry wasps. Halfway home, they ran into Uncle Richard, who'd been sent to get them. "This is bad," he said. "This is really, really bad."

The three siblings arrived home to find Grandpa and Grandma listening to the radio for any news of the attack. The children knew better than to disturb their parents so, after announcing their arrival with the customary "tadaima"—"I'm here"—they headed back outside to climb onto the roof of the family's two-car garage. There they watched in horror as ominous black smoked filled the sky over Pearl Harbor. Aunt June, who usually made light of things, was too frightened to even attempt to reassure Mom like she usually did. For Uncle Richard's part, anger replaced his earlier fear. "Damn you, Japan," he shouted to the faraway planes, "damn, damn, damn you!"

Mom knew then something catastrophic was going on, but she couldn't quite grasp exactly what it was. At six years old, all she knew was the Minatoya household changed overnight, her parents and siblings now constantly preoccupied with worrying thoughts beyond her comprehension. Little did she know just how tumultuous a dislocation her young life would suffer.

A couple weeks after the Pearl Harbor attack, three tall, burly FBI agents dressed in dark suits arrived at the Minatoya house and ransacked both floors, confiscating a camera and radio. "I was shocked," Mom recalled to me, "that they didn't even take their shoes off, and Grandpa and Grandma were too afraid to tell them to." The agents questioned Grandpa in the living room for more than an hour, and they took him when they left, allowing him to bring only his toothbrush. Mom fought back tears as she watched the agents' dark sedan reverse out of the driveway and turn onto Vineyard Boulevard. Grandpa, who was in the backseat, just stared straight ahead. "Not once did he turn to look at us as he was being driven away," Mom told me, her face stoic as she described the painful memory.

That evening, Grandma cobbled together some leftover food for dinner, and the family ate in silence. They knew that other prominent members of the Japanese community had already been picked up: Uncle Richard's aikido instructor, the Shinto priests at the temple down the street, and all the instructors at the Japanese-language school the children attended. But no one ever expected Grandpa to be targeted. At the end of dinner, as everyone cleared the dishes, Grandma finally said, "This is all a big mistake. I'm sure your father will be back with us tomorrow."

"But what if he's not?" Uncle Richard shot back.

"This is America," Grandma said, her voice suddenly turning hard. "People have rights here. Yes, your father will be back tomorrow. He might even be in time for breakfast."

But Grandpa didn't return the next day. Nor was he back the day after, or even the day after that. In fact, no one knew what had happened to him until Grandma was informed by phone that he was being detained on Sand Island in Honolulu Harbor. A neighbor said hundreds of other men of Japanese ancestry were being held there too, because of some vague suspicions they might be enemy spies or even saboteurs. Grandpa a spy? The idea was so absurd it might even have been funny had the circumstances not been so dire.

The weeks Grandpa spent at Sand Island weren't easy. He was a fastidious man who never broke from his habits of cleanliness, including his need to change his undergarments on a daily basis. With no laundry facilities at the detention center, he at first washed his underwear in the nearby ocean. But the salt water soon made the cotton fabric too sticky. Eventually, he ended up washing his undergarments in the communal toilets.

Things were no less hard on Grandma, who was overwrought with worry. A day after she learned Grandpa was being held on Sand Island indefinitely, she gathered anything in the house that was from Japan, especially items highlighting the Japanese culture—beautiful silk scrolls, woodblock paintings, books, a miniature hand-carved wooden pagoda, Japanese awards Grandpa had received—and dumped it in the backyard. She then doused the pile with kerosene and lit it on fire. Uncle Richard, Aunt June, and Mom watched as their many kimonos, dolls, and toys from Japan went up in a blaze. Although crushed by the loss of so many prized possessions, they knew better than to complain.

Months later, Grandma received a letter from the U.S. Department of Justice. Because she didn't understand the formal English of the text, Uncle Richard translated it for her. The letter informed the family that Grandpa was being sent to the mainland, to a detention center in Lordsburg, New Mexico. Grandma was beside herself with worry. "How is he going to survive there?" she asked. "What if the other prisoners don't like the Japanese and they attack him?"

"He'll be okay," Uncle Richard said, trying to reassure her. "I'm sure the guards there will protect him."

"How can you be so sure?" Grandma asked.

"They're not just going to let the prisoners do whatever they want. There'll be guards there to keep everyone in line."

"But he doesn't even speak a word of Spanish!" Grandma shouted, rushing out of the room in anger.

Uncle Richard, Aunt June, and Mom looked at each other, wondering if their mother was losing her mind. It was only days later, Mom told me, that they learned that Grandma had, in her overwhelming anxiety, heard only "Mexico" when Uncle Richard said "New Mexico." Even after the misunderstanding was cleared up and Grandma knew Grandpa wasn't being shipped off to a foreign country, she still feared the worst. "Why are they holding him for so long? And why did they send him to the mainland? What do they want with him, and what are they doing to him?"

Grandma's repeated requests to the local police and FBI field office yielded no new information. What's worse, the Minatoyas were treated with suspicion by many in their own community. Business plummeted at Grandpa's department store, which Uncle Richard and Grandma were trying to manage. Even erstwhile loyal customers who were sympathetic to the family's plight kept their distance for fear that they, themselves, might then be targeted. A close cousin of Grandma's who used to visit every Sunday morning, bringing two dozen eggs from his farm in Waianae, stopped coming over to the Minatoya house, each week making another excuse for his prolonged absence. And then there were those who weren't afraid of voicing their feelings. "Well, your father must have done something wrong, or else he wouldn't have been arrested," a classmate told Mom.

Slowly, the Minatoya family withdrew into itself, partly from simmering anger (they didn't do anything to deserve what was happening) and partly from inexpressible shame (maybe Grandpa did do something wrong after all). For months, the family felt like they were sleepwalking, just going through the motions of living, waiting for something to jar them awake. Finally, Grandma received a letter from the War Relocation

Authority stating the family could be reunited with Grandpa if she agreed to go with her children to a "relocation camp" on the mainland. For Grandma, the decision was easy. She quickly sold the department store and all its contents, accepting only cents on the dollar, and prepared to make the move.

After finalizing the paperwork for the relocation, Grandma received a letter with detailed instructions. The family would be allowed only one suitcase for each person. Uncle Richard was nearly hysterical. "What am I supposed to do with Pono?" he asked, referring to the beloved poi, or mutt, dog that he'd adopted as a tiny puppy. When Uncle Richard had snapped his leg on a bad slide into home plate while playing baseball, it was Pono who stayed with him night and day throughout his recovery, keeping vigil. Even after Uncle Richard had shed his cast and was finally off crutches, Pono continued to sleep with him on his bed, as if to guard him from future harm.

"We'll find another home for Pono, a good home," Grandma promised.

"No, if Pono can't go, then I'm not going," declared Uncle Richard, his anger and frustration barely contained. He was already leaving his good friends and the baseball team at McKinley High School; losing Pono would be the final indignity, and he wasn't going to submit to it.

Grandma looked at Uncle Richard with such sadness in her eyes. "What kind of son," she asked, "chooses a dog over his own father?"

Nothing more was said about the argument. Then, several days later, Aunt June and Mom came back from school to find Pono missing. Both knew better than to ask their brother what happened. Oddly, Uncle Richard didn't seem sad, sullen, or even angry about the loss of his cherished dog. If anything, he was all the more determined and serious. As Mom described it to me all these decades later: "It was like Uncle Richard grew up, literally overnight, to become the new man of the house. At the time, Aunt June and I didn't like it, his all of a sudden bossing us around, but I think Grandma would have completely fallen apart without his help."

One of the things Uncle Richard insisted on was converting all the family's wealth into tangible goods. The government had already frozen Grandpa's bank accounts, but Grandma gathered the cash he had stashed at home and at the store, and they went on a shopping spree at the jewelry stores in downtown Honolulu, buying everything they could: pearl necklaces, jade pendants, gold bracelets, and brooches encrusted with semiprecious stones. "We felt like we were some kind of royal family," Mom recalled. But that feeling was fleeting, as Uncle Richard wrapped all the jewelry in cloth, packed the items into tin cans, and then buried the cans deep in the backyard. "We'll get everything back when the war is over," he said.

Those few weeks before the big move to the mainland went by like a flash. And before Mom knew it, there she was—a year after the bombing of Pearl Harbor—boarding a ship with Grandma, Uncle Richard, and Aunt June. They knew they were headed from Honolulu to California, but they had no idea their final destination. All they were told was that they were being relocated to a camp somewhere on the mainland, where they would finally be reunited with Grandpa.

·   ·   ·   ·   ·

The U.S. concentration camps were mainly for people of Japanese ancestry who lived on the West Coast. Relatively few people from Hawaii were sent there, because the agricultural economy of the islands would have collapsed with the loss of all the Japanese labor needed in the sugar cane and pineapple fields. But anyone suspected of having strong ties with Japan was interrogated and detained. This included Buddhist priests, Japanese schoolteachers, and leaders of Japanese community groups. Unfortunately, this also included Grandpa, who, as a successful businessman, often entertained visiting Japanese dignitaries.

For the move to a camp on the mainland, the Minatoyas were assigned passage on the SS Lurline. As they boarded the ship in Honolulu Harbor, they were overwrought with such apprehension. They were leaving their lives behind and had little idea what the future would bring. All they knew was that they would soon be with Grandpa again.

The voyage to the West Coast took five days over rough ocean waters. Mom had never been on a boat before, and she was frightfully seasick throughout the entire journey. "I kept throwing up, over and over again," she told me, her face crimping at the unpleasant memory. "Finally, Grandma relented and stopped trying to force any food on me, and I only sucked on oranges for the rest of the trip."

After the ship arrived in San Francisco, the passengers were shuttled onto a ferry to Oakland, and from there they boarded a train. All the train's windows were covered with paper, so none of the passengers knew where they were headed. They didn't even know what direction they were going, although many thought they were traveling east to some unknown location. Rumors flew—were they going to be sent to Idaho? Or maybe somewhere in the Nevada desert? Or perhaps Texas?

The train chugged along for five days, with everyone crammed into the cars and many forced to sleep in a sitting position. The air became stale with the smell of soiled diapers and sour milk, but everyone did their best to keep to themselves, not wanting to bother or worry others. During the long journey, people were allowed outside just once, somewhere in the desert. Even then, they were watched by armed guards with bayonet rifles. "We were in the middle of nowhere," Mom recalled to me. "Where did those guards think we would go?"

When the train finally arrived at its destination, everyone disembarked to discover they were in Denson, a small town in rural southeast Arkansas. "Yikes," said Uncle Richard, "where in the world are we?" With a population of little more than a hundred people, Denson was located in one of the poorest regions of the United States. The Minatoya family had never seen such poverty—people living in tattered shanties with no electricity or indoor plumbing. The town was also heavily segregated, with very few (if any) of either the white or black residents having ever seen any Asians before. A couple of the townspeople watched with binoculars as the scores of "foreigners" disembarked the train. After Pearl Harbor, many Americans were understandably fearful of another attack, even in rural Arkansas, and these Southerners did not appreciate suddenly having thousands of people who looked like the enemy as their new neighbors.

Mom's expectation was that the family would live in a so-called relocation camp, but her image of a "camp" was little preparation for what they experienced. To her, a camp was where her family sometimes spent a weekend on the North Shore of Oahu, renting a one-story, three-bedroom wooden house right on the beach. For fun, Aunt June and Mom would pitch a canvas tent in the backyard and spend the night "roughing" it outdoors, sleeping with the cool trade winds blowing through the tent, the sound of the ocean waves gently lulling them to sleep. That property also had tall mango and lychee trees, and the sisters would gorge themselves on the abundant fresh fruit.

The Jerome relocation center was nothing at all like that. It was essentially row upon row of long, ugly, squat, rectangular one-story barracks, slapped together as fast as humanly possible. The walls were made of plywood and tar paper, held together by vertical straps of thin wood. Grandma, Uncle Richard, Aunt June, and Mom were assigned a single room, roughly twenty feet by twenty-five feet, with slender metal cots for everyone's beds. Their new makeshift home in Arkansas was a grim, depressing departure from the family's sturdy, wooden, two-story plantation-style house in Honolulu.

Earlier, when Mom repeatedly asked Grandma why they had to leave Hawaii, Grandma would tell her, "shikata ga nai." And when Mom then asked, "but why can't it be helped?" Grandma, nearing exasperation, would say it was for their own safety. The U.S. government wanted to protect them, because many of their fellow Americans might blame them for Pearl Harbor. To Mom, this was somewhat plausible, because after the bombing she heard snippets over the radio like, "those sneaky Japs," or "never trust a Jap," or, even worse, "the only good Jap is a dead Jap."

But when she arrived at Jerome, Mom saw a camp surrounded by barbed wire and wooden watch towers, with guards pointing their machine guns toward the inside of the camp, not the outside. "If the guards are trying to protect us," she asked Grandma, "why are their guns aimed at us?"

Throughout the long, arduous trip from Hawaii to Arkansas, the one thing that kept the Minatoya family going was the anticipation of reuniting with Grandpa. By then, it had been almost a year since they'd last seen him, and Grandma, Uncle Richard, Aunt June, and Mom eagerly waited for the entire family to be together again.

But Grandpa wasn't at the Jerome camp; he'd been transferred from Lordsburg to a different facility in Santa Fe, New Mexico. And, to make matters worse, it wasn't clear when—or even if—they'd ever see him again. The disappointment was crushing and, almost overnight, Grandma became a different person, so much frailer and increasingly despondent. There were long stretches of days when she barely got out of bed, and she caught one cold after another.

Still, everyone tried to make the best of things, even though life in the concentration camp was harsh, made all the more difficult by the severe lack of privacy. It wasn't just that entire families, some with six or more members, were crammed into a single room. It was also the inconvenience of the communal shower and toilet facilities, which were several blocks away. Mom loathed them. She and Aunt June always took their showers late at night, just to avoid others. The toilets, arranged in one long row without any stalls, presented a more difficult problem. Whenever Mom needed to use the latrine, she brought Aunt June with her so her sister could hold a sheet around Mom, affording her at least some tiny shred of privacy. And whenever Aunt June needed to use the toilet, Mom returned the favor. One of Mom's worst memories was of the night when the mess hall inadvertently served spoiled pork. A few hours after that dinner, a long line of people urgently waited to use the toilets; some were unable to hold back their diarrhea and soiled themselves. "It was beyond humiliating," Mom told me, shuddering at the memory of that night, "as if we weren't even human beings anymore."

It didn't help matters that the surrounding area was essentially swampland, with regular flooding from the nearby Mississippi River. The ground, which was basically red clay, turned to mush from the torrential rains and periodic flooding. To avoid walking in ankle-deep mud, the camp's residents laid down planks of wood between the buildings. But even those makeshift walkways disappeared in a heavy storm. They also had to beware of snakes and chiggers: parasitic insects that burrow beneath the skin. Everything was new to the Minatoya siblings, who quickly learned just how truly fortunate they'd been growing up in Hawaii.

It was a lesson underscored when, within a couple weeks of arriving at Jerome, Aunt June developed a terrible toothache and found out that, although the camp had a resident dentist, he lacked adequate equipment or supplies. Her only option was to have the tooth pulled. Fortunately for her, it was a molar and not one of her front teeth. Medical care was hardly any better. The doctor at Jerome was a middle-aged white man who'd spent time in Tokyo and spoke passable Japanese but was prejudiced against any non-white person. The camp internees would go to see him only as an absolute last resort, and they were treated brusquely, at best.

Perhaps the rudest shock, though, were the brutal Arkansas winters, with freezing winds that cut straight to the bone. Unfortunately, with walls constructed of unseasoned plywood that deformed over time, the barracks had large gaps through which the harsh, cold wind invaded, the tar paper that covered the walls offering little resistance. A single pot-bellied wood-burning stove in one corner of each room was the only source of heat. Thankfully, the American Red Cross issued sweaters, caps, and mittens, which Mom wore practically day and night, even while sleeping, that first winter the family spent in Arkansas. A group of Quakers also sent warm woolen blankets, and other internees from the West Coast pitched in to provide those from Hawaii with heavy coats, boots, scarves, and other winter necessities.

Initially, the Minatoyas and others from Hawaii were greeted warmly by their mainland counterparts, but friction eventually developed between the two groups. The internees from Hawaii thought the mainlanders were too Americanized in how they spoke and dressed. For their part, the mainland internees looked down on the folks from Hawaii because of their pidgin English and casual, uncouth ways. "The kotonks were so uppity," recalled Mom, using the derisive label to describe how she felt about the mainland Japanese Americans. Added to that mix was a small population of kibeis, those born in the United States but raised in Japan, usually by their grandparents, before then returning to the U.S. Because the kibeis didn't really fit in with either group they had the most difficulty adjusting to camp life. Many spoke heavily accented English and were deeply loyal to the Japanese Emperor. Some even proclaimed Japan would win the war, which only resulted in their being further ostracized by their classmates and others in the camp.

The bleakness of life in Jerome was punctuated one winter morning with the grisly suicide of a kibei teenager from Fresno, California. The young man, who was on a work detail clearing some thick brush outside the camp, somehow made his way to the railroad tracks about a half mile away. He had taken off his coat, folded it precisely in quarters, and placed it on the ground with his juzu in the front pocket, arranged so half the prayer beads hung outside in a perfect semi-circle. He then laid down with his body perpendicular to the tracks. On thin onionskin paper, he'd written a note in Japanese: "For the brief time I was here, I tried to lead a clean, honorable life. I have not purposefully hurt anyone or caused others to suffer. I have done my best to be a good, kind, and understanding person, as well as a respectful son, but life has now become pointless. I hope the gods will be forgiving; I ask my father and mother to excuse me for what I am doing; and I beg everyone to please disregard my life." That night, a train headed into town cleaved his body in two, leaving his parents inconsolable with grief.

• • • • •

As life in Jerome became increasingly difficult to bear, family units broke down. Children ate in the mess hall with their friends instead of with their parents, and Uncle Richard was particularly restless. He constantly hung out with his buddies, joining the family in their cramped quarters only to sleep. One day, he announced he had volunteered to fight in the 100th Infantry Battalion, a U.S. Army unit composed entirely of Nisei men from Hawaii. Many of these sons of Japanese immigrants had earlier served in the Hawaii Army National Guard, and Uncle Richard had gone to high school with a number of them.

Grandma wasn't particularly surprised or upset at Uncle Richard's enlistment, and that apparent indifference angered Aunt June. It was as if Grandma had already resigned herself to losing another family member. The more Aunt June thought about it, the angrier she got, not just at her mother but also her brother.

"How can you leave us, without Dad here?" she confronted him.

"You'll be fine," Uncle Richard said. "Nothing is going to happen here in the middle of Arkansas. But I can't just stay here doing nothing while we're at war. I gotta do something or I'll go crazy."

Cameras were officially forbidden at the camp, but Mom somehow had a single photo taken there. In it, she's standing with Uncle Richard outside their ugly barracks. He was no longer living in the camp, having just finished his basic training at Camp Shelby in Mississippi, and was allowed to visit his family before shipping off to Europe. Mom looks so proud next to her older brother. When she first showed me the photo, decades after it was taken, she spoke with such unabashed pride. "Just look at Uncle Richard," she told me. "Doesn't he look so handsome there in his uniform?"

I, however, saw a much different photo, one that captured so succinctly the hypocrisy of the United States, a country I'd grown up loving and respecting. From one side of its mouth, the U.S. government was saying, "People of Japanese ancestry, even U.S. citizens, can't be trusted and must be locked up." Yet from the other side of its mouth, that same government said, "Let's have Japanese Americans help fight this war and put their lives on the line for good 'ole Uncle Sam."

Uncle Richard did willingly put his life on the line for his country, and he was killed in Italy. Just seconds after returning to his foxhole it was shelled, his body blown beyond recognition. As it turned out, his company—the 100th Battalion of the 442nd Infantry Regiment—was given the most dangerous missions. The Nisei were considered expendable, even though these men were full U.S. citizens. At the Battle of Monte Cassino, the 100th Battalion lost almost eight hundred of its one thousand three-hundred troops. In one platoon, only five soldiers survived out of the original forty.

The bravery of the 442nd would later reach legendary status for rescuing "The Lost Battalion," an army infantry unit composed of men originally from the Texas National Guard. In October 1944, German forces surrounded The Lost Battalion in the Vosges, a mountain range in eastern France near the German border. Two U.S. battalions had tried but failed to rescue the Texans, forcing a fighter squadron to airdrop supplies to the two hundred seventy-five trapped soldiers as the situation grew increasingly desperate. U.S. military commanders decided the 442nd would make one final rescue attempt, although it was essentially a suicide mission. Miraculously, the Japanese American battalion broke through the German line and rescued more than two hundred of those Texans, but that victory came at a tremendous cost. For that mission, the 442nd suffered more than eight hundred casualties.

Given all that, I had to ask Mom, "Doesn't this photo make you angry?"

"What?" she said, turning from the photo to look at me, a puzzled expression on her face. "Why should this photo make me angry?"

I told her, "Never mind," not wanting to degrade the one seemingly happy remembrance she had of her time in Arkansas—and the last memory she had of being with her dashing older brother.

CHAPTER SEVEN

After Uncle Richard had left the Jerome camp, Aunt June and Mom made a pact with each other. "We decided to adopt a new mindset to be positive," Mom told me, "doing whatever we could to make life in Arkansas as bearable as possible." The two sisters eventually made friends among their classmates and even began to enjoy small moments and novel experiences: participating in their first snowball fight, gathering dandelions and the other wildflowers of spring, foraging in the nearby woods for kikurage mushrooms, and listening to the crickets at night.

To battle the boredom so prevalent in the camp, people immersed themselves in various arts-and-crafts projects, often using leftover materials and even trash. There was no shortage of ingenuity or creativity in what the internees could do. People carved beautiful birds from scrap wood or larger sculptures from the roots of the cypress trees growing nearby. Others created macramé from hemp fiber, crocheted doilies from cotton thread, made bracelets from tin cans, strung buttons into necklaces, and wove belts from electrical wire. A number of artists were able to order watercolors, chalk, and pencils from the Sears catalog, creating beautiful, if somber, drawings of the camp and adjacent woods. Popular among the internees were the handful of carpenters who could build bookcases, shelves, tables, chairs, and other furniture from wooden packing containers and other scraps.

Mom and Aunt June's specialty was constructing miniature, ornamental umbrellas from toothpicks and the paper wrappers of cigarette packs. The toothpicks became the individual ribs of the umbrella spine, around which Mom and Aunt June carefully twirled the cigarette wrappers before tying them together with thread to form a decorative circular pattern. The wrappers from Camel packs could be arranged so that, looking down at the top of the umbrella, an outer ring of gray appeared next to an inner circle of white, followed by a smaller ring of gold with brown borders. Four camels would stand equally spaced above those outer rings. The use of cigarette wrappers from other brands resulted in different geometric patterns. The red-and-green wrappers of Lucky Strike packs became an exploding star, and the colorful wrappers of Player's cigarettes transformed into a stunning spiral of blues and whites.

Like much of life at Jerome, obtaining those cigarette wrappers required shrewd bartering skills. For breakfast, all internees received one teaspoon of sugar to eat with their cereal. Mom and Aunt June saved theirs in a jar, to be used in exchange for the cigarette wrappers and other items they needed. As Mom recalled to me, "It became almost a fun game, seeing what we could get in return for a quarter cup of precious sugar."

Just as Mom and Aunt June was settling into their life in Arkansas, they suffered another wrenching dislocation. At the concentration camps, people had to sign a document that became known as "the loyalty questionnaire." The form asked two life-altering questions: whether people were willing to serve in the U.S. Armed Forces, and whether they would forswear any loyalty to the Japanese Emperor. Many Nisei like Uncle Richard answered "yes" to both questions and, to further prove their loyalty, enlisted in the U.S. Army.

Things were trickier for Grandpa at the Santa Fe camp. At the time, U.S. law barred Japanese immigrants from becoming naturalized citizens solely because of their race. So, if Grandpa renounced his Japanese citizenship, he risked becoming a stateless person. Who knew what would happen to him then, especially if the war dragged on for years? Also, Grandpa didn't particularly trust the U.S. government, given all that had happened to him. And, if the war did end soon, would he still be held prisoner against his will? Amidst all that uncertainty and distrust, Grandpa reasoned it would be better to remain a civilian citizen of Japan than a stateless man in the United States, so he answered "no" to both loyalty questions. Unfortunately, that response apparently only confirmed the U.S. government's worst suspicions of him, and he was transferred to the Tule Lake War Relocation Center in northern California, a maximum-security facility used to imprison those men considered troublemakers, dissidents, or security risks.

Life at Tule Lake was the harshest of all the facilities used to incarcerate people of Japanese descent. A curfew was strictly enforced, and barrack-to-barrack searches weren't uncommon. Shortages of food, hot water, and fuel to heat the barracks made life increasingly difficult to endure, and dissent festered among the prisoners. Feeling isolated and emasculated, Grandpa began to lose the hope and optimism that had driven him as a young man. On his bleakest days, he started to doubt he would ever see his wife and three children again.

For her part, Grandma wrote several letters to the War Relocation Authority and the Director of Alien Division in Washington, D.C., asking when she could be reunited with Grandpa. She could barely speak English, let alone write it, but there was a young Nisei man who lived just three units away in the same barracks at Jerome. A student at U.C. Berkeley when the war broke out, he was more than happy to help Grandma with her correspondence. As the months dragged on, Grandma's letters remained unfailingly polite yet increasingly desperate. "As it is decidedly unfavorable for my daughters to be separated from their father, and as I have been rather sickly of late," she pleaded, "I would appreciate any action you may decide to take to help facilitate our reunion with my husband."

Meanwhile, behind the scenes, a civilian exchange was being brokered. Although the United States and Japan were officially at war, the two countries were intensely negotiating a deal through diplomatic intermediaries from Switzerland, Sweden, and Spain. The U.S. government wanted the return of thousands of U.S. civilians who, when the war broke out, found themselves stranded in Japan, Shanghai, Singapore, and other parts of Japanese-occupied Asia. These individuals included not only diplomats but also business executives, missionaries, and their families. The U.S. State Department was especially anxious to repatriate these civilians, because rumors were swirling that they were being held in harsh captivity by Japan. In return, the U.S. government offered to "repatriate" to Japan an equal number of persons of Japanese ancestry. Unfortunately, the Minatoyas were included as part of that civilian exchange. Although Mom was still a child at the time, the government doublespeak didn't escape her. "I knew even then this was nothing but baloney," Mom told me, her face knotted in anger. "What did they mean, we have to 'go back' to Japan? We'd never even been to Japan."

Grandma did her best to stifle any feelings of disappointment, frustration, or anger she must have felt, and recast the upcoming move as an exciting adventure. She told her daughters about the beauty of her homeland: majestic Mount Fuji, the elegant pagodas, the dramatic waterfalls, the sublime cherry blossoms in spring, and the glorious Japanese maples in autumn. She also described in detail Iwakuni, a town in southern Honshu along the Inland Sea, where she and Grandpa were born and raised. She talked about the town's historic Kintai Bridge, a magnificent wooden structure with stone pedestals supporting five graceful arches spanning the winding Nishiki River. According to legend, it was on the Kintai Bridge that the famous swordsman Kojiro Sasaki developed his renowned tsubame-gaeshi fighting technique by studying swallows in flight. At night, cormorant fishermen in long slender boats with fire torches dotted the water, illuminating the river. During the day, Iwakuni Castle, perched atop Mount Yokoyama, was visible from the town, and the surrounding hills were said to be inhabited by fabled white snakes thought to bring good luck to the villagers.

Grandma repeated these stories almost nightly until August 1943, when she, Aunt June, and Mom were packed on a train headed from Arkansas to the East Coast. Their final destination was New York City, where they were finally reunited with Grandpa. At first, Mom didn't recognize the hunched old man with a cane and was shocked to realize it was her own father. "The thing I can't ever forget," Mom recalled to me, "was that Grandpa wasn't really walking anymore. Instead, he was shuffling his feet, and he was slightly stooped, like an elderly person."

The reunion was much more bitter that sweet, as the family soon boarded the MS Gripsholm, along with hundreds of other Japanese nationals and Japanese Americans who were being similarly repatriated or deported to Japan. The ship was painted white and would be lit with bright lights at night to signify it had safe passage throughout its journey. And on September 2, 1943, the Gripsholm pulled out of New York Harbor with the Minatoya family on board. It was a warm, clear day, and as the diesel-powered ocean liner made its way past Liberty Island, Mom's family stood on the top deck and watched the Statue of Liberty, her pale verdant robe and upraised torch gradually receding. No one said anything, but Aunt June clutched Mom's hand tighter and tighter as they watched Lady Liberty disappear in the distance, the two sisters saying a silent goodbye to the country of their birth.

From New York City, the Gripsholm headed south, down the coast of North America and then along South America, stopping briefly at Rio de Janeiro. There, the ship picked up South Americans of Japanese descent and loaded a replenishment of water, food, and other supplies. The Gripsholm then crossed the Atlantic Ocean, rounded the Cape of Good Hope, and stopped at Port Elizabeth, South Africa, to restock its supplies. From there, the ship crossed the choppy Indian Ocean and headed for Mormugao, Goa, an Indian port city that had been a Portuguese colony but was then occupied by the British Army.

During the forty-day journey aboard the Gripsholm, Mom and Aunt June attended daily classes to improve their Japanese. Although the Minatoya girls spoke the language fluently, learning to read and write Japanese was a different story. The crash course, taught by a Peruvian Japanese woman, was intended to bring all the children up to a minimum level so they could attend schools in Japan without having to be dropped more than a grade or two. Aunt June, in particular, had trouble learning all the difficult kanji, the Chinese ideograms used in written Japanese, that a teenager of her age should know. Whenever she had to write an essay, she frequently fell back on hiragana, using the Japanese alphabet to phonetically spell out words because she didn't know their proper kanji. The teacher would shake her head, wave a wooden ruler, and chastise her. "You should be embarrassed. You write like a small child!" Aunt June was fourteen years old at the time, and she dreaded every class.

But life aboard the Gripsholm wasn't all intensive schoolwork. For one thing, dinners were a special event, because the family got to eat together on a regular dining table, instead of the long wooden tables and benches in Jerome, and everyone was given elegantly printed menus. The ship also had three small movie theaters where Mom and Aunt June saw "Yankee Doodle Dandy," starring James Cagney and Walter Huston, several times. After each viewing they left the theater singing "I'm a Yankee Doodle dandy. Yankee Doodle, do or die." Even with the song's upbeat tempo and cheerful melody it must have released a strong undercurrent of sadness for the Minatoya sisters, as each day propelled them that much farther from the U.S. and that much closer to Japan.

At Goa, the Gripsholm docked alongside the Teia Maru, an armed merchant cruiser the Japanese had seized from the French and quickly converted into a civilian ship. Over the course of a week, people and baggage were exchanged between the two vessels. On one side were about one thousand four hundred U.S. and Canadian citizens who'd been living in Japan, Shanghai, Hong Kong, Saigon, and Singapore. And on the other side were an almost equal number of people of Japanese descent, including the four Minatoyas. The actual exchange of passengers was conducted as if trading livestock. One by one, people left their old ship and boarded their new vessel, each person matched with a counterpart transferring in the opposite direction. It didn't escape Mom's attention that all the people she and her family were exchanged for were white. "Some things you never forget. They stay seared into your brain, like a hot iron branded into tender flesh," she told me, as she shook her head. "All those people were so happy to be returning to America, and all I could feel was fear and unrelenting sadness, despite Grandma's efforts to make me excited about Japan."

The Teia Maru was a much smaller ship than the Gripsholm, and many passengers were forced to sleep on the deck and in the lounge areas. Mom's family was fortunate enough to be assigned a small cabin with two sets of bunk beds on a lower level of the ship. The cabin was cramped, but at least the Minatoyas had some privacy, and they tried to adjust to their new surroundings as best as they could. Gone were the beautiful dining room, the printed menus, and the three theaters. Instead the passengers suffered various deprivations. Water was in short supply, both for drinking and washing, and at many meals neither water nor coffee was served.

From India, the Teia Maru sailed to Singapore, where a number of passengers disembarked because the Japanese Army needed English speakers to act as interpreters. The ship then headed to Manila, and from that port people were allowed to leave the vessel for a day of sightseeing on buses. Mom and Aunt June saw hibiscus flowers and mango trees, and those sights made them inconsolably homesick for Hawaii.

"I can't believe we're going to Japan," Aunt June said, as the bus rounded a curve and opened onto a view of the Port of Manila.

"Shikata ga nai," Grandma said.

"But I don't understand," Aunt June replied. "How could this even be happening? It's so unfair."

Grandpa, who'd been silent during the entire bus ride, kept on looking out the window and said, "Some things are not for you to understand. Some things are well beyond you, and well beyond your mother and me as well."

Mom recalled to me how frightened she was at that moment, not so much by what her father said but more by the way he said it. Grandpa was utterly resigned, as if he no longer had a say in how his life would unfold, and there was just enough anger and bitterness in his voice to silence Aunt June for the remainder of the bus ride.

After a few days in Manila, the Teia Maru sailed for Japan and arrived at Yokohama Port in mid-December. The trip from New York City to Japan had taken a little over two months, leaving everyone exhausted and eager to be on land again. But as people disembarked in Japan, they were aghast at what they saw. The port city was clearly under siege, with burnt structures and a few buildings reduced to rubble, and the Japanese looked like they were dressed in ragged pajamas, their faces so dour and their bodies underfed. Even Grandma could no longer put on a brave face, and it was more than clear that she, too, was distressed at what she saw.

"I thought Japan was winning the war," Mom whispered to Aunt June.

"I told you not to listen to those kibei at the camp," Aunt June responded. "They don't know anything. If life were fair, they should have been the ones sent here, not us."

The immigrant processing center in Yokohama wasn't heated, and the Minatoyas had to sleep on the floor, fully clothed with their overcoats. Food was scarce, and whatever could be found by either paying or bartering for it was barely edible, mostly dried fruit or salted dried seafood.

Grandpa and Grandma had siblings who still lived in Iwakuni, so the family took a series of trains to get there. Every train was packed to the hilt, leaving the Minatoyas to stand for most of the journey, which took three days because of all the frequent stops and delays in service. Today, that trip on the bullet train can be done in under five hours.

In Iwakuni, the Minatoyas were greeted with considerable curiosity, mixed with no small amount of suspicion. Were they really in Honolulu when Pearl Harbor was attacked? How much did they know about the industrial capacity of the United States to build more ships, airplanes, and tanks? And why had they left the U.S.? Were they sent to learn about conditions in Japan and the country's resolve to continue fighting?

The daily language instruction aboard the Gripsholm and Teia Maru had certainly helped improve Aunt June and Mom's Japanese, but it didn't prepare them for the discrimination they faced in school. The sisters spoke with a slight accent, which their classmates teased mercilessly, and even their teachers had little sympathy for the two new immigrant girls. In math class, Aunt June was asked for the answer to a word problem involving fractions and she said "three-fourths" in Japanese, indicating three-quarters. Her teacher, an elderly man with piercing eyes, railed at her because, in Japan, the denominator is given first, so the answer should have been "fourths-three."

"Don't you know you're not in America anymore?" the teacher asked, rapping his wooden pointer against the top of Aunt June's desk. "If you like America so much, please return there."

"Obviously, I would if I could," Aunt June shot back, and with that, the teacher slapped her across the face with such force she flew off her chair. The teacher then continued with the lesson as if nothing had happened.

Throughout 1944 and into 1945, as it became increasingly clear to even some of the most ardent Japan loyalists that the country would lose the war, hostility toward Aunt June and Mom intensified. "You smell funny, like stinky cheese," one classmate told Mom. Another girl who used to be her friend announced one day, "My father said I'm not allowed to talk with you anymore because you're a spy." The most hurtful blow, though, came when a popular girl had a birthday party at her home and invited everyone except Mom. Recalling those painful times, she told me, "I was just grateful people weren't aware I had a brother who was fighting in the U.S. Army."

Indeed, perhaps it was best that everyone in town didn't know about Uncle Richard when, on August 6, 1945, the United States dropped its first nuclear weapon on Hiroshima, the neighboring city to Iwakuni. Mom and Aunt June were in school when that unprecedented weapon of mass destruction was unleashed, its blast and firestorm killing tens of thousands. The two sisters watched the resulting mushroom cloud rise high in the blue sky before opening like a dark, malevolent umbrella. Later they would experience the horrific black rain that cloaked the region. "I really thought the world was coming to some hellish end," Mom recalled to me. "And part of me felt guilty, as if I were somehow responsible for what the U.S. had done." Ironically, Mom added that she had also felt guilty when Pearl Harbor was attacked, even though she had no loyalty or allegiance to Japan. "I know it doesn't make sense," she said, "but that's how I felt as a young child."

The atomic bomb leveled Hiroshima. For weeks after the blast, people who had survived but been rendered homeless straggled into Iwakuni. Many of them suffered excruciating pain, patches of their skin sloughing off from the extreme heat of the blast while the resulting radiation poisoned their internal organs. One elderly man who approached Mom and Aunt June near the Kintai Bridge looked like a charred animal. "At first, we didn't even realize it was a man," Mom said, "he looked like a walking scarecrow. We were overwhelmed by the sight of his face, his eyes bulging and his skin charred and smothered with pus. And that horrible smell of blood and creosote. I think he might have just wanted water, but we were so frightened we just ran away as fast as we could." After another atomic bomb had destroyed Nagasaki and Japan had finally surrendered, Mom and her family felt some sense of relief mixed with crippling despair. How was the country ever going to rebuild itself?

While describing those post-war years in Japan, Mom recalled to me an odd, painful assortment of memories: not being able to bathe for days, riding buses converted to run on burning charcoal, and eating dried persimmons, smoked fish, and tiny portions of rice and barley. But what she remembered most was the day when she and Aunt June were walking home from school and a small gang of teenage boys began bullying them, taunting them with crude, lewd insults and trying to yank their skirts down as they hurried home. Thankfully, a shopkeeper saw what was happening and chased the boys away. Decades later, Mom vividly recalled what he said, kind words that helped her understand all the chaos and jarring dislocations of her young life. After the shopkeeper sat the two sisters down and gave them some rice crackers to eat, he told them, "You have to understand something important. It's not people who are at war with each other; it's governments. But it's ordinary people like us who get swept up in it, and we all pay the price."

CHAPTER EIGHT

After World War II had ended, the Minatoya family continued to live in Iwakuni, but Aunt June and Mom desperately wanted to return to Hawaii. Grandpa, however, was dead set against it. As Mom explained to me, "Given all Grandpa endured in the war, he wanted absolutely nothing to do with Hawaii, let alone the United States." He wasn't only angry about his imprisonment, the son he lost to the fighting in Europe, and the family's deportation; he was bitter about all the property and bank savings he lost. Adding insult to injury, the Hawaiian economy was booming after the war ended, with Honolulu becoming a major international city. As jet travel brought tens of thousands of tourists from the mainland, Waikiki became a major destination for rest and relaxation. Grandpa, meanwhile, struggled to provide for his family in war-torn Japan. Missing out on the most prosperous years on Oahu only made his antipathy toward the U.S. fester into full-blown enmity: "Americans took my home. They took my business. They took my freedom. They even took my son. But I will not let them take my daughters too."

For Aunt June and Mom, it wasn't just that life in Japan was so difficult, with chronic, lingering food shortages, a lack of young men suitable for marriage, and businesses struggling to rebuild; they also missed Hawaii's warm climate, beautiful beaches, and easy-going lifestyle and culture. They longed to be back on the islands where they were born and spent their early charmed childhood together, blissfully unaware of the outside world's ugliness. For the Minatoya sisters, Hawaii was a beautiful, idyllic land that wasn't really a part of the United States, even if it was then officially a territory. That is, Hawaii was its own separate place, with its own distinct culture, whereas Arkansas, San Francisco, and New York City were the United States. The two sisters were also acutely aware they might never fully fit in with the Japanese, even as they equally endured all the suffering of a country devastated in war.

Those post-war years dragged on, seemingly with little hope, until one day pure serendipity struck. A neighbor heard through the grapevine that a young, single man from Oahu would be visiting Hiroshima to attend his grandmother's funeral. He was a kibei, born in Hawaii but raised in Japan by his grandparents while his parents toiled long hours in the sugar-cane fields on Oahu. When he was twelve and old enough to help out around the house, he returned to Hawaii.

A blind date was arranged between the young man and Aunt June, but the two failed to hit it off. It was more than a lack of physical chemistry. He thought she was too outspoken and opinionated, and she thought he lacked drive and ambition.

So that's how Dad then met Mom, who'd just turned seventeen. The attraction was immediate and mutual. They took long walks along the Nishiki River, talking about their upbringing, their desire to have a family, their hopes for the future. A few days before Dad was scheduled to leave on his return ship to Honolulu, he asked Grandpa for permission to marry Mom.

Initially, Grandpa was adamantly opposed, "Who is this stranger from America who wants to take my daughter away?" But Grandma, Aunt June, and Mom pleaded with him, arguing that Dad wasn't really from America; he was from Hawaii. And, according to the village nakodo, the matchmaker who checked Dad out, he came from an honorable family in Hiroshima with strong roots throughout the Ohtake neighborhood. Moreover, because of the war, there weren't many eligible bachelors waiting in line to woo the Minatoya daughters, especially because the two young women were born and partly raised outside Japan.

Mom told me that, for two excruciatingly long days, Grandpa thought things over. He had to admit that his wife and daughters made some excellent points. As he mulled things over, he realized if Aunt June and Mom should fail to get married, then he would need to support them throughout his life. And what would happen to them after he died? Already, he was struggling, doing odd jobs to earn a living. How much longer could he continue to support a family of four? And although he hated to admit it, even to himself, he had to acknowledge that Mom stood a much better chance of happiness in Hawaii than in Japan, and that the children she would bear, his grandchildren, might even prosper there, because America was still the land of opportunity. In addition, Dad had been raised in Japan and was polite and pleasant enough. Another reason came to mind too. Grandpa hoped that, with Mom's return to Hawaii, she could pursue trying to get back the property taken from him after the bombing of Pearl Harbor. At the very least, she would certainly stand a much better chance in Honolulu than he would in Japan, appealing to the federal authorities to right a terrible injustice. Given all that, Grandpa sent word of his approval of the marriage to the nakodo, who then relayed the message to Dad's relatives in Ohtake.

The next day, Dad took Mom on a ferry to Miyajima, a small island just off the coast of Hiroshima. There, in the early evening, with the waning sunlight striking the giant red torii, or "floating" gate, in the shallow waters just off the coast, he proposed and Mom accepted.

The plan was for Dad to return to Hawaii, with Mom following several months later. Dad would set up the small house he lived in, located on the same property as the home of his oldest brother and his family. Back in Honolulu, Dad and his brother worked long days painting the two-bedroom house, replacing the corrugated-aluminum ceiling with a tar-and-gravel roof, and sanding and polishing the wooden floors. With no small amount of elbow grease, working for weeks well into the late hours of night, they transformed a bachelor's ramshackle house into a small home fit for starting a family.

When Mom arrived back in Hawaii, though, she was abruptly detained by the immigration officials. Much to her abject horror, she learned she had somehow been stripped of her U.S. citizenship. In stunned silence, she listened as an immigration official explained that she had unwittingly renounced her citizenship by moving to an enemy country (Japan) during the war. To make matters worse, the Japanese government later declared her a non-citizen as well, even though she was the child of Japanese nationals. The terrifying reality of the situation was that Mom had become a stateless person—literally a woman without a country.

For days, she was held at a detention center on Sand Island, in Honolulu Harbor, while the authorities tried to sort out what to do with her. Ironically, Sand Island was where Grandpa had been imprisoned more than a decade before. Mom was incredulous that history was repeating itself, in a variation of a theme that had earlier brought her family so much grief and hardship.

During the time she was held on Sand Island, Dad visited Mom every day, pleading with her to register as a resident alien. Then, later, she could apply for U.S. citizenship based on their marriage. But Mom would have none of it. She wanted to reclaim her citizenship, which she felt had been unfairly stripped, and she wanted to do so based on the merits of her own case. "I did not renounce my citizenship," she told me adamantly, her face flush with indignation. "And how dare the government say I did?"

As Mom's case dragged on, Dad's brothers and sisters took turns accompanying him on his visits to Sand Island, trying to convince Mom to give up her ostensibly quixotic battle. They were all worried about her because she was so young, still a teenager really, and appeared so delicate. Also, they were afraid for her after hearing that many of the Sand Island detainees had lice, tuberculosis, and other communicable diseases. Eventually, even Dad's mother went to visit Mom in hopes of convincing her to change her mind. What my paternal grandmother must have thought! In all likelihood, she expected her future daughter-in-law from Japan to be a dutiful, docile young lady. And yet there was Mom, waging a headstrong battle against the U.S. government over her citizenship.

It must've been so tempting for Mom to compromise her principles. After all, her future husband was waiting for her and she was eager to begin her new life back in Honolulu. But she resisted the easy path and stood her ground. How could the U.S. government, she asked, claim she had forsaken her citizenship? She was just seven years old at the time she boarded the MS Gripsholm, and she didn't have a choice in the matter. After all, what was she to do, remain in Arkansas while the rest of her family sailed to Japan? And then there was the matter of how Mom, a U.S. citizen by birth, was essentially deported to a foreign country. The uncomfortable truth was this: The incarceration of ethnic Japanese without due process, followed by the deportation of many of those individuals to Japan during the war, was likely an ugly chapter the federal government wanted closed for good. So, perhaps to avoid the exposure of such a shameful (and, really, quite un-American) act committed by the

United States, the government did eventually concede that, because Mom was a minor at the time, she had not in actuality renounced her U.S. citizenship.

It was a sweet victory. Following Mom's release from Sand Island, she and Dad married in a small civil service in Honolulu. A few years later, Aunt June applied for and was granted a reinstatement of her U.S. citizenship, because she too had been a minor during the war. As Aunt June made plans to repatriate to Hawaii, the U.S. government may even have felt somewhat guilty for the deportation that had sent the Minatoyas and others like them to Japan, because she received a loan for the one-hundred fifty dollars she needed to purchase a ticket aboard an American President Lines ship for passage back to Hawaii. Aunt June made sure to pay back every cent of that debt, although at times she must have been tempted to tell the U.S. immigration officials they could find the payment for her loan just outside of Aala Park, buried in the backyard of the Minatoya family's former home. There, they could find compensation in the form of an array of expensive jewelry—worth exceedingly more than their one-hundred fifty dollars—all stashed in an assortment of tin cans.

CHAPTER NINE

Both my parents spent a large chunk of their childhoods in Japan. For me, though, the country was a mysterious place, a land where countless generations of my ancestors lived, and yet I'd only seen it in movies and on TV. Growing up in Honolulu, I thought of Japan as distant and foreign. At the same time, there was something indescribably familiar about the land of the rising sun, even though I'd yet to set foot on its soil.

A huge part of that familiarity came from the many Japanese fables Mom read to me as a young child. I didn't learn about the Golden Rule, the value of perseverance and hard work, and the dangers of overweening pride from stories like "The Tortoise and the Hare," "The Fox and the Crow," and other Aesop's Fables. Instead, I learned those important life lessons from the Japanese counterparts of those Western stories, tales like "Momotaro" ("The Peach Boy") and "Shita-kiri Suzume" ("The Tongue-Cut Sparrow"). Some of my earliest memories are of Mom reading those fables to me after lunch, right before my nap. A hyperactive, moody child, I'd bargain with her and agree to sleep for at least an hour if she would read me a story. And as I lay on the living-room sofa, listening to her gentle, soothing voice, I'd stare at the large silk tapestry that hung on the wall above. In the foreground of that tapestry stood the famous Kintai Bridge, with its five elegant arches. In the center arch were three women dressed in resplendent kimonos, holding paper umbrellas to shield themselves from the bright sunshine. In the background stretched a broad mountain, on its summit Iwakuni Castle: a three-story tiered structure, with each level marked by dormer gables and roof corners that turned slightly upward in a graceful curve.

Mom often pointed to the serene, pastoral scene and told me, "Grandpa gave me that tapestry when I left Japan to set sail for Hawaii. He told me, 'Do not ever forget where you came from.'" And she always said that one day she'd take me to Japan to see the Kintai Bridge for myself and finally meet my grandparents.

Unfortunately, we didn't make that trip soon enough. When Grandma was stricken with stomach cancer in 1970, Mom and Aunt June flew to Japan to be with her throughout her final weeks. During that time, they also reconnected with their many aunts, uncles, and cousins. "It had been such a long time since we'd last seen our family," Mom recalled. "I couldn't believe how much things had changed, and how little they hadn't. It was the oddest thing, like time had accelerated yet also remained frozen." What had changed wasn't only how much older everyone was—a few childhood cousins had become grandparents—it was also how modernized Japan had become. Gone were the outhouses, replaced by flush toilets, while kitchens now boasted modern electrical appliances. Among the things that hadn't changed, though, was Grandpa's attitude toward America. As he aged, his bitterness remained an angry presence in his life, alienating neighbors and relatives.

After Grandma died, Grandpa's mental health deteriorated at a frightening pace. He was at a total loss without her and seemed to have relinquished all purpose in life. Then, late one night, Aunt June got a call from a relative in Japan saying Grandpa had passed away suddenly from a heart attack. This was in the early spring of 1975, when I was a junior in high school. Coincidentally, our spring break was just about to start, so Dad applied for permission to extend my vacation by a few days. With the approval of the vice principal at my school, Mom, Dad, Aunt June, and I all made the trip to attend Grandpa's funeral services.

For the first leg of our journey, we flew from Honolulu to Tokyo and stayed overnight at a hotel in the Ginza area. This time it was Dad who couldn't believe how modern Japan had become in his absence. As we walked around the city looking for a place to have dinner, he was amazed by the constant flow of cars, the glowing neon lights, and the throngs of people rushing about. "I feel like I'm Rip Van Winkle just waking up to a new Japan," he exclaimed.

The next morning, we caught a cab to Tokyo Station and bought tickets for the bullet train to Iwakuni. As I waited on the main floor for Mom and Aunt June to buy bento lunches to take with us on the ride, I watched Dad strike up a conversation with a construction worker who was having a snack while on his break. I couldn't quite make out exactly what they were talking about, something regarding a new building going up near the station. I'd heard my father speak Japanese before, of course, but never quite like this. The language sounded so rough to my ears, and I realized it was because I'd never heard Dad speak Japanese in such a colloquial manner, using so much slang. Just then, Mom and Aunt June returned, so I called out in English, "Dad, we gotta go to the platform. Our train will be here soon."

The man to whom Dad was speaking was so startled that he dropped the riceball he was eating as he watched Dad pick up his bag and rush toward me. Apparently, the man had mistaken Dad for a Japanese retiree with ample free time to talk to strangers, rather than a tourist from the United States with an American teenaged son. It was the first time I realized just how Japanese my father was, even after all his years living in Hawaii.

On the bullet train, we stored our luggage and kicked back in the comfortable, roomy seats. Dad began reading some Japanese newspapers he'd picked up, and I played Solitaire with a deck of Western cards I had brought with me. As the train sped south and the Japanese countryside unfolded, I couldn't help but watch Mom as she stared out the window, lost in her thoughts. She could have been thinking of a million things. Of course, she must've been weighed down by grief, but did she also regret not having seen Grandpa before he died? Or was it maybe a larger guilt, for leaving Iwakuni after the war to pursue a new life in Hawaii? She also could've been wondering how her life might have turned out had she stayed in Japan. Would she have gotten married, and to what kind of man? Or maybe her thoughts were more mundane. Mom may simply have been thinking about how fast the bullet train was racing southward along Honshu, just one more sign of how Japan had recovered from the war and was now a fully industrialized country.

Around noon, a woman with a rolling cart came down the aisle offering various treats and either hot or cold ocha. We all ordered hot ocha to have with our bento lunches, which were a delicious mix of sushi, tempura, and broiled eel. As we ate, Mom told me, "Grandma was such an excellent cook. She made the best tempura, the batter so light and crunchy. And Grandpa was such an intelligent man, with a brilliant mind. Did you know he learned English by himself from reading the daily newspaper?"

"Wow, I had no idea."

"In fact, he could negotiate complex contracts with haole businessmen in English. I wish you could have known him. But we never had the money to take this trip before, and now it's too late."

I didn't know what to say, so I muttered, "Shikata ga nai."

· · · · ·

When we arrived at the Iwakuni train station, we were greeted by Isamu, a cousin of Mom's with whom we'd be staying. He offered his condolences for Grandpa's passing, and Mom and Aunt June thanked him for helping to take care of their father after Grandma had died.

We all squeezed into Isamu's Toyota, with Dad in the front passenger seat and me in the back, sitting between Mom and Aunt June. As Isamu drove us to his home, we passed alongside the Kintai Bridge, silently spanning the Nishiki River in the waning late-afternoon sun. Mom stared out her window and Aunt June leaned across me to see the breathtaking structure, the two sisters soaking in the sight. I, myself, was surprised at how much longer and more elegant the five arches were. In Mom's tapestry, the artist had foreshortened the bridge horizontally to make it fit a certain perspective, and that manipulation didn't do justice to the graceful, flowing arches. I was also surprised by the massive stone pedestals supporting the long wooden arches.

"Do you remember when Typhoon Kijia washed out the bridge?" Mom asked.

"That was terrible," Isamu replied, as he navigated the narrow streets of the town center. "I heard part of the problem was that, during the occupation after the war, the U.S. Marines took away a lot of gravel from around the foundation, weakening it. Apparently, they needed the material for a runway they were building."

"How did people get from one side of the river to the other?" I asked.

Everyone was quiet for a while, trying to remember post-war life in Iwakuni. "Well, there was another bridge for cars," Aunt June said, "but they also built a temporary, rickety wooden bridge for pedestrians. Remember that?" she asked Mom.

"Yes, of course," Mom said. "I was so afraid whenever I had to cross that bridge. I held onto the railing for dear life."

"Not only the railing," Aunt June added. "You would also grab my hand so tightly I sometimes thought you'd pull it off." The two sisters laughed heartily, joined by their cousin.

When we arrived at Isamu's house, we were greeted by his wife, Sachiko, and their teenage daughter, Akiko. "I've prepared a hot bath for you," Sachiko told us, as Aunt June, Mom, Dad, and I entered the warm, cozy home.

•　　•　　•　　•　　•

The next day, most of Grandpa's family—his sister and her family, and his brother and his family—arrived at Isamu's home to help with the funeral arrangements. Amid the growing buzz of activity, as everyone helped plan the service, selecting the caterer, running errands, and making calls, it was decided that Dad and I should take a day trip to Hiroshima to catch up with some of his distant relatives there. In particular, Dad was eager to see his cousin Takeko, with whom he'd grown up during the childhood years when he was sent from Hawaii to live in Japan.

To get to her home, Dad and I took a short train ride to Hiroshima, and then caught a taxi to the Ohtake neighborhood. As we entered that area, Dad looked totally perplexed. "Are you sure this is Ohtake?" he asked the taxi driver.

"Yes, but what is the address of your cousin's home?" the driver replied.

"I don't have the address," Dad said, "but she lives a couple blocks from the high school."

As we drove around the neighborhood of one- and two-story wooden homes, trying to find the right house, I learned it wasn't just that Dad didn't have Takeko's address; he also didn't have her phone number, so we couldn't call her for directions. What's worse, Dad also said she wasn't even expecting our visit. "You mean we're just going to pop into her home, as if we're a neighbor?" I asked, incredulously. "Why didn't you let her know?"

"It'll be fine," Dad said, annoyed with my question. "She and I are very close."

This was just one of the many ways my parents differed from each other. Mom would never have imagined dropping in on a relative in Japan unannounced. She'd have wired or called Takeko in advance to let her know of our upcoming visit. For Mom, visiting relatives in Hawaii unannounced was one thing; doing the same with a cousin she hadn't seen in decades was unimaginable. In a way, I was glad she wasn't with us, because she and Dad surely would have argued over his questionable lapse of propriety.

Finally, Dad vaguely remembered a street we were on and told the cab driver to stop at a narrow alleyway. "This is it," he said, as he paid the driver. We exited the taxi, and right before it drove off I realized we'd forgotten a small package of omiyage Dad had brought. Thankfully, we were able to stop the driver in time. We got the package, and then headed down the alley.

"What omiyage did you bring?" I asked.

"I don't know," he replied. "Mom got it for me."

We arrived at Takeko's home, a small, one-story wooden structure raised a couple feet off its foundation. "Takeko-chan," Dad called in Japanese. "Anyone home?"

We heard footsteps in the house before the front door swung open, revealing an elderly woman, slightly stooped, with short gray hair. Almost instantaneously, her expression changed from curiosity to shock to utter joy.

"Oh my, it's really you," she exclaimed. "After all these years!"

Takeko waved us into her home, leading us to a living room decorated with beautiful silk scrolls, wooden carvings, and rows of ningyo (miniature lifelike Japanese dolls). After a few minutes of conversation, Takeko excused herself to make a quick phone call. She returned with freshly brewed ocha and an assortment of rice crackers.

Takeko and Dad were soon immersed in conversation, talking about various relatives and friends in the neighborhood, many of whom had since passed on. At times, I had trouble following their conversation. It wasn't just that they were speaking only in Japanese; I also wasn't familiar with the Hiroshima dialect and its informal slang. Several times they used the word hibakusha, which I'd never heard before, but before I could ask the meaning the conversation had moved on to something else.

Around noon we were interrupted by someone calling "tadaima" before quickly entering the house. It was Fumiko, Takeko's daughter, arriving with two large bags, one of which contained an assortment of prepared food.

"I hope you like Japanese cuisine," Takeko told me, half apologetically.

"Oh yes, very much so," I said.

"Don't worry about him," Dad added. "He'll eat anything Japanese. He even loves natto."

Takeko smiled and laughed, amazed someone from America could actually tolerate, let alone like, the pungent fermented soybeans. "Even my own grandchildren won't eat natto," she said, as she and Fumiko began unpacking the takeout food onto beautiful ceramic serving dishes. It was a veritable feast—nigiri sushi, grilled mackerel, broiled eggplant with miso sauce, steamed fishcake—quickly materializing almost from nowhere.

After lunch, Takeko told me, "I want to show you what your great, great grandparents looked like." I was more than curious as she rummaged through a closet, found what she was looking for, and then unfurled a scroll onto the coffee table in the living room. The scroll depicted a man sitting opposite a woman, with the young couple wearing matching black robes covering their yukatas. Between them was a round plate of mochi, or rice cakes, set on a small, low, square red table.

While I was busy soaking in the details of my ancestors, Takeko talked about the history of the scroll. I quickly got lost in the conversation, though, because the years she cited were all with respect to the eras of Japanese emperors. Dad had to explain that the scroll was painted around the end of the Edo period. "Wait, does that mean this scroll is from around the mid-1800s?" I asked. As Dad nodded his head, Takeko continued to explain how my great, great grandparents had moved to Hiroshima from a very rural area on the west coast of Japan, becoming successful farmers during the tail end of the Tokugawa Shogunate's rule.

The scroll was beautifully rendered, but the faces of my great, great grandparents weren't painted with very much detail. I'd hoped to see what they looked like in real life. As Takeko rolled the scroll up and inserted it back into a rectangular wooden box, I thanked her for showing it to me and asked if she might also have photos of those ancestors. Dad laughed. "I don't think cameras were invented yet when this scroll was painted."

To my embarrassment, it hadn't even occurred to me just how old the scroll really was. Not only was it painted before the invention of modern photography; it might also have been rendered before the U.S. Civil War had ended. And it might even have preceded the year Commodore Perry sailed into Tokyo Bay and forced Japan to end its strict isolationist policy. After Japan had opened itself to the outside world, shiploads of Japanese— including my grandparents—emigrated to Hawaii in the late 1800s and early 1900s.

•   •   •   •   •

Later that afternoon, after saying goodbye to Takeko, Dad and I walked a few blocks and then up a long, steep flight of stairs to visit the Shinto shrine where his grandparents' ashes were interred. We prayed for a few minutes to pay our respects, and then we took a taxi to the Hiroshima Peace Memorial Park, where we walked the grounds of that somber memorial to see the A-Bomb Dome. What was once a large, impressive three-story exhibition hall with an elegant copper domed roof was now a shattered shell of concrete, brick, and twisted exposed metal. We also visited the Memorial Cenotaph, a concrete monument in the shape of an upside-down "U" meant to protect the souls of those who perished there, and we walked through a long museum containing various artifacts, like a wristwatch forever stopped at the time of the blast and myriad graphic photographs showing not only the flattened city but also the radiation effects suffered by the unfortunate victims. There were photos of people with patterns from their kimonos seared into their skin, with their hair falling out and their skin sloughing off.

On the train ride back to Iwakuni, I asked Dad what hibakusha meant, and he explained it was a word used to describe those who had survived the atomic bomb. Fragments of his conversation with Takeko reentered my mind, and then things began to make sense. "So, did Takeko's sister die in the blast"? I asked.

"Yes, Mieko-chan died," Dad replied. "She was at school when the bomb exploded. Takeko was supposed to be at school too, but she was sick that day."

It then dawned on me that I'd never asked Dad an important question about his boyhood: "When you were in Hawaii and heard that the U.S. had bombed Hiroshima, how were you able to find out which of your relatives survived?"

Dad looked at me, and I could tell he was struggling to remember. "It was so long ago," he said. "We were so poor; we didn't have phones, and sending a telegram was much too expensive. Also, the mail was so unreliable. I don't think I found out that Takeko's sister had died until much later, well after the war had ended."

As Dad continued to talk, those tucked-away memories slowly unfolded. "We used to check the Hawaii newspapers to learn whenever a ship from Japan would be arriving in Honolulu. Then we'd go down to the harbor, wait for the passengers, and try to find whoever was from the Hiroshima area. And if we found folks from the Ohtake neighborhood, they would probably know something about my family. So, little by little, over months, we were able to piece together who had died and who survived."

"I can't imagine what that must have been like," I told Dad.

"I know," he laughed. "You get so impatient when the newspaper doesn't have all the baseball scores for yesterday's games."

•　　•　　•　　•　　•

Although I'd attended a few Buddhist funerals in Honolulu, I was unprepared for Grandpa's service. In Hawaii, Buddhist priests might chant in Japanese for a few minutes, but they would then conduct the rest of the service, which typically includes a homily, in both Japanese and English. A family member or friend might also give a short tribute to honor the deceased.

The chanting at Grandpa's funeral lasted for at least half an hour, with everyone sitting Japanese-style on tatami, our legs tucked under our butts on the mats. I understood only a word here or there of the chant, and after a while my legs began to stiffen. And yet, I didn't dare move, so still was the room. Eventually, my mind floated into a trance-like state, partly from my legs going numb but also from the smell of the incense and the priest's hypnotic chanting.

Just when I thought I might nod off, the chanting stopped, and the priest rose to address us. Several of the younger people shifted their bodies to sit cross-legged, so I did the same. It amazed me that Mom and Dad could continue sitting in the traditional Japanese style.

The priest talked about how Grandpa would be reborn into a new existence and how we shouldn't grieve much, because he would always be with us. "Don't worry about him," the priest said. "He will be fine. In fact, he will be watching over you to protect you." I listened closely to the priest, trying to follow what he said, but my emotions were somewhat detached; I'd never had the chance to meet my maternal grandfather, so I knew him only from how Mom and Aunt June spoke about him. From the corner of my eye, I watched the two sisters and could see they found some comfort in the priest's thoughtful words, which made me grateful we'd all made the trip.

After the service concluded, we retired to a large reception area at the rear of the temple. The room contained a half-dozen long, low tables set with an assortment of food displayed in beautiful lacquered wooden boxes and porcelain dishes neatly arranged. Dad, Mom, Aunt June, and I sat next to Grandpa's brother's family.

"It's too bad you never got to meet your grandfather. He was a very interesting, accomplished man," Mom's uncle told me.

"Yes," I replied, "I heard he taught himself English."

"There's an interesting story about that," my great-uncle said. He paused, took a gulp of ocha, and continued. "Late one night during the war your grandfather was awakened by someone pounding on his gate door. It was the local police. They wanted his help to interrogate two U.S. servicemen. The men had been captured after their plane was shot down in the hills outside Iwakuni. You see, at the time, our town was small enough that people knew your grandfather spoke English fluently, and the police needed his help to find out if any other Americans had survived the crash. The interrogation went on for hours, while your grandmother was at home frantic with worry. Finally, the next afternoon, your grandfather returned, much to everyone's relief. But here's the really interesting thing: Your grandfather refused to speak English ever again."

"Did he ever talk about what happened that night?" I asked.

"Not really, but this was just a week or so before the U.S. dropped the atomic bomb on Hiroshima, so I think the plane was doing some kind of reconnaissance work, trying to figure out exactly where to drop the bomb."

I couldn't believe what I'd just heard. Only the day before, Dad and I were at the Hiroshima Peace Memorial and saw the devastation of that nuclear weapon. It was mind-boggling to think Grandpa had been involved in the interrogation of those captured servicemen.

After we finished eating and were saying our goodbyes, my great-uncle pulled me aside. "There's something else I wanted to tell you," he said, speaking almost in whispers. "Years after the war ended, your grandfather did tell me something about those U.S. servicemen. Apparently, during a break in the interrogation, one of them secretly passed him a piece of torn toilet paper. Your grandfather took the paper and stuffed it into his pocket. Only later did he look at it. That American had written someone's name and an address in Massachusetts. He wanted your grandfather to contact his family to let them know he was alive but had been captured."

"Did Grandpa contact them?" I asked.

"No, he didn't dare. You have to understand—this was during war. As soon as your grandfather saw what that American had written, he threw away the paper. He didn't want to get in any trouble."

A thought then crossed my mind, and I wasn't sure how to ask my great-uncle about it. I couldn't think of the Japanese word for torture, so I asked, "Do you know if the servicemen were harmed during the interrogation?"

My great-uncle looked at me without saying anything, and I could see my question slowly sinking in. "I really have no idea," he finally said, "but your grandfather never mentioned anything of the sort."

A small wave of embarrassment hit me as I realized I might've offended my great-uncle by asking what may have been an impertinent question. I tried to explain myself in my flailing Japanese: "I'm sorry to have asked, it's just that you said earlier Grandpa never spoke English again after that night, so I thought he might have seen things he wanted to forget."

"Oh, I didn't get to finish the story," my great-uncle said, as we exited the temple's reception room. "You see, those Americans were later transferred to a military prison in Hiroshima, probably for further questioning by the kempeitai, the military intelligence. But then the atomic bomb was dropped just a few days later, and they all died. Your grandfather felt so guilty that he was unable to contact the U.S. serviceman's family, to let them know what had happened to him, and I think that's why he stopped speaking English."

⋅　⋅　⋅　⋅　⋅

On the flight back to Honolulu I asked Aunt June about Grandpa, what his feelings might've been regarding the United States. She looked at me, not sure why I was asking. I explained I was curious, because Grandpa had lost everything during World War II and then had to restart his life in Japan, which couldn't have been easy. I imagined that, when he immigrated to Hawaii, he was full of hope for a better life, only to have that optimism crushed. Also, because Grandpa grew up in feudal Japan, the U.S. principles of democracy might've had some attraction to him. For years, he lived the American dream, building up a business from scratch through hard work and sheer determination, only to have all of that stripped from him, merely because of his race. I wanted to know how Grandpa felt about what had happened to him. Did he hate the U.S. for turning its back on its own principles during the war? Or, perhaps, even after all that happened, did Grandpa still believe in America and its shining promise as the land of opportunity?

Aunt June paused a while before answering, her mind deep in thought. Finally, she said, "Your grandfather was a very complicated man. I really don't know how he felt about the U.S. after he returned to Japan." Aunt June then returned to the Time magazine she'd been reading, prompting me to retrieve my school textbook to study. But my mind kept drifting back to the conversation I'd had with my great-uncle. How ironic that Grandpa, who himself was interrogated for months after the Pearl Harbor bombing, would find himself having to help question those U.S. servicemen after their plane was shot down.

I was half asleep on the flight when Aunt June suddenly started talking about Grandpa again. She told me that, when he was a young boy growing up in Japan, he once went to the train station just to watch as the train carrying Emperor Meiji, the grandfather of Hirohito, passed through the town. People had to lower their gaze as the steam train approached—no one was allowed to actually look at the train—because, at that time, everyone truly believed the Emperor was divine. Many decades later, as President Richard Nixon's administration began to unravel, Grandpa followed the Watergate hearings intently from across an ocean. He was intrigued by the U.S. government's system of checks and balances, and he was also incredulous that a Japanese American—Senator Daniel Inouye from Hawaii—could play such a major role in the proceedings. When Nixon finally resigned, Grandpa wrote to Aunt June, telling her half in awe and half in disbelief, "It's really true in America. No man, not even the President, is above the law!"

I asked, "So, Grandpa still admired the U.S., even after everything that happened to him?"

"Yes, I guess you could say that. On some level, I think Grandpa was always fascinated with America. He certainly respected it, especially for its economic might and vast resources."

CHAPTER TEN

The trip to Japan was a milestone in Mom's life. Just before her fortieth birthday she had essentially become an orphan. Although she enjoyed being in Iwakuni, which allowed her to reconnect with her relatives there, she must have felt a great sense of loss—of not just her father but also the old culture and traditions of our ancestors that, even in Japan, were slowly giving way to a modern society.

For me, the trip marked the end of my carefree childhood. I was about to enter my senior year in high school, and from that time forward an invisible barrier slowly emerged between my parents and me. It was an obstacle we would find difficult to overcome as we increasingly began to talk at, instead of with, each other.

Up until that time, I'd led an easy, untroubled life, growing up in Honolulu. Although my parents may have struggled financially—Dad worked at his brother's bakery and Mom was a part-time seamstress—I never felt disadvantaged; there was always money for anything important. When my permanent teeth emerged and crowded my mouth, pushing my lateral incisors behind my front teeth, my parents somehow found the money for the braces I needed so I'd eventually be able to smile without being self-conscious. And from my first day in kindergarten, there were always ample funds for anything related to school: notebooks, book bags, three-ring folders, slide rules, protractors, and class excursions.

Fortunately, for me, schoolwork always came easily, especially in math and science. From elementary school on, I could race effortlessly through my homework and assigned projects, leaving me with virtually limitless free time to hang out with the other neighborhood kids. We caught tadpoles and fish in the stream that cut behind our backyards and sped our bikes over the hilly, winding streets of our quiet neighborhood.

Then, in junior high, I became obsessed with playing the oboe.

Ironically, when I first joined the school band, I didn't even know what an oboe was and insisted on playing the trumpet, because it seemed like all the cool guys chose brass instruments. But after struggling on the trumpet for almost a year, the band director diplomatically, yet rather firmly, encouraged a switch to a woodwind instrument, probably because I was small and slight for my age. At first, I was frustrated with the oboe's tiny double reed, which is so fragile—and expensive. Even being extremely careful, I frequently chipped and ruined a reed. At well more than a dollar a piece, the expense of continually having to buy new reeds cost my parents a small fortune. To make matters worse, I wasn't even sure what an oboe was supposed to sound like. I practiced after school, but I was only able to honk out angry sounds rather than anything resembling music.

Then, my band director arranged for me to take a private lesson with Mr. Yoshimura, an oboist with the Honolulu Symphony Orchestra. At the start of the lesson, Mr. Yoshimura listened to me for a few minutes, and then said I needed to form a softer cushion with my lips around the reed. He also said I had to open the back of my mouth, as if I had a tennis ball lodged there, in order to achieve a rounder, fuller sound. To demonstrate what he meant, he played a short, lyrical passage. As soon as I heard him, I was immediately captivated by his rich, warm, fluid tone. There was such complexity in the sound he produced. In a single short phrase, Mr. Yoshimura was able to capture an astonishing range of color, different hues I never would have thought possible from a single instrument.

After that lesson, I was hooked. Every day after school I practiced in the band room, and my closest friends became the other kids who'd been similarly bitten by the music bug. The neighborhood friends with whom I'd grown up began to feel slighted as I became a veritable "band geek," more interested in practicing than in hanging out.

Soon enough, the highlight of my week became the Boston Pops concerts the local PBS station regularly broadcast on TV. And I saved every cent from my allowance to buy vinyl albums of Pierre Pierlot, Leon Goossens, Heinz Holliger, and other renowned oboists. I spent afternoons playing those recordings repeatedly, mesmerized by the oboe's plaintive tone, so pure and expressive, as it sang to me with an emotional power I'd never encountered before.

At the time, my junior high school had only three entry-level oboes for students to borrow. The instrument assigned to me was serviceable, but it was made of plastic and didn't have the full complement of keys; I had to use workaround fingerings to play certain difficult technical passages. Even so, when I entered music competitions and auditioned against kids who had their own expensive professional-model instruments, which were made of wood with a full set of keys, I placed at the top. These early successes encouraged me to practice even harder, and my playing soon became a huge source of pride, confidence, and self-esteem. When I was just a high-school freshman, I started learning major concertos in the oboe repertoire, works by Haydn, Mozart, Saint-Saens, Strauss, Poulenc, and Vaughan-Williams. These are quintessential pieces all professional oboists must have "under their fingers," and I was learning them as a teenager.

All along, though, I knew my parents could never afford to buy me a top-of-the-line Loree oboe. That type of professional instrument, which at the time cost around one thousand dollars, might as well have cost one million dollars as far as my parents' finances were concerned. Fortunately, before my sophomore year, I auditioned for the Honolulu Youth Symphony, was accepted, and was loaned a Loree oboe from the orchestra. That professional wooden instrument was a huge step up from the plastic oboe I'd been using, and my tone matured almost overnight, becoming much warmer and more resonant, with subtle overtone shadings. I also started to make my own reeds, so I could really begin to hone my sound to exactly what I wanted. And when I learned vibrato and developed a wider dynamic range, I found I could communicate through music, expressing myself in ways I couldn't always articulate in words. On certain days, I almost felt like I was singing through my instrument instead of playing on it.

Toward the end of my junior year in high school, Mr. Yoshimura paused in the middle of a lesson and said we needed to talk. "I've been teaching oboe students for almost thirty years," he told me, "so I don't say this lightly: You have the talent to make it professionally." Furthermore, Mr. Yoshimura said he felt confident I could not only get into a top music school like Juilliard, Eastman, or Oberlin, but also receive a scholarship.

I was speechless, even though deep down inside I suppose I already knew I was good enough to pursue music as a career. But to hear Mr. Yoshimura say those words out loud confirmed those nascent feelings. I deeply trusted and respected him, and I knew he wasn't the type of person who would give any student false hope.

After that talk, Mr. Yoshimura and I began strategizing which numbers to prepare for an audition tape. He recommended selecting pieces from different periods that would highlight a variety of musical styles and techniques. We settled on works by Marcello, Mozart, Strauss, and Bozza, and I practiced several hours every day, including the weekends, to perfect those pieces. The Strauss concerto, in particular, contains many long tricky passages that require rote learning, countless repetitions before muscle memory takes over. Soon enough, I found myself dreaming about that concerto, and I'd often wake up with one of its melodies swirling in my head.

Throughout this time I knew my parents wouldn't be able, financially, to send me to a mainland college. In fact, they could barely afford the resident tuition at the University of Hawaii. But my plan was to record the audition tape and send it to my dream schools. If I was fortunate enough to receive a full scholarship at any of them, I'd go there. I'd also apply to the University of Hawaii as my backup school.

When I told my parents about my plans one Sunday afternoon, though, they had a meltdown. "You can't be serious," Mom said. To her, the only acceptable profession for me was one of four: doctor, dentist, lawyer, or engineer. Of course, I had suspected they'd disapprove of my plans, but I had optimistically hoped that, with time, I could slowly change their minds. I was surprised—shocked, really—by the vehemence of their objections, especially Mom's. "We can't have you throwing your life away like that," she declared.

I countered my parents with typical teenage rebellion. I told them it was my life to waste if I wanted to and, as my parents, they should support me in pursuing my dream instead of trying to derail it. They were flabbergasted. "How dare you talk to us like that," Mom said, her voice rising in anger. "We're your parents. Show some respect!"

That heated battle ended in a stalemate, with the three of us retreating to separate corners of the house. Mom went to her sewing room; Dad did some gardening in the yard; and I played the oboe in my bedroom. As I practiced those tough passages in the Strauss concerto, I disregarded the piece's dynamic markings and played everything as loudly as I could, banging out the music like I was playing the tympani. I wanted to ensure my parents heard every note of anger in my playing. I guess I was waiting for them to eventually barge into my room and tell me to knock it off, which would have precipitated round two of our battle. Instead, they ignored me. Soon, exhausted from blowing my lungs out, I decided to take the bus to the main library in town, a historic, stately building situated adjacent to Iolani Palace.

From my earliest days in school, libraries were always my sanctuary, the place outside my home where I felt safest. I took such comfort being among countless books, each one promising an escape to an exciting world. Sometimes I went to the library just to walk among the endless rows of tomes, occasionally stopping to pull out a random book that piqued my interest. And it wasn't just the subject matter that caught my attention; I was also fascinated by the ancillary information: where and when was the book published, what was the author's background, to whom was the book dedicated, who qualified for a mention in the acknowledgments? All that information helped transport me to a different, wondrous world, a place far from my life in Honolulu.

That day, after the bruising fight with my parents, I found myself on the second floor of the library, in the music section. There, I happened to come across the complete score to Stravinsky's "Rite of Spring." This landmark masterpiece was years ahead of its time, with the premiere in Paris said to have caused a near riot, the music and accompanying ballet apparently too avant-garde for early twentieth-century ears. As I studied the score, hearing the music in my head, trying to make sense of the wild dissonances, bizarre meters, and novel rhythms, I increasingly longed to be a part of this arcane world. I was so entranced that, had a librarian not come to warn me they'd be closing shortly, I might have stayed well into the next day.

Back at home, over dinner, Mom, Dad, and I continued our battle, this time in a less heated, almost emotionless fashion. It was clear to me they'd talked while I was at the library and, in my absence, agreed on how they'd proceed—by mounting a united front. Mom's voice was soft and cool, but absolute in its firmness. "If you were having trouble in school," she said, "we would be okay with you becoming a musician. But you have other options. You could be so successful in lots of other areas."

"But those aren't areas I'm interested in," I said. "This is the rest of my life we're talking about, and I don't want to be stuck in a boring job." I looked at Dad, my eyes pleading for some assistance.

"Your mother's right," he said. "Do you know how tough it is to make it as a professional musician? We don't want you starving out there."

I resisted telling them about Mr. Yoshimura's encouragement, afraid they'd take things out on him for swaying me in a direction of which they disproved. Instead, I responded by mentioning all the music awards I'd won, including becoming the first-chair oboist with the Honolulu Youth Symphony when I was just a sophomore. "Why don't you have more faith in me?" I asked.

Mom's patience began to fray, but she remained calm and switched to a different offensive tack. "Have you ever really looked at the New York Philharmonic? Or the Philadelphia Orchestra? Or any major U.S. symphony? How many of those musicians do you think are Japanese American? You watch the Boston Pops all the time on TV. Do you see any Oriental musicians?"

I was taken aback by what she said. I guess I'd never noticed that about the Boston Pops. And yet, to me, that was hardly the point. There was so much I wanted to say, but Mom's tolerance for further debate had dwindled rapidly and her next words made it clear that, as far as she was concerned, the discussion was over. "This is what your father and I have decided. Yes, you're free to pursue whatever you want in college. But if you choose music, then we can't help you financially. You'll be on your own."

·　·　·　·　·

For the next several weeks I brooded. Part of me felt defiant and wanted to stick it to my parents and flagrantly disobey them. And yet, I was terrified of the prospect of making it without their help. I wasn't yet eighteen. I had never been to the mainland. If I didn't have the necessary talent, then what would I do? How would I make a living if I couldn't hack it as a musician? I could touch type around sixty words per minute and knew the Dewey Decimal system inside out from my summer jobs at the neighborhood library, but how far would those skills take me in the real working world?

As my anxieties mounted, each fear feeding the next, I caved. I met with my guidance counselor at school to review my academic record. I had a near perfect score on the math section of the SAT, as well as an unbroken string of "A's" in my math and science courses. In addition, I'd taken the highest levels of chemistry and physics and was excelling in AP calculus. Given all that, the counselor strongly recommended I study engineering.

Even as I gave up my dream of becoming a professional oboist, I still knew I wanted to study at a mainland college. It wasn't just that I wanted to experience the wider world, which I knew only from the movies and TV. I longed for some separation from my parents, especially after our latest bitter fight. And there was something else: I was becoming increasingly aware of my sexuality, that my attraction to men wasn't merely some adolescent phase. I foresaw another major battle with my parents when I eventually came out. I guess that's why, even though I wasn't even old enough to vote yet, I had the overwhelming desire to become financially independent as soon as I could. That way I could live life the way I felt I needed to.

Thanks to my guidance counselor, who steered me through the college application and financial-aid process, I received a full engineering scholarship to attend the University of Southern California in Los Angeles. The scholarship took care of my tuition, a student loan covered my room and board, and I could work part-time to have some spending money for incidental expenses. This way, I wouldn't have to depend on my parents for any financial help. I was ecstatic.

My excitement, though, did little to prepare me for my freshman year at USC. It was the first time I'd lived away from home, and I was terribly homesick. I longed for everything that was Hawaii—not just my family and my high-school friends, but the food, culture, and aloha spirit of the islands. Nevertheless, I was determined to plow through. Not long after classes started, I found work as a part-time lab assistant, conducting stress tests of different materials. Between schoolwork and those lab experiments, I was so busy I rarely had any free time, which was probably a good thing and prevented me from wallowing in my yearning for Hawaii.

I suppose I could have made an effort to continue playing the oboe, a couple hours here or a few minutes there. I might even have tried to make the time to join the university's orchestra. But once I'd performed my final concert with the Honolulu Youth Symphony, I said goodbye to the oboe. I wouldn't even consider continuing to play for fun as a hobby. I suppose this was all some misguided attempt to spite my parents—see what you forced me to do, wasting all those years of practice and lessons?

Thankfully, given how busy I was, the first three years at USC flew by. I excelled at schoolwork and earned enough cash in my part-time work to cover all my expenses. During the summers, I was fortunate enough to be selected for internships with General Electric and Martin Marietta. Those summer jobs paid me enough that I actually saved some money, all while burnishing my future resume with experience that would make me more desirable as a young engineer looking for a full-time job. Everything was going my way. Then, all of a sudden, in the middle of my senior year, doubt crippled me.

This happened during the time I began interviewing with different companies, not just GE and Martin Marietta, but Exxon, Bechtel, Fluor, Morrison-Knudsen, and others. Through those interviews I realized I just couldn't see myself doing engineering work for the rest of my life. I felt trapped, like I was being boxed into somebody else's life. In near panic, I called my parents for some advice—or at least for some reassurance.

"You're so close to graduating, why not just finish up?" Mom said. "Once you have your degree, nobody can ever take it away from you. You'll always have it."

"But what if I hate being an engineer?"

"Well, with a bachelor's degree," Mom said, "you can always go back to school and get your master's in something else."

Her reassuring words helped me push through the uncertainty. I finished up my senior year, graduating summa cum laude, and took a job with Armstrong Construction in downtown Los Angeles. I worked in the computer department, writing programs to analyze how different skyscraper designs would withstand an earthquake or heavy winds. At first, I enjoyed the job, particularly because I got along well with my boss and co-workers. We had a nice camaraderie and would go out for drinks at the end of the week. After the first few months, though, the daily grind of sitting in an air-conditioned room, running software models of different proposed buildings, began to wear me down.

We had one particular client, a major real-estate developer in Southern California who kept insisting we lower the cost of a steel skyscraper he was planning to build in San Diego. We repeatedly overhauled the design, investigating one alternative after another. We tried traditional tube concepts (using the twin towers of the World Trade Center in New York City as an inspiration) and diagonal-bracing frames (similar to the John Hancock Center in Chicago). We also looked at unconventional options, even exploring somewhat whacky solutions in one brainstorming session after another. I worked overtime through several weekends. Then, finally, we arrived at our "eureka" moment: a three-dimensional space frame with diagonal cross-bracing at various angles, with the lower floors seemingly pushing (and supporting) the higher floors upward. It was like a bamboo shoot, with each new growth propelling the main stalk higher and higher. The elegant structure would not only withstand large earthquakes but also be very cost efficient, requiring considerably less steel than conventional alternatives.

After the client approved our preliminary concept, we began developing and finetuning the design. This required additional weekends of overtime, but everyone on the team was stoked to be working on such an innovative solution, one that would push the state of the art in structural engineering. And yet, at every turn, the client continued to ask us to shave additional costs, until we'd cut every possible corner. Finally, when we were right at the margin of safety mandated by government code, we received another request for a further cost reduction. This led to a tense meeting where we tried to explain to the client that we'd gone as far as we could and that it would be dangerous to push the design any further. Ignoring our advice, the client's team kept asking whether we'd investigated this option or that alternative, the discussion going back and forth with no progress made. I could tell my boss was struggling to maintain his composure, even as his exasperation rose, until something gave in him. In a voice a couple levels higher in volume than his usual affable manner, he told the client, "Apparently, you don't understand what we've been saying. We've already squeezed as much blood from this turnip as we can."

83

There was a long pause as people in the room fidgeted, adjusting positions in our chairs while avoiding eye contact with one another. I, myself, was fearful for my boss, whom I liked and respected. Then the manager of the client's team got up, closed the leather folder he was scribbling in, and said, "Well then, if you've reached the extent of your capabilities, we'll just have to find another firm to help us." And with that, the meeting was over.

Back at our office, my boss assembled everyone who'd worked on the project and thanked us for all the tireless hours we'd spent. He was incredibly composed after the earlier meeting, betraying not even a hint of frustration or resentment, and he tried to get us excited about another project in the pipeline. After that pep talk, I followed my boss to the office kitchen, where we both refreshed our mugs of coffee.

"It really sucks that our space frame will never be built," I sighed.

My boss stood there, staring into his coffee. Finally, he looked at me and said, "Ethan, maybe I shouldn't be telling you this, because you're just out of college, but perhaps it's good if you learn this now. In our profession, people don't care a hoot about technical brilliance. They just want to know how much money you can save them." It was precisely at that moment when I realized I couldn't be doing what I was then doing for the rest of my life.

That night, sitting on the wooden barstool at the kitchen counter in my apartment, I thought about all the ways in which my life had gone off track. It was all too easy for me to blame my parents, but I knew the fault lay mainly with me. I lacked the courage and confidence to pursue my youthful ambitions. Whereas I'd been just a teenager when I let fear thwart my dreams, I was now a young adult who needed to take control of a life derailed. I knew that if I didn't do something soon to alter the momentum of my current trajectory, I would end up living someone else's life. My inertia would continue pushing me on the wrong path until it was too late to correct my course.

After much painful introspection, I gathered an assortment of colored pencils and a pad of legal-size paper so that I could begin charting the path for the rest of my life. Red was for my current situation, including an accounting of my meager financial resources. Green (my favorite color) was for what my desired destination looked like. And blue was for all the steps I needed to take to get from "A" to "B." I knew I needed to rekindle my earlier ambition of becoming a professional musician, but I had to plot a course for getting there. Soon, the blue items filled more than a page. To organize myself, I arranged those actions in roughly chronological order. Number one on that to-do list was simple enough: call my mentor and former oboe teacher in Honolulu.

Mr. Yoshimura was only too thrilled to hear that I would be playing again. He said he would talk with his friend Tom Janoski, the assistant principal oboist with the LA Philharmonic, and ask him to take me on as a student. Mr. Yoshimura also told me that a student of his had recently bought a new oboe and wanted to sell her old instrument. He said he'd send the oboe to me and, if I liked it, I could buy it from her.

When the oboe arrived, I immediately tried it with a soft reed that Mr. Yoshimura had thoughtfully sent along with the instrument. From the first note I played—a middle "A," the exact pitch used to tune an orchestra—I was transported back in time, my breath making its way from my lungs through my mouth and into the small double reed, the resulting vibrations amplifying into the oboe and resonating throughout my living room. A warm blanket of pleasure enveloped my body as the sound of that note reawakened something deep within me that had been hibernating, waiting for this very day to be summoned. I will never forget that moment—the way the afternoon sunlight was filtering through the window of my apartment, the faint murmur of a neighbor's TV, the smell of someone grilling hamburgers across the street. I literally had not even touched an oboe for more than four years and, all of a sudden, there I was, playing again. It was like being reunited with a cherished love. But the feeling was even more than that; it was as if I'd recovered the use of a limb I'd thought lost for good.

Over the next couple weeks, I rushed home from work, eager to play. At first, I could sustain my embouchure for only ten minutes or so before my facial muscles tired. But slowly, so slowly, I regained my stamina. For a while, my fingers were somewhat rusty. Soon enough, though, I found I could play all the difficult passages I'd spent my youth studying. That muscle memory surprised me and, before I knew it, I was eager to push myself by learning new, complex pieces.

My first few lessons with Mr. Janoski went well, and I could tell that both he and Mr. Yoshimura had studied with the same teacher—Ralph Gomberg, the legendary principal oboist with the Boston Symphony Orchestra—because the two men had the same style of playing and reed making. Fortunately, I'd kept all my reed-making tools and was able to start fashioning my own reeds again, almost as if I'd never stopped.

Eventually, I talked with Mr. Janoski about my goal of pursuing a career in music. He suggested I look into studying at USC, where he was on the faculty. Deep down inside, though, I still harbored nagging doubts about whether I could succeed as a professional oboist, so I hedged my bets. I applied to USC for a master's degree in music as a non-performance major. This would allow me to continue studying with Mr. Janoski, as well as take various orchestra and chamber-music classes. But I could also enroll in a number of other types of classes—in nonprofit administration, entrepreneurship in the arts, and bringing music into local communities—that would provide me with a different skillset if a performance career didn't pan out.

I was accepted into USC, and that fall I started my eighteen-month program. I was like an arrow launched: focused on a singular, well-defined goal. It didn't bother me that many of my fellow musicians were much younger than I, some yet to even have a job in the real world. It also didn't bother me that I had to continue working part-time at Armstrong Construction. Although USC had offered me a generous financial-aid package of grants and loans, I still needed to make enough money for food and rent.

During those eighteen months, I was utterly engrossed. If I wasn't in class, studying at the library, practicing, or working at Armstrong, I was usually eating, sleeping, or driving to get somewhere I needed to be. The concept of free time had little meaning for me. All my hours were occupied, even on the weekends. It hardly mattered, though, because every day was bringing me that much closer to my goal.

Then, a milestone: I got my first paying gig. When Mr. Janoski heard through the grapevine that the orchestra for the San Diego Ballet needed a substitute oboist for several performances, he kindly recommended me. It was also through his connections that I was able to get my musician's union card. I could hardly believe I was actually going to be paid to play the oboe!

After subbing for the San Diego Ballet, other part-time gigs began trickling in. A regional production of "Fiddler on the Roof" needed musicians for the orchestra pit; Paramount Recording Studios was looking for an oboist to record some music for a TV commercial; the Long Beach Symphony Orchestra needed an emergency sub for a few concerts. And then Emily, a flutist and fellow USC student whom I'd gotten to know through playing in the school orchestra, asked me to join her woodwind quintet. Emily wasn't only an excellent musician, she was a tireless promoter, and soon we had frequent gigs playing at weddings, birthdays, company functions, and other events.

By the time I graduated, I was fortunate enough to already have my union card, along with a number of important contacts in the local music scene. I was well on my way to achieving my dream, thanks to two invaluable teachers and mentors: Mr. Yoshimura and Mr. Janoski. Despite this promising start, though, I knew the road ahead would require even more determination and perseverance.

In retrospect, it was so easy to blame my parents—especially my mother—for diverting me from my dream. Really, it was just too tempting to say it was their fault I quit playing the oboe. It was also far too easy to fester resentment toward them for those lost years of playing, when I could—and should—have been studying at a music conservatory. But at seventeen I just didn't have enough faith in myself, and I was too susceptible to having my parents talk me out of pursuing the path I desired. At the time, I wanted to be like Stravinsky, bold enough to launch a "Rite of Spring" years ahead of its time. I thought I could become the first Japanese American oboist in a major U.S. orchestra. But I let my parents' fierce resistance scuttle my plans. Faced with my own rioting Parisian audience, I caved. I lacked the self-belief I needed and, truth be told, I was almost relieved when Mom and Dad lowered the boom on my plans to attend a conservatory. A secret part of me was afraid I wouldn't be able to cut it, because I'd no longer be the proverbial big fish in a small pond. At Juilliard or Oberlin, I'd likely have been a tiny guppy in a very big lake. It's difficult for me to admit that, even now, but it's the truth.

CHAPTER ELEVEN

Throughout my two-year transformation from engineer to musician, I kept things secret from my parents. I told them I was going back to school at USC for my master's degree but let them blissfully assume I was continuing my studies in engineering. Then later, after I graduated with my master's in music, I told them I'd started playing the oboe again and was getting some part-time gigs. The few details I gave weren't outright fabrications, but my many omissions of crucial information left my parents with an overall impression that was basically one huge lie. They thought I was a professional engineer who happened to play the oboe, when actually the truth was the reverse: I was a professional musician who did some part-time computer programming to help pay the bills.

I wasn't proud of leaving my parents in the dark, but I was happy I'd taken control of my life, that I'd somehow found the courage, confidence, and wherewithal to pursue my own course. True, I'd amassed a significant amount of debt in graduate school. And my future was far from certain. I might eventually learn I'd made a huge mistake pursuing a career in music, but at least it would be my mistake, not someone else's. And I told myself I would much rather regret having tried something and failed than have allowed fear to keep me frozen in an unsatisfying life.

I also had to admit that a petty part of me was secretly delighted in my rebellion. I'd put one over my parents, dramatically altering the course of my life without their having any knowledge. But what I didn't realize then was that my secret would become a wedge between us, an obstacle our relationship might've overcome except for one huge complicating factor: my being gay.

Throughout my college years and into my mid-twenties, I'd had my fair number of crushes, but I hadn't really pursued any of them. I was still in the closet and, besides, I was too busy concentrating on my studies and my career. Or at least that's what I told myself. Interestingly, all the men with whom I'd become infatuated during this time were straight, which might very well have been a self-protection mechanism at work in my subconscious, keeping me in the closet until I was ready to accept my sexual orientation.

In particular, I fell hard for a fellow student who played the trumpet in the USC orchestra. From the first time I saw Patrick walking on campus, I was immediately attracted to his tall, lean body; his tousled brown hair; and his tanned face, so handsomely framed with a light beard and mustache. And I became all the more smitten with him because of his fearless trumpet playing. Patrick was from Ann Arbor, Michigan. He'd grown up there and attended the University of Michigan for his undergraduate degree before applying for his master's at USC. In the fall semester, we were in the same music theory class and often studied together at the library. Occasionally, I'd invite him over for dinner and nervously struggle to prepare one of the few dishes I could cook well at the time, either a lasagna or a beef stew. We'd eat, drink beers, and talk for hours about music, asking each other an endless series of hypothetical questions. Will orchestras still be performing Beethoven's Ninth Symphony centuries from now? If electric guitars and synthesizers had been invented in Mozart's time, how would he have used those instruments in his compositions? Which of Tchaikovsky's symphonies is his masterpiece: the Fourth, Fifth, or Sixth?

"I can't believe you'd say it's the Fifth," Patrick argued. "Think of the first movement of the Fourth Symphony. That alone is a masterpiece. And then you have three more movements!"

"But that's part of the problem," I countered. "The long first movement of the Fourth should have been a standalone piece, not part of a larger work."

"Seriously? But then what about the gorgeous oboe solo in the second movement? Would you really just get rid of it?"

"Okay, you have a point," I conceded, "but even I have to admit that that solo can't hold a candle to the horn solo in the second movement of the Fifth. That melody is divine."

And back and forth we'd go, drinking beer after beer as time seemed to melt away. Then, one day out of the blue, Patrick started dating Laura, a violinist in our school orchestra. Although I'd long known that he was straight, I was still devastated. I felt so betrayed, even though I knew I had no right to. Over the course of our friendship, I hadn't allowed myself to think of Patrick in a sexual way, but my affection for him had nevertheless grown so deeply entrenched in my being, like the taproots of a giant oak tree. I surprised myself with how desolate I became, as Patrick and I went from hanging out regularly to seeing each other only occasionally. I longed for his easy companionship and engaging conversation, and it seemed that nothing could fill that aching void.

As Patrick's relationship with Laura deepened, he would sometimes invite me to concerts or dinners with them, but I always politely declined. I just couldn't bear the thought of seeing them together. Once, though, the three of us did go out for drinks after our orchestra performance. I found myself simmering in an odd combination of both jealousy and envy: jealous that his girlfriend had become the primary focus of his attention, and envious that he'd found someone so lovely and intelligent. When Laura had excused herself to use the restroom, Patrick beamed, "Isn't she great?"

"You're a lucky guy. I'm happy for both of you."

"And, by the way, she agrees with you."

"What?"

"She thinks Tchaikovsky's Fifth is a better symphony than the Fourth, and for pretty much the same reasons that you did."

I had no idea how to respond to that. Laura's liking the Fifth only made me prefer the Fourth, peeved as I was. So, Patrick was in love with a woman who might share my musical tastes. Was he implying that she and I might have other things in common, that we might eventually become close friends? I couldn't fathom that possibility. Instead, all I could think of was that, had Patrick been gay, he might have fallen for me the same way that he had fallen for Laura. Of course, that thought only depressed me further.

At that moment, in that restaurant as we waited for Laura to return from the restroom, the only thing I could say was, "Well, Laura certainly has good taste." Patrick chuckled and raised his beer toward me, as if to concede victory in battle to superior troops. I knew that he was assuming that I was talking about Laura's taste in music, but in my mind I was actually referring to her taste in men. After that night, I saw Patrick (and Laura) only in orchestra rehearsals. I just couldn't get past the pain and bitter chagrin I felt, and I let my friendship with him wither into nothing.

It was right around this time when I first began hearing about a gay-related illness. I hadn't seen the initial, foreboding New York Times story—"Rare Cancer Seen in 41 Homosexuals"—that had appeared in the summer of 1981, but I soon heard the scary rumors: that maybe the "gay cancer" could be transmitted through deep kissing, that poppers were the cause, that mosquitoes could transmit it. Later, as stories about gay-related immunodeficiency (GRID) began to circulate widely in the media, I became terrified, and it forced me even deeper into the closet, where I sublimated all my sexual desires into my oboe playing.

For a while, the burgeoning epidemic stayed at least two degrees of separation away from me. The closest people I knew who were affected were friends of friends whom I'd heard had become seriously ill. Soon enough, though, the epidemic hit much closer to home. I noticed that Nick, the French horn player in Emily's woodwind quintet, was becoming ill with increasing frequency. At first, he missed a rehearsal here or there, but then, as he became thinner and frailer, he had trouble making many of our gigs, leaving us to scramble to find a sub for those performances. The last time I saw Nick was when Emily and I visited him at his apartment. We were shaken to see that purple lesions had spread to his face, and he looked like he'd aged at least 20 years. "I have lesions inside my mouth too," he told us, "and the last time I tried playing my horn I sounded horrible. I couldn't make a decent tone and was so out of breath."

"Don't worry," Emily said, "I'm sure it'll all come back to you."

But Nick wouldn't accept her baseless optimism. "I heard that some people are losing their sight. I actually wouldn't mind that, just as long as I could still play, but that's just not going to happen." A month later he moved back to his parents' home in Wichita, Kansas, where he died not long after.

Emily and I, along with the two other musicians in our quintet, offered to play at Nick's funeral, but his parents politely (yet firmly) demurred. They also made it clear that perhaps it would be best if we didn't make the trip to Wichita for the services or, if we felt we had to, it might be best if we sat at the back of the church. We got the distinct impression they didn't want any reminders of Nick's life in California, where their son had come out as a gay man and contracted HIV. So, we held our own memorial in Los Angeles with a non-denominational service attended by more than a hundred of Nick's friends and classmates.

With Nick gone, Emily's quintet drifted apart. I suppose none of us could even think of having another French horn player take his place, so we were all content to just let the group dissolve. This was okay with me because Emily, who had initially enlisted all of us and was essentially our group manager, booking all of our performances, was fine with moving on to other musical ensembles. She and I still got together to play duets once in a while, purely for fun, and it was during one of those sessions she told me she'd sent Nick's family a copy of the program from his service in L.A., along with a book in which we'd all written about our fondest memories of him. She'd also included a few recordings from our quintet's performances. No one from his family ever sent back a note to even acknowledge they'd received the package.

I wasn't as close with Nick as Emily was, but I was still deeply hurt that his family tried to erase an essential part of his life. "I suppose," Emily told me, "I shouldn't have been surprised, but I was still disappointed. It makes you wonder whether they really, truly loved their son. I mean, what is wrong with them?"

What was wrong with Nick's family was the growing contagion of homophobia, more virulent in some ways than the HIV virus itself. First, there was Anita Bryant and her "Save Our Children" campaign. Next, there was the Briggs Initiative and its attempt to ban gays from teaching in public schools in California. And then there was the cold-blooded brazen assassination of Harvey Milk, the first openly gay elected official in California, right in San Francisco's City Hall.

As thousands died, the AIDS epidemic raised homophobia to a whole new level of fear and hate. It became open season for mocking and persecuting gays, with religious fundamentalists outrageously claiming

AIDS was god's punishment for homosexuality. Truly unforgettable were the cruel, vicious jokes. Question: What does GAY stand for? Answer: Got AIDS Yet? Or even worse: What do you call a fag in a wheelchair? Answer: Roll-AIDS. Homosexuals became society's latest scapegoats, to be reviled with impunity.

Up until then, my entire sex life had been limited to restrained kissing and episodes of mutual hand jobs with guys I met at gay bars in the Silver Lake neighborhood and West Hollywood. Later, as doctors accumulated a rudimentary understanding of the disease—that it's transmitted by a virus in semen and blood and that the use of condoms could significantly help prevent infection—I finally felt I could allow myself more sexual freedom. And thus began my journey, as I slowly made my way out the closet.

CHAPTER TWELVE

Meeting Lucas wasn't "love at first sight"—I don't even know what that is—but there was definitely an undeniable, irresistible attraction. When I first saw him, I was with a couple friends at the Studio One disco in West Hollywood, enjoying a carefree night of celebration. I'd just finished playing in the orchestra pit for the final performance of the Pasadena Playhouse's revival of "Carousel" and was in the mood to blow off some steam by dancing into the early morning. I'd already had several beers when, while waiting in line to use the men's room, I noticed a tall, medium-build guy, maybe a little older than me, with straight black hair in a neat side part, accenting the strong features of his handsome face. He saw me and smiled, but I quickly turned my gaze away, embarrassed that he'd caught me staring. Lucas had the most endearing smile, his slightly crooked grin and soft brown eyes seeming to light up with kindness and intelligence. Before I knew what to do next, though, one of Lucas's friends grabbed his arm and pulled him toward the dance floor, and they were quickly swallowed by the crowd of shirtless men.

After I used the restroom, I looked everywhere for him. There must've been at least a thousand men crammed into Studio One, and it took me a good hour just to circle the dance floor. In the process, I lost the friends I was with, and then my mind started its usual descent into pessimism: Lucas was smiling at someone behind me in line, not at me; if he'd indeed been interested in me, he'd have stopped to talk; one of the friends who'd dragged him off was really his boyfriend. All that negativity still cluttered my head two hours later as I stood in line to use the men's room again.

And then, just as I neared the front of the line, Lucas came walking out of the restroom. I caught his eye, and he walked directly over to me. "We've really gotta stop meeting like this," he said. We both laughed, and then quickly introduced ourselves.

Throughout the night, as we danced together, I learned that Lucas didn't live in Los Angeles. He was from New York City, where he worked as an editor with Warner Books. He was in L.A. that week for a publishing conference and was flying back home the next day. Because Lucas was returning to the East Coast so soon, it made that night all the more special. I felt like I was in a dream, one I knew would end soon, so I wanted to savor every second before returning to reality. All my senses were heightened to the vivid colors of the laser lights on the dance floor, the blaring sound of the music reverberating through every cell in my body, the visceral smell of men perspiring while packed on a dance floor, the electric charge I felt every time Lucas's body brushed lightly again mine; and the sweet, intoxicating taste of his lips when he reached over and kissed me as we danced to Taylor Dayne's "Tell It to My Heart."

•   •   •   •   •

I wasn't sure what would become of that night. I was very much smitten with Lucas, and I thought the feeling was mutual. But we'd each had a few beers and were in a mood to have fun—it was Lucas's last night visiting L.A. and I'd just finished a gig. Would the time we spent together lead to anything, or were those few hours of magic an isolated moment, never to be repeated?

At the end of that night, Lucas needed to head back to his hotel in Century City to finish packing for an early-morning flight. As we left Studio One, we exchanged phone numbers, kissed, and then walked off in different directions to our separate cars. I allowed myself to look back at him just once, as if to confirm that he did indeed exist.

Unfortunately, none of my friends knew any of the friends Lucas was with that night, so I didn't have any mutual connections I could tap to learn more about him. And, of course, the rational part of me was more than aware of the major obstacle of geographic distance, what with our living on opposite coasts. Still, I kept thinking about him.

If I hadn't known better, I'd have assumed Lucas was straight, given my strong attraction to him, so wary had I become of my painful habit of falling for heterosexual men. But I'd met him at a gay nightclub, he had a bunch of gay friends who lived in L.A., and he'd told me he was doing a lot of volunteer work for the Gay Men's Health Crisis in New York City. And, more to the point, the sensual way he danced with me and the two kisses we shared should have left little doubt in my mind. So, I was reasonably sure he was gay. But then I wondered if I had replaced one type of obstacle (sexual orientation) with another (geographic separation).

A few days later, I was still trying to muster the courage to phone Lucas when, much to my delight (and considerable relief), he called first. I was ecstatic. We talked for nearly an hour, and that conversation was followed by numerous phone calls in the weeks that followed. Talking with him was effortless; we never ran out of topics to discuss—movies, books, magazine articles, and current events—each of us so eager to learn more about the other's tastes and general worldview. After a few months of our budding long-distance relationship, which began to strain my meager phone budget, Lucas told me he'd soon be back in Los Angeles on business to work with an author at UCLA.

I was thrilled, yet somewhat nervous. In addition to those long, easy conversations over the phone, Lucas and I had also sent each other letters, some with goofy photos of ourselves and touching anecdotes of our quotidian lives. I was falling in love with him, and a part of me was afraid that our being together again might not live up to our growing expectations of each other. To be frank, I wasn't sure how much of my memory of that magical night at Studio One was real and how much had been embellished by my imagination.

Lucas told me that he'd be flying into LAX on Wednesday evening for all-day meetings on Thursday and Friday. He also had to attend a business dinner on Thursday night, but otherwise he'd be free from Friday evening until Sunday, when he'd booked a red-eye flight back to New York City. We planned dinner together on Friday, and then figured we'd play the rest of the weekend by ear.

When Friday evening finally arrived, I nervously drove to the Italian restaurant in West Hollywood where I'd suggested we meet for dinner. I planned to be there early, just to make sure I wasn't late. But when I arrived, fifteen minutes ahead of time, Lucas was already there. As I headed toward our table and he got up to greet me, I felt like I'd stepped back in time—as if the intervening weeks of separation hadn't happened and we were simply continuing where we'd left off on that wondrous night when we'd first met.

Even though we had talked so much over the phone and corresponded through numerous letters, we were still starving to learn more about each other. We talked about our work—the books Lucas was working on and the gigs I was playing—and about all the interesting and funny things that had recently happened to us, our conversation ricocheting from one topic to the next with hardly a moment's pause. The waiter had to return three times, seeking to take our order, before we finally forced ourselves to stop talking and actually look at the menu.

The next day we had brunch at a café in Westwood before catching a matinee showing of "Cinema Paradiso." I was mesmerized by Ennio Morricone's lush score, which made me want to get an album of the soundtrack. So, after the movie we browsed around the shops in Westwood Village and stopped at a record store there. The soundtrack hadn't yet been issued but, while we were there, one of the clerks had selected to play a new-age album—William Ackerman's "Passage"—over the store's sound system. That album happened to include a song with a soulful English horn solo, accompanied by an acoustic guitar. The English horn's mellow, melancholy tone resonated through the store, singing a simple but haunting melody. "There, that's the instrument I play," I told Lucas.

"Wow, that's sublime," he replied. "You'll have to play for me sometime."

"Well, actually, that's a tenor oboe and my main instrument is the oboe, but I also double a lot on the English horn."

"Then I have to hear you on both," he said, his beautiful smile beaming at me from across a long row of record album bins.

That night, back at my apartment, we had sex for the first time. Unfortunately, even though I was totally engaged on an emotional level, I couldn't remain physically aroused. Through my embarrassment, I started to explain to Lucas that my performance anxiety had nothing to do with my attraction to him, but before I could mumble out how I was feeling, he stopped me. "Don't worry about it," he said. "I think I already know how you feel about me."

We smiled at each other in the dim light of my bedroom and, as we hugged, I could feel his heartbeat from his chest through mine. We fell asleep in each other's arms and then later, in the middle of the night, we awoke and made love. Before then, my only experience had been mutual masturbations with other guys. Lucas was the first man I had ever had oral or anal sex with, his calm, soothing voice and manner putting me at ease. When he tore open a condom package and slipped on the latex so effortlessly, I said, "This is just a guess, but I'm thinking you've done this before?"

"Well, practice does make perfect," he laughed. "So, lets you and I get some practice in." That was one of the many awesome things about Lucas. He always seemed to know what to say to relax me, even as I fought my myriad anxieties and insecurities.

The entire weekend was like a thick but pleasant haze, and I found myself feeling the world through my senses rather than thinking (or, more to the point, overthinking) about what I was experiencing with my brain. The thing I'll remember most about that time was how Lucas made me feel. Up to that point in my life I'd never really felt good about being gay. On my worst days, I felt like a dirty aberration, a mistake. And even on my best days, when I could tell myself I was basically a decent, well-intentioned (but flawed) person, I still often felt like there was a major glitch in my sexual being, that some wires had somehow gotten seriously crossed. On an intellectual level, I knew I had every right to be who I was. And yet on an emotional level, I harbored the insidious feeling that I had unwholesome, unnatural desires. I hate to admit it now, but before meeting Lucas, if someone had offered me a pill that would have miraculously made me straight, I'd have gladly swallowed it without hesitation. Actually, I'd have gulped down an entire bottle of that prescription.

But everything that weekend with Lucas felt so good, so right, so natural. It changed me on a fundamental level. From that point on, I left the closet and never looked back. And if ever I would then be offered those magic straight pills, I'd have immediately flushed them down the toilet.

·　　·　　·　　·　　·

After Lucas returned to New York City, the next few weeks for me were a mix of longing, desire, and anticipation. He and I talked on the phone at least every other day, and we mailed each other small, thoughtful gifts. I sent him the William Ackerman album we'd discovered on his last visit, along with another recording of oboe concertos. He sent me a copy of a book he'd just edited on evolutionary psychology, telling me I might find interesting the middle section on the origins of music. He was right; those chapters were fascinating, and we talked about them for well over an hour one night.

And then there were the constant reminders Lucas had left for me. When we'd been at that café in Westwood for lunch, he made a point of telling me he very much preferred the small, individual white packets of sugar rather than the cylindrical glass dispensers coffee shops typically use. "These packets are so much more convenient," he stated, "because you know exactly how much sugar you'll get. For example, Ethan, you appear to be a one-packet kind of guy, whereas I usually use one-and-a-half packets for a standard mug of coffee."

"How fascinating," I teased him.

"No, seriously, think about how clumsy those big glass dispensers are. Sometimes just a pinch of sugar pours; other times it's an avalanche, and you've ruined a perfectly fine cup of coffee."

I had no idea why Lucas was making such a big deal about such a mundane thing. Later, though, after he had returned to New York City, I discovered those individual sugar packets in the oddest of places: stashed inside my oboe case, tucked behind the phone in my living room, hidden underneath my TV remote control, lodged inside a book I was reading. Lucas must've swiped a whole bunch of those packets and hidden them, like Easter eggs, throughout my apartment. When I asked him about that over the phone, he said, "Now every time you discover one, you'll think of me."

"I already think about you constantly," I told him. "I really don't need any reminders."

"Well, just in case," he said, and in my imagination I could see him smiling at me, with his slightly crooked grin and those endearing brown eyes.

•   •   •   •   •

The next time I saw Lucas was when I flew to New York City to stay with him for a week. It was early December and the city was festive, with department store windows decorated for the upcoming Christmas holiday and the air in Midtown filled with the smell of roasting chestnuts from sidewalk vendors. It was a time of pure magic on Manhattan—the city wildly exceeding my expectations from the many movies I'd seen.

Lucas laughed at me every time I looked up at yet another tall building to admire its audacious height. And it wasn't just the height and magnificent architecture of skyscrapers like the Empire State Building or the Chrysler Building; it was the sheer density of those many structures congregated so closely together. That, combined with the crowds of pedestrians and the constant flow of cars, taxis, and buses, energized me to a heightened level of awareness. I felt as if electricity was constantly coursing through my body.

And then, most certainly, there was Lucas. I enjoyed every minute of the time we'd spent together in Los Angeles, but there was something about my being with him in Manhattan, where he was clearly in his own element. He seemed all the more self-assured, confident, and, well, irresistibly attractive.

We had sex two or three times a day—wild, uninhibited couplings, our bodies intertwined in new, imaginative ways. At one point, we were both so completely spent from the intensity of our carnal activities that we slept during the day for nearly ten hours straight. And for a long stretch we didn't even leave his apartment on the Upper West Side, not until we had run out of food to eat. Eventually, though, Lucas began to feel guilty and said he wasn't being a good host. "What will your friends say when you go back to L.A. and they find out you didn't even see the Metropolitan Museum, a Broadway play, or the Statue of Liberty?" he asked.

"Well, I would just have to tell them the truth. We spent the entire week in bed having wild monkey sex."

"No," Lucas laughed, "you can't do that. They'll get the wrong impression of me."

"You mean the right impression?"

"Well, that too," he grinned.

So, toward the end of my stay, we crammed a ton of activities and sights into a couple days. We saw the "Phantom of the Opera" on Broadway, we immersed ourselves in the ethereal beauty of Monet's renowned "Water Lilies" at the Museum of Modern Art, and we lunched at a café in Rockefeller Plaza, admiring its lavish Christmas tree in all its outrageous splendor. We even went ice skating in Central Park. It was the first time I'd ever done so, but after several ungainly falls I was able to maintain my balance and begin pushing off with small, awkward strokes. Lucas, who'd learned to skate while growing up in central New York, was surprised I picked it up that quickly. But I explained to him that I frequently went roller skating as a kid growing up in Honolulu and that the basic motions were relatively the same, although skating on ice was so much tougher on the ankles.

Later that night, as we lay in his bed, his warm flannel sheets and down comforter insulating us from the world, Lucas asked me what it was like to be a Japanese American boy growing up in exotic Hawaii. I explained that I hadn't really appreciated Hawaii while I was there, because it was always just home to me. "I never thought that being able to go to the beach for a quick swim in the ocean after school was anything special. It's just the way I grew up," I told him. "Exotic to me wasn't Hawaii. Exotic to me was Paris, or Rome, or right here in New York City."

Lucas was born and raised in Syracuse. And just as I'd grown up in a culturally and racially homogeneous neighborhood, so had he. For me, it was Honolulu, where Asians were the majority, while he'd spent his entire childhood in an Irish Catholic neighborhood of his hometown. I was surprised—and yet not surprised—when Lucas told me I was the first Asian guy he'd ever dated. In some subconscious way, I knew he hadn't been with other Asian men before he told me so, and perhaps that was part of my attraction to him. In the past, I'd been hit on by guys who were interested only in Asian men. Derisively called "rice queens," they typically had preconceived notions of who I was and how I should act. More often than not, I wasn't as submissive, either sexually or in general, as they'd assumed I'd be, and they quickly lost interest. This was just as well, because I invariably found those types of men and their Asian fetish somewhat unnerving, if not downright creepy.

Lucas didn't harbor any of those preconceptions, and I liked that he was eager to discover the person I really am. And, in turn, he seemed to derive much pleasure knowing how much I enjoyed learning every new thing about him. I was fascinated to hear about the young man who put himself through college at Brown University, with a double major in English literature and French, and then moved to New York City with limited funds but abundant self-confidence, somehow knowing he possessed the talent, education, and drive to make it in the hyper-competitive publishing industry.

CHAPTER THIRTEEN

After returning to Los Angeles, I promptly entered a deep funk. I missed Lucas terribly, and the need to be with him slowly began to unsettle me. Until then, I'd thought of myself as supremely independent. After all, as a teenager I'd moved to Los Angeles for school and supported myself. And I remained fiercely self-reliant even as I changed careers, never once asking my parents for a single penny. But now I was becoming a different person, overly concerned with the likes, dislikes, thoughts, and actions of someone else. Where was all this headed, I wondered.

Then something happened, completely knocking me out of that post-vacation funk. The events that would eventually upturn my life started inauspiciously enough, with a call from Mr. Janoski, my oboe teacher and mentor, asking if I'd been contacted by Alicia Avilla, the arts reporter from the L.A. Times. I told him I hadn't, and he said to let him know if she did call and that I should simply decline to speak with her. When I asked him what this was all about, he said, "She's working on a story that's a whole lot of nothing. Just tell her you have no comment."

The next day I got a call from my flutist friend Emily, from USC, also inquiring if Alicia Avilla had contacted me yet.

"What's this all about?" I asked.

Apparently, Avilla had been working for weeks on a story about Project Music for Kids, a nonprofit association with the mission of bringing classical music to inner-city schoolchildren. I was somewhat familiar with PMK because, through Mr. Janoski's recommendation, the organization had hired Emily's quintet to play at different schools in L.A.'s poorer neighborhoods. I always enjoyed those small concerts, because the kids were genuinely interested in our performances. Of course, we were careful to pick the right kinds of numbers, usually short arrangements of music with which they'd be familiar: TV theme songs, movie soundtracks, and hyperkinetic music from Saturday-morning cartoons. Emily was a natural for these performances, with her bubbly, engaging personality. She always held the kids' attention when describing the different pieces we were about to play and when talking about classical music in general.

Through the grapevine Avilla had heard that someone at PMK was cooking the books. Evidently, money earmarked for concerts, private music lessons, and rental instruments for schoolkids had somehow been diverted to lavish fundraising events and other questionable expenses. Avilla had gotten a copy of some of PMK's financial records, and our quintet had repeatedly shown up as a line item. When Avilla met with Emily and showed her the information, Emily was shocked to learn that we'd supposedly performed far more gigs at the schools than we had, and that we'd charged PMK for them, even though we usually played for free as a service to the community.

Emily didn't know what to do. She really believed in PMK and didn't want to bring scandal to the nonprofit because it might turn off private donors. Without their generous money, PMK could potentially collapse, as the organization received only a small fraction of its funding from government sources. The result would be hundreds of schoolkids no longer benefitting from an exposure to classical music in the classroom. And yet, on the other hand, Emily didn't want to be implicated in a financial fraud in which we had no part, so she told Avilla the truth of what she knew.

A few days later, when Alicia Avilla phoned me, I told her I didn't think it was a good idea for us to talk. Before I could hang up, though, she pleaded with me, saying all she needed was for me to confirm what Emily had already told her. Apparently, the two other members of our former quintet had refused to talk with Avilla, and now some of the executives at PMK were claiming that Emily was simply a disgruntled musician who'd once applied for a grant from the organization and been denied.

That did it for me. I couldn't let a good friend be disparaged in that way. Avilla read to me what Emily had told her, and I confirmed every bit of that information. Avilla thanked me for my assistance and reassured me I'd done a good thing by helping to bring the truth to light.

After I got off the phone, my heart was racing. I'd never been interviewed by a reporter before, and I didn't particularly like being swept up in a breaking scandal. To calm my nerves, I tried to play some soothing music on my oboe but had trouble concentrating on the music in front of me. I lost track of what key I was in or made silly fingering mistakes, which only frustrated me and heightened my anxieties. Eventually, I just started playing from memory, pieces I'd learned years ago with Mr. Yoshimura.

Avilla's exposé made the front page of the Sunday arts section, and in it were several quotes from Emily, along with a mention that I'd corroborated what she said. The story also mentioned that Mr. Janoski's wife was a senior executive at PMK, something I hadn't known but perhaps should have suspected. This was why he was so easily able to get us those gigs in the first place, and also apparently why he was so vested in impeding Avilla's investigation.

I'd just finished reading the story when I got a call from Mr. Janoski. "You have no idea how much trouble this is causing," he said, barely containing his anger. "Do you know what you've done? Powerful people sit on the PMK board, and they're not happy with this story."

After he hung up, I felt like I'd been holding my breath throughout the entire call. In the two years I'd known him, Mr. Janoski had always been a gentle, supportive teacher and invaluable mentor. He'd never ever come close to uttering one harsh word to me, choosing instead to coax my best playing through detailed instructions and soft reassurances. It was Mr. Janoski who'd taught me how to overcome my habit of succumbing to nervous, shallow breathing whenever I was tense, especially before a big performance or important audition. "Breathe deeper until you feel like you're filling the lowest part of your diaphragm," he'd say, "and then take a few breaths even deeper than that." Ironically, after our phone call, I had to force myself to remember his invaluable advice to help calm my nerves from the angry words he'd just spoken to me.

•   •   •   •   •

After the L.A. Times story broke, several of the top executives at Project Music for Kids resigned, including Mr. Janoski's wife, and the entire board was later replaced. This helped restore some confidence in the organization, and the widespread publicity of PMK's financial difficulties actually led to an eventual increase in private donations.

But things were never the same between Mr. Janoski and me. In the past, he'd call at least every few weeks to refer me to a gig, tell me about a new supplier of oboe cane, or simply ask if we could get together for lunch to catch up with each other. Those calls all stopped. Finally, after not talking with him for several months, I mustered the courage to phone him.

He was polite but painfully curt as I tried to make small talk, and after a few tortuous minutes we ended the call.

I later wrote him a letter saying I hoped his wife was doing okay, that I was sorry the L.A. Times story had put us at odds with each other but felt I had to support a good friend whose credibility and reputation were being assailed. I also thanked him for being such an encouraging, supportive teacher and told him I'd forever be grateful for all the help he'd given me. Mr. Janoski never answered the letter, which didn't surprise me but was nevertheless painful. I knew I was being idealistic and naïve to expect a response. Still, I hoped that he and I could, perhaps with time, return to some form of our previous relationship. Then even those hopes were dashed when I talked with Mr. Yoshimura, my former oboe teacher in Honolulu. Mr. Yoshimura was more than just my teacher and mentor; he'd been like a second father to me. Even he couldn't offer any advice, and his words were hardly reassuring. He told me Mr. Janoski had called him and was furious at what he perceived to be my appalling lack of loyalty and pitiful paucity of gratitude. "The word 'ingrate' was used repeatedly," Mr. Yoshimura said.

During this time, I couldn't help but notice my gigs were dwindling. It wasn't just that I was failing to secure new engagements; I was losing standing ones. I'd played in the summer outdoor concert series of the La Jolla Symphony for the past couple years, but when I called my contact in April to confirm that I'd be available to play with them again, he apologized and said they'd already filled the two oboe spots.

Fortunately, at the same time that my music gigs were evaporating, demand for my computer skills was picking up. Armstrong Construction had received a huge contract to build a skyscraper and adjoining mall in Atlanta, and the firm needed me to work on a new type of sophisticated computer model. Without that side job, I would have depleted the meager savings I'd accumulated and might even have had to default on my student-loan payments.

Emily wasn't so fortunate. Her gigs had also dried up, and she'd taken a part-time retail job at the Santa Monica mall. When I told her the same thing was happening to me, she apologized and said she was sorry to have dragged me down with her.

"Don't be ridiculous," I told her. "This isn't your fault. And besides, you'd have done the same for me."

"I know," she said, "but it still stinks. Remind me to keep my mouth shut the next time a reporter comes snooping around."

So, knowing what you do now, you wouldn't have spoken with her?"

There was a long pause before Emily said, "I honestly don't know. What about you?"

"I don't regret what we did, but it sucks being punished for doing the right thing."

"Let's face it," she told me. "We're done here in Southern Cal."

Not long after that talk Emily moved back to her hometown of Chicago to see if she could have a fresh start there. Her sister had just graduated from college and gotten a job with a downtown firm in the Loop when one of her housemates decided to move out, so the timing was perfect. The rent was cheap, and Emily's sister could even loan her some money until she got settled.

I, too, needed a fresh start. As my music gigs in L.A. became fewer and fewer, Lucas encouraged me to move to New York City. Through his volunteer work with the Gay Men's Health Crisis, he knew a few people who might be able to open some doors for me. One was a Broadway musician, who said he could get me on the sub lists that would get my feet in the door, and another friend was an officer with the local musicians' union, who told Lucas he could expedite the processing of my membership application. Lucas also said I could live with him until I found a place of my own.

Given all that, the decision was simple, and I moved to Manhattan in the summer of 1986. At first, to earn whatever I could, I worked various odd jobs, temping for companies and waiting tables. I also started getting one-off music gigs, usually subbing for another oboist who was ill or on vacation. And then, almost a year after my big move, fortune struck. I'd been regularly subbing for the oboist in the Broadway production of "Cats," and when she decided to move on after having played in the orchestra for two years, the conductor asked me to take her place. The music wasn't the most satisfying to play, but I was thrilled—not only would I get a regular paycheck, I'd also receive health benefits and contributions to my pension.

Moving in with Lucas went smoothly too. Perhaps things were so easy with him because, thanks to our different schedules, our relationship never came close to reaching the "familiarity breeds contempt" phase. With his day job and my work, either waiting tables or running off to a night gig, we always just missed each other. And then, when I was fortunate enough to land that full-time job with "Cats," we became the proverbial two ships regularly passing each other in the early evening.

In a way, our different schedules worked out better than if we'd planned things that way, with neither of us feeling guilty about the time we spent away from each other. I was busy trying to establish myself in the New York City music scene, and he was focused either on his job, trying to sign promising young authors he would cultivate throughout their careers, or on his activism at the Gay Men's Health Crisis. The large amounts of time we spent apart only made the time we did share that much more precious. We'd take a day off here and there to explore a new museum exhibit, take the train to Philadelphia, swim at Jones Beach, or visit the Bronx Zoo. And every so often we'd plan a long weekend, rent a car, and drive to Syracuse to visit Lucas's family and friends.

Initially, I planned to stay at Lucas's place for just a few weeks or a couple months at most. I hoped to find an affordable studio apartment in Brooklyn or Queens. The last thing I wanted was to crowd him, so I was surprised at how quickly we settled into a comfortable routine. During the day, I'd look for a job or an apartment, stop at a grocery store on the way back to his place, and then start cooking dinner before he returned from work. Everything seemed to come so easily, so effortlessly, that neither of us felt any rush to change anything. The months accumulated, and we continued to live together. At first, it was the practical thing for us to do, saving rent money, then it became the only thing for us to do. We'd reached the point that neither of us could imagine a home without the other's daily presence.

CHAPTER FOURTEEN

As my love for Lucas intensified, so did a nagging feeling in the back of my mind. I needed to tell my parents about my relationship with him, but in doing so I would have to officially come out to them. I knew that both Mom and Dad must have at least suspected I'm gay, but I never confirmed that with them. I lacked the courage to be upfront, and I rationalized this by telling myself it was much kinder to leave them with some hope I might be straight. The Japanese have a saying—fukusui bon ni kaerazu—that literally means you can't return spilled water to the bowl. In other words, what's done is done. Once I told my parents I'm gay, there'd be no turning back. They'd be confronted with the cold truth, and then they'd have to deal with it.

Lucas joked with me that at least I was spared from the devastating "triple reveal": Hey Mom and Dad, I'm gay, I have a boyfriend, and I have AIDS. He'd heard about the triple reveals of numerous friends, and many of those family relationships couldn't weather the ensuing upheaval. It was only through sheer fortuitous timing that I was HIV negative—thankfully I'd already known about safer sex before I came out. Still, the double reveal was going to be bad enough with my parents, and I dreaded it.

The truth was this: Telling Mom and Dad I'm gay was one thing; informing them that I had a boyfriend was an entirely different matter. My parents might accept my being gay if they didn't have to deal with that fact, if I quietly pursued a "don't ask, don't tell" life of discreet existence. They would regret that I wasn't straight and wasn't likely to marry or have children, but they would eventually accept that as the way things were going to be—shikata ga nai. Having a boyfriend and living with him, though? That would, especially for my mother, be too much to countenance. Spilling water from a bowl might be tolerated, but only if the mishap could be ignored as if it'd never happened.

It wasn't that my parents had any inherent deep-seated animosity toward homosexuality. After all, they were raised by Japanese parents and, before the opening of Japan to the West in the mid-1800s, the country condoned a wide range of human sexuality. Samurai warriors frequently took adolescent boys as their lovers. Kagema (male prostitutes) were known to have a thriving business with both male and female clients. Attractive young Kabuki actors often moonlighted in prostitution for wealthy patrons of both sexes. And ukiyo-e (Japanese woodblock prints) depicted no shortage of erotic couplings and sexual gymnastics. So it was ironic that my parents, who resisted assimilation into the United States in many ways, would adopt its puritanical views on sex, including a taboo on homosexuality.

For Lucas's part, things were far less complicated. Although his parents were Catholic and he and his siblings were raised in that faith, his older sisters helped pave the way for him to come out. They gently threw out hints about Lucas's sexual orientation to their parents until, finally, his mom and dad sat him down and told him they knew he was gay and would always love him unconditionally.

I liked and admired Lucas's parents, who welcomed me into their family so wholeheartedly. But in a perverse way I secretly resented them for being so accepting, because that only made it more difficult for Lucas to comprehend why I couldn't be as open with my own parents. "Doesn't it ever bother you," he once asked me, "that your parents don't even know who you really are?"

I tried to explain to him why I led such a subdued life. First, my relationship with my parents was already strained and had been ever since I'd changed course and decided to become a professional musician. Second, although I wasn't sure about their personal views toward homosexuality—whether, for example, they thought it was mainly a product of nature or a consequence of nurture—I was sure their initial reaction would be to think about how others would react. Regardless of their own feelings toward homosexuality, they would be more concerned about relatives and friends viewing my being gay as something that would bring dishonor to the Taniguchi name. And lastly, I knew my parents, especially Mom, desperately wanted grandchildren to continue our bloodline.

I delayed the inevitable until, finally, Lucas's patience had worn paper thin. He wasn't one to issue ultimatums, but I knew we were reaching a point at which I had to do something or risk irreversibly undermining our relationship. So, I told Lucas I would take him to Hawaii to meet my parents.

•　　•　　•　　•　　•

Before the trip, I talked with Mom and Dad, explaining that I wanted them to meet Lucas, that we'd been living together for several years, and that I hoped to spend the rest of my life with him. "So, he's not just a friend but a special friend?" Mom asked, haltingly, in Japanese. I responded to her in Japanese that, yes, Lucas was a very special friend. And in those words, as simple as that, I officially came out to her.

My parents were less than enthusiastic with the news, to say the least. But, when I mentioned that Lucas and I were looking into staying at a hotel in Honolulu, Mom was offended that we would even consider doing so. "My son will not stay at a hotel when he comes to visit me," she declared over the phone. So, after talking it over with Lucas, we decided to stay at my parents' home—the same house where I grew up. In retrospect, I should've realized that Mom wanting us to stay with them didn't really indicate her acceptance of my relationship with Lucas; it was more her reluctance with my being in a hotel, because relatives and friends might wonder why I was back in town but not saying with my parents. After all, what would the neighbors think?

The week in Hawaii got off to an uneasy start. Upon entering my childhood home, Mom made it clear that Lucas and I would be sleeping in different rooms. She had made up my old room as the guest room for Lucas and set aside bedding for the sofa in the living room for me. Lucas looked at me, hoping I might say something, but I didn't. Later, when he and I were alone, I tried to explain my earlier silence: "If you and I were a straight couple but not married, Mom wouldn't allow us to sleep together either." But I knew, and I knew he knew, that that was just a weak rationalization.

I expected everything to be awkward at first, given that my parents suddenly had to deal with not only a gay son but also his boyfriend. Of course, I assumed they'd be discomforted initially. What I didn't anticipate was the role that race would play. To this day, I'm not sure what made my parents more ill at ease, the fact that the person with whom I wanted to spend my life was a man or that he was white. My parents didn't believe that any race was innately superior to another, but I do think they'd have much preferred if Lucas were Asian. Their unfamiliarity with whites resulted in their maintaining an arms-length distance from him. It was a bad situation all around. Mom and Dad were uncomfortable in their own home, Lucas felt like an intruder, and I was remorseful for being the linchpin of everyone's distress.

Thankfully, Aunt June provided a much-needed respite. Ever since I'd moved to the mainland, she and I had established a tradition that, whenever I was home for a visit, we would spend an entire day together to catch up, just the two of us. I was heartened when, for this trip, I asked whether it would be okay to include Lucas and she said, "Of course, he should join us!"

The three of us spent a morning visiting the Pearl Harbor National Memorial. It'd been years since I was last there, and I'd forgotten the historic site's devastating power to conjure the past. As we stood on one of the walkways overlooking the sunken USS Arizona, where more than a thousand sailors and Marines perished, I was struck by the number of Japanese tourists among us, all solemnly paying their respects. Lucas kept staring at the submerged battleship, as if trying to grasp the sheer magnitude of its historic significance. "Look," he said, "You can see oil still leaking from the ship."

Later that day we drove to Manoa Valley to have lunch at the Waioli Tea Room. Set in a lush, verdant valley, the one-story restaurant with stone columns and ceiling fans had a large patio for outdoor seating. Opened in the 1920s, the tea room was like a capsule in time—the perfect setting for the reflective mood we were in that day.

"It must have been terrible to be living in Honolulu when Pearl Harbor was bombed," Lucas said, probing to see whether Aunt June would be receptive to talking about the past.

"Well, the attack on Pearl Harbor was one thing," she said, after a slight pause, "but it's what happened after that, that was truly tragic. I'd never have thought a mighty country like America could so easily turn against its own values." It was obvious to me that Aunt June was referring to the U.S. incarceration of Japanese Americans in concentration camps. But Lucas, knowing little of our family history, misinterpreted her response.

"I recently edited a book on World War II," he said, "and the author, a historian at Harvard, argues that the bombings of Hiroshima and Nagasaki weren't necessary. Japan was about to surrender, but the U.S. wanted to show its military might to the Russians, to discourage them from expanding into Asia and Europe."

Aunt June, polite as ever, didn't let on that she wasn't referring to America's use of nuclear weapons, and soon the conversation moved on through a variety of topics: the Soviet crushing of the Hungarian Revolution, the McCarthy hearings, the Cuban Missile Crisis, the nuclear arms race. Yet again, I was amazed at the breadth and depth of Lucas's knowledge. I was also fascinated by Aunt June's take on different topics. She told us that, even given the horrific devastation of the atomic bombs on Japan, at least they ended the war before the Soviets could invade. "Can you imagine having a North and South Japan today?" she asked.

After lunch, as Aunt June and I waited for Lucas to use the restroom, I thanked her for spending time with us and apologized if the intense, weighty conversation over our meal had worn her out. "When Lucas gets nervous, he tends to ramble a bit," I explained.

"What are you talking about?" she said. "I thoroughly enjoyed our lunch together. You deserve to be with someone like him, who's so passionate about his work and as intelligent as he is. Otherwise, you'd get bored too easily. And besides, it's obvious he thinks the world of you."

As Lucas exited the restaurant, spotted us, and walked our way, Aunt June touched my left cheek with her hand and said, "I'll see what I can do with your Mom."

· · · · ·

Toward the middle of our visit to Hawaii, Dad thankfully started to relax. It helped immensely that he and Lucas shared a fanatic obsession with baseball, although Dad was a lifelong supporter of the Dodgers and Lucas, like me, was a diehard Red Sox fan. Both men had a facility for stats and could talk for hours about hypotheticals: Who would win in a seven-game series, the '65 Dodgers with Don Drysdale and Sandy Koufax, or the '53 Yankees with Mickey Mantle and Whitey Ford? Would Ted Williams have been able to hit Nolan Ryan's fastball? Would the Red Sox have won the '86 World Series even with Bill Buckner's hideous error if the designated-hitter rule hadn't been changed that year? Baseball gave Dad and Lucas a common language, but what really broke the ice between them was learning that they agreed on things with far greater resonance outside the sport.

Both men greatly admired, for example, the same type of person: someone who isn't naturally gifted but who makes the absolute most of his talents. And they vehemently disdained the exact opposite type of individual, someone who is preternaturally gifted but squanders his talents. Dad and Lucas were also stout supporters of the underdog, in everything from sports to countries to business. If I could point to any one moment when Lucas won Dad's approval, it was this: After Lucas returned from the supermarket with a few items, Dad noticed a six pack of Pepsi and said, "I thought everyone liked Coke instead of Pepsi." Without any hesitation, Lucas responded, "That's why I like Pepsi. I always go for number two."

Dad smiled, then thought for a moment and said, "Hey, what are you saying about my son? He's not number two. He's always been number one!"

"Yeah," Lucas replied, "sometimes you gotta go for number one. Well, I didn't say I never made any exceptions." And with that, Dad laughed heartily, squeezed Lucas's shoulder, and exited the room.

With the ice broken between them, Dad let his natural curiosity overcome any initial wariness. He asked increasingly personal questions, about not only Lucas's upbringing but also his views on potentially touchy subjects like politics and religion. On the last night of our stay, Dad and Lucas were sitting outside on the lanai, enjoying a beer. A cool, pleasant breeze wafted through the house, carrying the sweet, intoxicating scent of the neighbor's plumeria tree in full bloom. From the living room, I overheard their conversation. "There's something I don't understand about Catholics," Dad said, prompting my body to tense up. "Why don't you like Protestants, and why don't Protestants like you? This whole situation in Northern Ireland is just terrible."

After a long pause, Lucas replied, "Well, it's very complicated, with centuries of bad blood, like a family feud that's been going on for far too long. I'm not sure I could explain it."

"But what I don't understand the most is that you're both white, right? Can you even tell if someone's Protestant or Catholic by looking at them?"

"No, you really can't," Lucas replied.

"So, why all the hatred? It's not like how the Japanese can't stand the Chinese and the Chinese can't stand the Japanese."

I wish I could've seen Lucas's expression but, from the living room, I could make out only the silhouette of his body sitting in the patio chair. Was Lucas incredulous or just nonplussed? Whatever his reaction, I could almost sense his nervousness, unsure of what to say, not wanting to be impolite toward my father. I was just about to get up to interrupt their conversation in hopes of changing the subject when I heard my father say, "I'm sorry to ask. It's just something that I could never understand."

"No problem at all," Lucas replied. "I, myself, don't really understand it, because we both believe in the same god and in Jesus Christ."

"You see, that's the thing. I can understand the conflict between Jews and Christians, but not between Protestants and Catholics."

"I know it must seem so odd from the outside looking in, especially for anyone of Japanese descent, because people in Japan are so accepting of different religions, from Shintoism to Buddhism to Christianity."

"Oh, so you know that," Dad said, and I imagined him smiling, impressed with Lucas's knowledge. "Hey, let me get you another beer."

As Dad slid open the screen door, I pretended to be asleep on the sofa. I heard him walk into the kitchen, open the fridge to grab a couple beers, pop their tops, and then head back outside. I smiled to myself as I heard them continue their conversation, which slowly migrated to the economic recession and the savings-and-loan crisis.

•   •   •   •   •

Although Dad eventually relaxed, Mom never did. She constantly worried about one thing or another, at times almost irrationally. One night for dinner she decided to serve a rib roast, one of her signature dishes, but then she wasn't sure what else to prepare. I told her Lucas wasn't a fussy eater. He was, in fact, the one who introduced me to Indian, Hungarian, and Venezuelan cuisines. But when she was cooking, I heard her struggling, banging pots and closing cupboard doors noisily, so I went to help. Mom looked so lost and defeated, something I'd never seen before, especially in the kitchen, where she excels in her culinary proficiency and creativity.

"Help me," she said, holding a potato in each hand. "I have no idea how to mash these."

I almost laughed. There she was, an amazing cook who could easily turn out the tastiest nishime and the most delectable hamachi kama, and yet she struggled with as simple a task as mashed potatoes. I stifled a chuckle, because the last thing I wanted to do was make light of her distress.

"Don't worry about the potatoes," I told her. "Lucas eats rice."

She looked at me with amazement, as if I'd just told her Lucas had mastered the Japanese poetry form of tanka. "But I thought he was Irish," she said.

"Yeah, but he doesn't have to have mashed potatoes. Really, he likes rice."

"Well, why didn't you tell me that in the first place!" she snapped, her face saturated with irritation.

Unlike Dad, Mom never quite allowed herself to be herself in Lucas's presence. Her mind was constantly preoccupied, as if there was always far too much for her to do and precious little time to complete those tasks. And her emotions were constantly on edge, like she was sure she'd forgotten something important but couldn't, for the life of her, remember what it was. Toward the last day of our visit, I hoped she might finally let herself relax and maybe even be a little sad, knowing she wouldn't be seeing me again for a while. But, if anything, she appeared more relieved than sentimental, and this made me feel guilty for pushing her so far outside her comfort zone.

The morning before our flight, I helped Mom hang a load of laundry on the outdoor clothesline. "Osewa ni narimashita," I told her, acknowledging everything she'd done to welcome Lucas into their home. She looked at me, and I felt her wanting to say something, but she held back and merely told me to take good care of myself when I returned to New York City.

Throughout the entire week in Honolulu, Lucas had been a trooper. Whenever I'd suggest going somewhere to meet Aunt June, spend time with cousins from Dad's side of the family, or hang out with a group of high-school friends, he was always game without hesitation. Even early on, when we were still jet-lagged and he was just getting accustomed to staying at my parents, he didn't once express any impatience or annoyance at having to adapt to the lifestyle and rhythms of a different culture. I suppose he sensed some of the anxiety I felt, having to deal with my parents, and he didn't want to add to that stress.

On the long overnight plane ride to Los Angeles and throughout our connecting flight to New York City, I was drained and slept most of the way, while Lucas read a book and watched the in-flight movies. Later, when we were back on Manhattan having dinner at a neighborhood restaurant, both of us struggling to stay awake as we forced ourselves onto East Coast time, I asked him whether, overall, he'd enjoyed the trip. Lucas put down his fork, looked squarely at me, and said, "Let me put it this way: Now I think I understand you so much better." And then he reached over the small circular table, squeezed my shoulders, and kissed me on the lips with such tenderness that, had I been standing, my knees would have surely buckled.

CHAPTER FIFTEEN

I had hoped that, with time, the four of us—Dad, Mom, Lucas and I—would gradually find a way to become what we ostensibly were: two couples, separated by a generation but connected through the strength of a family bond. I even imagined we might travel together. Lucas had long wanted to go to Japan (he'd never been), and I was eager to return there to see Mom's relatives again. I was so curious as to what Lucas's reactions would be: what he would think as he experienced the hustle and bustle of Tokyo; how he might marvel at the clean and punctual trains; what he would say when he first saw the Kintai Bridge. I also thought of Mom and Dad explaining to him the subtle aspects of Japanese culture: how people constantly try to infer what you're really trying to say; how even young schoolchildren have such respect for the property of others; how crimes against tourists are virtually nonexistent; how the Japanese, especially older ones, respect and admire Americans. Unfortunately, we never had the pleasure of such a trip.

Just four months after we returned from Hawaii I got a late-night call from Aunt June. As soon as I heard her voice, I braced myself for the worst. For whatever reason, I thought something terrible had happened to Mom. Instead, it was Dad. He'd been working outside, trying to clear a clogged roof gutter of debris from a recent storm. Somehow, he lost his balance and fell, hitting the ground at just the wrong angle, snapping his neck and killing him instantly.

"I'm so, so sorry," Aunt June said.

My brain couldn't fully comprehend the finality of what I'd just heard, but my mind clearly envisioned my father up on his creaky, lean-to wooden ladder, precariously propped against the side of the house.

Working to dislodge the leaves and branches, he was probably listening to his trusty transistor radio, which he relied on to follow the Dodgers games whenever he did yardwork. As he cleared the debris, he might've accidentally knocked the radio over and, as he tried to catch it, lost his balance, sending his body crashing to the ground below.

"Was Mom home?" I asked.

"Yes, she was cooking in the kitchen and heard him fall."

I couldn't imagine what it must have been like to rush outside and discover Dad's lifeless body, sprawled on the ground. I knew Mom was a strong woman, but I feared this horrible accident would be beyond her inner steely strength.

"How is she?" I asked.

"Not too well. How soon can you get here?"

• • • • •

The next few days were a blur. Aunt June picked me up at the airport in Honolulu and drove me to Mom and Dad's house. When I entered the living room, Mom got up from the sofa and we hugged. She looked utterly exhausted, like a worn-out shell of the woman who'd raised me.

"Have you slept at all?" I asked.

"No, not really. I've been waiting for you."

Staying with Mom those first few days was surreal. It was like we were both in a deep trance, merely going through the motions of being alive. The only thing I really remember is going to Hasegawa Mortuary to arrange Dad's service. Mom and I had an appointment, but when the time came, she said she didn't have the strength, so I drove into town myself.

Hasegawa Mortuary kept meticulous records of the funerals for Dad's parents, so it was basically a straightforward process to arrange a similar Buddhist service for him. The information was so detailed that I was even able to order the exact same urn for Dad that he and his siblings had ordered for both their parents. Then I ran into a snag. The funeral director needed to know how Dad's name was written in kanji, because the Buddhist priest would then derive his new name from those specific Chinese ideograms. The new name was a crucial part of the service, symbolizing how Dad would be reborn into a different being.

Although I knew my father's Japanese middle name, I didn't know how to write it in kanji. I barely knew how to write my own Japanese middle name, Kenichi, in kanji. And, as it turned out, according to the mortuary's reference book, there were four different ways to write Dad's Japanese name.

"Do any of these kanji look familiar?" the funeral director asked.

I had to admit that none did. I'd never really seen Dad's name written out, except when he spelled it phonetically in English. This gap in my knowledge was embarrassing, my ignorance exposing me as an ungrateful son who hadn't even bothered to learn the kanji for his own father's name. I felt myself sinking from a sea of grief into the deeper waters of guilt. The funeral director, probably sensing I was close to an emotional breakdown, did his best to keep me afloat.

"Don't worry about it," he reassured me, "Lots of Sansei don't know the kanji for their parents. Maybe you can find out from your mother or another relative and let me know?" The funeral director himself appeared to be Sansei, or the grandchild of Japanese immigrants, and I greatly appreciated his calm demeanor and charitable efforts to rescue me from feeling any worse than I already did.

When I returned home, Mom was in her bedroom with the door shut. I wasn't sure if she was trying to catch up on her sleep, or if she was awake but wanted to be left alone. Either way, I didn't want to disturb her. I was also hesitant to ask her about Dad's name. I feared she might take affront at my lack of knowledge of something so important. And yet, how would I have learned the kanji for Dad's name? It wasn't something that ever came up in conversation, even when we were in Japan. I also feared that, after professing my ignorance about Dad's name, Mom would then quiz me about her own name, which I didn't know either. Mom was already on a razor's edge of emotions. The last thing I wanted to do was to tip her over.

I was about to call Aunt June to ask for her help when it suddenly dawned on me. At the time of my parents' marriage, a relative in Iwakuni gave them a beautiful tea set custom-made by a famous potter there. The set consisted of a teapot and five cups, made from the town's clay. All six pieces were impossibly light, as if the potter threw each item as thin as possible while still maintaining enough strength and sturdiness for everyday use. (My parents, though, would never think to actually use the valuable set, instead choosing to display it on a wooden credenza in the living room.) Years ago, when I was just in elementary school, Dad showed me the tea set and said each of the pieces had his and Mom's names hand painted in Japanese, written in elegant calligraphy. At the time, I had little interest in what he was saying, even as he tried to impress on me just how exquisite the calligraphy was.

Over the years, I never really paid much attention to the tea set. It was, to me, a mundane fixture of our house, like the silk scroll of a tiger hanging in the living room or the miniature wooden pagoda sitting on the TV console. But now that I looked at the teapot, sure enough, I could make out both Mom's and Dad's names written by a fine-tipped fude, or Japanese ink brush, with the graceful black kanji standing out against the crackled celadon glaze. I felt such triumph (and relief). I could almost see Dad smiling and saying, "So, you were listening to me after all!"

●　　●　　●　　●　　●

Three days after I had arrived in Honolulu, Lucas joined me. We'd talked over the phone and agreed that, given Mom's delicate state, it would probably be best for him to stay at a hotel in Waikiki. I would sleep with him at the hotel but spend the days with Mom until the funeral. Several high-school friends offered to take Lucas sightseeing during the days, but he said he'd be perfectly fine just reading and lounging by the hotel pool.

At first, Mom seemed uninterested in Lucas's presence. I was somewhat surprised by this, and a bit annoyed. I just kept telling myself that, while I'd lost my father, she'd lost her husband, the man to whom she'd been married for more than thirty years and with whom she'd planned to live out her twilight years, making the transition from middle-aged couple to elderly soulmates. Yet, as much as I reminded myself of her tremendous, life-altering loss, I later realized that I was, in actuality, suppressing a growing resentment toward her.

Everything came to a head the day before the funeral. Mom and I were having lunch, trying to force down some food because we hadn't really eaten anything substantial since Dad's death. Aunt June had brought over some takeout food from Gulick Delicatessen and I was actually able to smell the delicious aromas, as if my senses were slowly returning to normal. The containers of shoyu chicken, pork long rice, and grilled ahi had me salivating.

"We have to eat," I told Mom. "We're going to really need our strength for tomorrow."

As Mom picked over the food on her plate, she looked so distracted and fidgety. I tried to calm her, telling her that all the planning and preparations for the funeral were done. We'd gone over the service with Dad's siblings and the Buddhist priest. I'd picked up the programs from the printer yesterday. Aunt June had ordered all the food for the reception that would follow the service. But none of my reassurances had a soothing effect, so I tried distracting her by making small talk about the state's proposed plan to build the controversial H-3 freeway, connecting Honolulu with the windward side of the island. I could tell, though, that she wasn't listening to me at all. Something was clearly on her mind.

"Mom, try not to worry," I told her, "we'll get through tomorrow."

She looked at me, her brow furrowed, and said, "But will Lucas be there?"

It took me a few seconds to fully grasp what she was saying. I really didn't want to believe she'd just asked what I thought she had.

"What do you mean?" I said, trying to keep my voice as level as possible. "Of course, he'll be there. He came to pay his respects to Dad, and he wants to be there to support me."

I watched as Mom pushed her food around her plate. She eventually dipped a piece of ahi into a small plastic container of sauce but then put it back onto her plate without taking a bite. Finally, she said, "But where will he sit?"

So that's what was troubling her! Buddhist funerals in Hawaii are very hierarchical, with the family members of the deceased always sitting in a specific order. First, of course, comes the spouse. After that are the children, with their respective families, in descending order from the eldest to the youngest. Then, in the next row, the deceased's siblings sit with their respective families, again in descending order according to their ages.

Dad came from a large family, with three boys and four girls, but that wasn't the problem. The big question was, where would Lucas sit in the hierarchy? I'd already anticipated the issue and discussed it with him. The night he arrived, we had cocktails in the hotel's outdoor bar, beneath a huge banyan tree. After Lucas started his second whiskey on the rocks, I broached the subject with him, asking if he wouldn't mind sitting at the funeral several rows discreetly behind where Mom and I would be. I told him that a good friend from high school had volunteered to sit with him, and she would explain what was going on during the service. "That's fine," Lucas said. "Anything to make things easier for your mom."

So, everything was already worked out. I suppose the compassionate and understanding thing to do at that point, sitting there having lunch with Mom, would have been to simply tell her that Lucas would be with my friend the whole time during the service, and that they would be a few rows behind us. I could have calmly explained all this to her, but I didn't. Instead, something in me cracked.

"Why are you so worried about where Lucas will sit?" I said, my voice quickly rising in anger. "After all, didn't your husband just die? Shouldn't you have other things on your mind?"

Mom looked at me, her expression both hurt and incredulous. Then outrage flooded her face. "Don't talk to me like that. How dare you talk to your mother like that? What kind of son are you?!"

I resisted the urge to shoot back, instead taking a deep breath to try to steady myself. "I'm sorry," I told her, "I just don't think you should be worrying yourself about where Lucas will sit."

She looked at me as if I'd failed to understand the simplest of things. "But won't people wonder who he is?"

I braced myself. "So, are you trying to say you don't want Lucas at the funeral at all?"

She turned away from me and her silence was maddening, unleashing a torrent of fury from somewhere deep inside an ugly part of my being. The words came hurling out of my mouth, my voice dripping with anger and contempt: "Lucas flew five-thousand miles to be here. There's no way in hell I'm telling him he's not welcome at Dad's funeral. You got that? No fucking way in hell. And, while we're at it, what kind of mother are you, not wanting her son to be comforted by his partner after the death of his father?"

"I told you not to talk to me that way. See what living on the mainland has done to you? No son should be this disrespectful. What would your father say? He would be so disappointed in you, so ashamed to have raised a son like you."

I was livid that she'd tossed Dad into the argument. Summoning every ounce of restraint I had, I told her, in a low, flat voice that surprised even me in its quiet, visceral intensity, "If Lucas isn't welcome at the service, then I'm not going either. So, you better decide what's gonna be worse for you: having people wonder who Lucas is, or having to explain to everyone why I'm in Hawaii but not at my father's funeral."

I left the dining table, marched through the kitchen, and slammed the back door as I exited the house. I got into my rental car and tore out of the gravel driveway, leaving behind a furious cloud of dust. My heart raced as I drove back to the hotel, flipping through radio stations but unable to find anything that would register itself as music in my highly agitated state. I knew that, at some point, I would deeply regret the virulent words I'd just spewed, yet still I seethed. Any guilt I might've felt then for speaking to my mother so harshly was overshadowed by the intense, red-hot anger coursing through my body.

· · · · ·

When I got to the hotel, I found Lucas at the pool, basking in the soothing Hawaiian sunshine. He'd been in Honolulu for only a couple days but was already beginning to turn a light shade of brown, the freckles on his shoulder becoming more prominent. He looked so peaceful, lying there napping, that I didn't want to disturb him. I quietly pulled up a chair and sat next to him, watching the waves in the distance gently lapping onto the white-sand beach, my mind trying to empty itself of the memory of my blowout with Mom. I wasn't sure how much time had passed when Lucas eventually woke up.

"What's up?" he said.

"I'll tell you over dinner. Let's go clean up, and then grab a drink somewhere."

Back at our hotel room, while Lucas took a shower, I called Aunt June. Apparently, she hadn't heard anything about my earlier fight with Mom. Or, maybe, Mom had already told her, and Aunt June thought it best to feign ignorance. Either way, I didn't want her to get caught having to choose sides between her only sister and her only nephew, so I downplayed what had happened. I said just that Mom and I had argued, and I asked her to do me a big favor. "Could you please go to Mom's house before the funeral tomorrow to help her get ready for the service?"

"Oh, don't worry about that," Aunt June said. "I had planned on doing that anyway."

After we hung up, I couldn't help but think how different the two sisters are. Aunt June never married, choosing instead to devote herself to her career. A woman ahead of her time, she put herself through business college, learning shorthand and how to type. Her first job was as a secretary at the Honolulu Advertiser, the city's morning daily paper. Over the years, she received one promotion after another until she became vice president of business operations. Now, she manages a staff of dozens of employees, overseeing the paper's marketing, advertising, and classified-ad operations.

Mom took an entirely different path. She married Dad and focused her life on being the best mother she could. My earliest memories are of her reading to me, and before I started kindergarten I already had the vocabulary of a child several years older. Even after I started school she took only part-time jobs that enabled her to be at home to greet me when I returned from classes, always with a cheerful welcome, "Okaerinasai!"

When I was in junior high, Aunt June had saved enough money and accumulated sufficient vacation time to finally take her dream trip—an extended tour of Europe. She spent three weeks hitting the major cities: Amsterdam, Copenhagen, West Berlin, Venice, Florence, Rome, Madrid, Paris, and London. After she returned, she stopped by our home to drop off a shopping bag of omiyage, including an elegant 18-karat gold bracelet from Venice for Mom, a stylish leather wallet from Paris for Dad, and a small wooden cuckoo clock from Germany for me. She spent the entire afternoon with us, showing photos she'd taken and telling us about her many adventures.

After she left, I asked Mom if she wished she'd gone with her sister. "Not me," Mom answered, "I have no desire to be any place where I can't speak the language."

Her reaction surprised me. Just a little earlier she had marveled at all the photos Aunt June had taken, oohing and aahing at the canals of Venice, the Colosseum in Rome, the Eiffel Tower in Paris. Mom must've inferred what I was thinking. "I know we're sisters," she told me, "but your aunt and I are two very different people. Ever since we were little girls, Aunt June wanted a career and excitement, and I wanted a family and a quiet life."

Growing up I always felt closer to Aunt June; she understood me in ways Mom didn't. But maybe that was just because my aunt always had the luxury of being the "good cop," constantly there to support and cheer me on. I could confide in her without feeling the weight of any judgment bearing down on me. Mom was necessarily resigned to the role of "bad cop." Because Dad was usually busy working, it was left to her to assume the disciplinarian duties, and she and I had bitter battles, often resulting in silent treatments lasting days. At my worst moments, I secretly wished Aunt June was my mother. But if the two sisters exchanged lives, would Mom have been my confidant and close ally instead of Aunt June?

·   ·   ·   ·   ·

Before dinner that evening Lucas and I decided to have a cocktail at the Royal Hawaiian Hotel. Famous for its pink stucco exterior, the hotel had an outdoor bar that served legendary Mai Tais, concocted with rum, Cointreau, Amaretto, and a blend of freshly squeezed orange and pineapple juices. Lucas and I sat side by side along a small wooden table, both of us facing the ocean while enjoying our drinks. On a small stage on the patio two men played slack-key guitar and sang classic Hawaiian songs as we watched the sun slowly descend into the ocean, a cool trade wind rustling through the palm leaves above us. The setting was too perfect to leave, so we decided to have dinner there, ordering from the bar's pupu menu.

When we returned to our hotel room after that meal I finally felt relaxed. But as I undressed, I noticed a large rash on the right side of my torso. I'd seen the beginnings of it earlier, when I showered, but thought nothing of it. Now, though, it covered a much larger area, stretching from my waist all the way to my shoulder. Moreover, the mottled skin had turned a bright red. I called Lucas into the bathroom to have a look.

"Oh geesh," he said, "where's the nearest emergency room?"

In the taxi ride over to Queen's Hospital, my anxieties started to get the better of me. What if the rash kept spreading, reaching my face? The last thing I wanted was to show up at Dad's funeral with ugly red blotches covering my cheeks and forehead, pulling people's attention unnecessarily toward me when the focus should be on Dad.

"Relax," Lucas told me. "You're gonna be fine."

I'd just managed to calm myself when we reached the waiting area of the emergency room. Then, as we sat there, I was overcome by a wave of intense sentimentality. I was born at Queen's Hospital, and it dawned on me that, at the time, Dad was around my age now. What was he thinking as he waited for me to be born? What dreams did he have for his first child? Did he hope I'd become a famous scientist one day or a lawyer who would argue a case in front of the Supreme Court? Or did he think I'd invent a vaccine against cancer? So many questions swirled in my head, and I had no idea of the answers to any of them. But I was fairly certain of one thing: Dad probably wouldn't have imagined that his only child—a son—would be gay, live with another man in New York City, and fail to bear him grandchildren. All of a sudden, I felt my composure give way, as if a trapdoor opened and plunged me into an emotional nadir. All I knew was that I needed to leave the waiting room, fast. Lucas followed and grabbed me just as I was about to exit the double doors.

"What's wrong?" he asked.

I was at a complete loss for words. There was so much I wanted to say, and yet I didn't know where to begin. My mind was overwhelmed; I couldn't process any of my tangled emotions into coherent English. I just stared at Lucas and shook my head helplessly. He'd never seen me anywhere near this state of raw vulnerability. Not sure what else to do, Lucas reached for my right hand, brought it to his mouth, and kissed it. He was just about to say something when we heard the admitting nurse call my name.

The attending doctor took one look at my torso and asked if I'd eaten anything unusual recently, been hiking, or used a different laundry detergent. I answered "no" to those questions and then said that I really didn't think I was having an allergic reaction because, throughout my life, I'd eaten all kinds of food, come into contact with different plants and animals, and used whatever detergent happened to be on sale. But after noting I now lived in New York City, the doctor was all the more certain it was an allergic reaction, even after I told him I'd grown up in Hawaii.

"Sometimes when you move away," he said, "your body 'forgets' and your immune system reacts to something that was benign to you when you were younger."

But I insisted I'd never been allergic to anything in my entire life. I also let the doctor know that my father's funeral was tomorrow and that earlier I'd had a huge fight with my mother. "Do you think the rash could be stress related?" I asked.

The doctor looked at me, his level face giving way to sympathy. He then gave me a prescription for a corticosteroid he said would help with the allergic reaction I was having.

Later that night, as Lucas and I went to bed, I told him about what'd happened earlier, during my knockdown battle with Mom. "It's no wonder you have that rash," he said, "I'm sure it's stress related."

The next morning the rash had spread but, thankfully, it had yet to reach my face, so no one at the funeral would see it. Even so, the raw redness was concerning. After carefully inspecting my body under the harsh fluorescent lights in the bathroom, I needed to get some fresh air and stepped outside onto the small lanai of our hotel room. The warm early-morning sunlight felt so soothing, gently caressing my body, but inside I was depleted. I knew I had to be at my father's funeral later that day, and I dreaded it. Just as I was about to head back into the room to take a shower, Lucas joined me on the lanai. He put his arm around my shoulder, and we both watched a small group of tourists with oversized surfboards taking a surfing lesson. Their instructor was showing them how to make the transition from lying on the board to standing on it in a crouched position. One of the students had a lot of difficulty with that maneuver, so the instructor broke it down into simple, exaggerated steps for her—all to no avail.

"I'm worried about you," Lucas said. "I've never seen you looking so worn out."

"I just want to be back in our apartment, curled up in bed with you, watching an old black-and-white movie on TV."

Lucas turned my body toward his and hugged me. I felt like I didn't have the strength to fully hug him back, so I just let my body be absorbed by his. He held me like that for a couple minutes, and then he said, "If I ask you a question, will you promise to answer it truthfully?"

"Sure," I nodded.

"Would it be easier for everyone if I didn't go to the funeral today?"

Something in the way he asked, his concern and compassion so sincere, overwhelmed me with emotion. I kissed him on his cheek as tears began to roll down my face and onto his chest.

"I'm not going to the funeral if you're not going," I told him, my voice shaking.

"You didn't answer my question," Lucas said, as he gently pushed my body from his so he could look directly in my eyes.

"I want you there," I told him. "This funeral is about Dad, not her."

"But you still didn't answer my question. Look, you're all going through so much pain right now, and I didn't come here to add to anyone's distress, especially your mom's. No offense, but I barely knew your father, so I really don't have to be at his funeral. I only want to be there for you. But now I don't want to go, because I think I'd be hurting more than helping the situation."

I couldn't really find fault with what Lucas said. And even if I could, I didn't have the strength to argue with him. After the blowout with Mom, I felt so drained I just wanted the funeral to be over with. What I wanted most was to spend the day only with Lucas, maybe driving over to the North Shore of Oahu, hiking on a trail, and quietly remembering my father as I absorbed the sights and smells of the lush greenery of the island he loved so much. But I worried about the repercussions I'd face for avoiding his funeral. And I wondered what Dad, himself, would think about the whole situation, whether he'd want me to stick to my guns or acquiesce. Much as I tried, I couldn't imagine how he'd advise me. The thing I couldn't escape, though, were the words I always heard so clearly in his voice: What would the neighbors think?

Years later I would look back at the decision I made that day and feel such shame and regret. But that morning, as I struggled with a tangled skein of emotions, I lacked the strength to do what I knew was right. I was a coward and took the path of least resistance. I left Lucas at the hotel and went to my father's funeral alone.

·   ·   ·   ·   ·

I don't remember much about the service, just isolated moments here and there. Of course, Mom and I were cordial to each other. For once, we were in perfect agreement: We just wanted the service to be over and done with so we could each grieve in private.

Thankfully, the Buddhist priest kept the chanting to a minimum and delivered much of the service in English. I was touched by so many things: the beautiful memorial board Dad's favorite niece had assembled from our family photos; the presence of so many of Dad's longtime friends, including his monthly poker gang, whom I hadn't seen in years; the huge bouquets and flower wreaths; the touching eulogy by Dad's oldest nephew.

I was especially moved by the many stories I heard at the reception following the service. A woman about my age told me that, years ago, Dad used to give her grandmother a ride to church every week. A high-school kid who worked at the bakery with Dad described how my father did everything by feel and taste, never using any measuring cups, and how he had an internal clock that knew exactly when the sheet cakes, pies, cupcakes, and other assorted pastries were done. Perhaps the most touching story was that of a woman who told me that Dad had once baked and personally delivered a birthday cake for her young son, even though she hadn't ordered one that year because her husband had just lost his job and money was tight. "To dis day," the woman said, her thick pidgin English like music to my ears, "I no can believe dat he would even rememba my son's birthday. Even I get hard time rememba his birthday."

I was also touched to see Mr. Yoshimura, who'd seen Dad's obituary in the paper. We talked about the different gigs I'd been getting in New York City, the declining quality of French oboe cane, and the new recording of the famous Nielsen woodwind quintet that critics were raving about. Not once, though, did either of us mention Mr. Janoski or the scandal in Los Angeles.

At different times throughout the reception, several people inquired about Lucas. When I told them he thought it best that he didn't attend, they all gave me a knowing look and sympathetic smile, unsure how else to respond. Even my good friends who'd met Lucas on our previous trip were at a loss for what to say. Only Aunt June mustered any words. "I'm so sorry about Lucas," she told me, as she clasped my hands tightly.

CHAPTER SIXTEEN

Back in New York City, I felt gutted. I woke in the mornings with so little energy that even getting out of bed to shower felt like a daunting chore. Thankfully, the oboist who'd been my temporary replacement while I was in Hawaii was only too happy to continue subbing for me as I struggled to reclaim myself. Initially, I thought I was suffering from depression over my father's death. But when my rash lingered and I developed a boil near my elbow, I decided I needed medical help.

My primary care physician took one look at the boil and told me I might have contracted a staph infection. He said I needed to go to the emergency room of a nearby hospital to have the boil drained and biopsied, and then undergo a two-week regimen of strong antibiotics. The biopsy revealed I'd somehow contracted Methicillin-resistant Staphylococcus aureus (MRSA), maybe from the locker room at my gym. Evidently, the misdiagnosis in Hawaii had only made things worse, because the corticosteroid the doctor had prescribed lowered my immune system, allowing the staph infection to spread unchecked like kudzu in a forest.

The lanced boil healed. And, thanks to the antibiotics, the rash eventually cleared, although the right side of my torso remained permanently discolored to a dark brown. To this day, whenever I look at my body in the mirror, I'm reminded of not just the MRSA infection but my father's death and the painful clash with Mom. And, even after my body recovered physically, my mind never quite healed from everything that had happened in Hawaii. A year after Dad's death, I still felt like I was in a daze, as if I had become a bystander to my own life.

At first, when I returned to playing in "Cats," the orchestra pit was a haven where I could immerse myself and forget everything. But then, after several months, things began to feel so episodic. It didn't help that I'd played in that musical for so long I'd memorized my entire part and could all but play it in my sleep. At times, I left a performance not even remembering actually having played in it. A part of me knew I should begin looking for another gig, yet I lacked the energy and motivation to do so. Also, there was some comfort in getting paid for a job that wasn't stressful, enabling me to maintain a minimal status quo existence.

Unfortunately, the months after my father's death were a terribly difficult time for Lucas as well. The publisher he worked for was acquired by a British firm, and his department suffered a round of distressing layoffs. Lucas was unscathed in the downsizing but found himself with a new boss who ended up hiring a round of editors from her previous job. This created an us-against-them dynamic in the workplace, with a line firmly drawn between the pre-acquisition veterans and the post-acquisition hires. The result was a constant clash: how things had traditionally been done versus new approaches that would supposedly increase productivity and cut costs.

Within weeks, Lucas dreaded going into work. It wasn't just that he'd been moved from an outer office to an inner cubicle and seen his travel and expense account slashed. It was that every manuscript he wanted to acquire suddenly had to pass through rounds of quantitative analyses, leaving no room for his editorial instincts and astute judgment. He was also ordered to offload the actual editing of manuscripts to cheap freelancers. But the hands-on editing was what Lucas liked best about his job; it was also a part of his work at which he excelled. He wasn't only adept at reshaping a manuscript, often re-conceptualizing and restructuring a book while fine-tuning the language to make it sing. He was also deftly skilled at the type of author handholding that's often required, massaging the delicate egos of writers while coddling them so that they'd accept his proposed changes, revisions that would ultimately improve the finished product. He prided himself that the books he brought to print were true collaborations between editor and writer, and his stable of authors adored working with him.

It didn't help that Lucas clashed frequently with his new boss, whom he said was very lowbrow, with little interest in the types of books he found most appealing. "She has such a simplistic 'women's magazine' view of the world," Lucas complained to me one night over dinner. "Everything to her has to be distilled down to '7 ways to keep your marriage alive' or '10 surefire tips for a romantic evening' or '5 reasons why husbands stray.'" Instead of a book about string theory that would offer an elegant treatise, describing the efforts of scientists to unite Einstein's theory of relativity with quantum mechanics, she'd rather Lucas be acquiring books more along the lines of "Physics for Dummies."

I wish I could say I was a caring, supportive partner to Lucas throughout his annus horribilis at work. But I'm ashamed to admit that, at the time, I was far too wrapped up in my own head to really be of much help to anyone, even the man I loved so dearly. Lucas was drowning at his job, and I wasn't able to throw him a life raft. I couldn't even find it within myself to offer words of constant support to guide him safely to shore. I knew what I should have been doing, but I couldn't summon the wherewithal to do it. In essence, I was too emotionally bankrupt to be of any help. That's a pathetic excuse, I realize, but it was the stark reality of my dismal state.

As work became increasingly intolerable for Lucas, he channeled his energies elsewhere. He put in the bare minimum number of hours at his cubicle, and then headed to the Gay Men's Health Crisis office. Even there, though, he eventually grew restless and joined the more militant AIDS Coalition to Unleash Power (ACT UP), becoming active in the group's numerous protests and even once getting arrested for public disobedience. Throughout this time, he repeatedly asked me to join him so that we, as a couple, could fight the government's appalling intransigence toward AIDS research and funding. Lucas's activism, which I greatly admired, should have inspired me. It should've helped me look beyond my own sorry state of funk to a much higher, worthier cause. Instead it had the opposite effect, making me retreat more tightly into my shell. I told him I was still mourning for Dad and the last thing I wanted was to be around others, especially people I didn't know. Lucas accepted my explanation, although I know he was deeply disappointed in me. He wanted me there alongside him, demonstrating to protest the government's inaction during such a catastrophic health crisis.

But the truth behind my reluctance to join him went far beyond a son's grief for his dead father. It's still difficult for me to admit this, but I was afraid of being photographed or filmed at a protest and then having that footage appear on the national news. I envisioned my mother, sitting on her comfortable sofa in her living room in Honolulu, watching as Peter Jennings or Tom Brokaw cut to video of an ACT UP protest, and seeing her son being handcuffed by police officers. Her mind would immediately race to what our relatives and family friends would think, many of whom weren't yet aware of my sexual orientation. Since returning to New York City after Dad's funeral, my relationship with Mom had grown increasingly strained, even though we still maintained at least a minimal level of infrequent contact. But I was afraid to disturb the fragile mother-son détente we'd settled into, and the possibility of an outing on national TV was, at that point, too big a risk. What I didn't realize was, deep down inside, my cowardice was eating me from within—and it was alienating Lucas.

Eventually, I did join the battle in the fight against AIDS, albeit in a behind-the-scenes role. A neighborhood group needed people to deliver meals to those too ill to shop or cook for themselves. The group especially needed volunteers around lunchtime on weekdays, which was perfect for my schedule as a Broadway musician. Still, I knew Lucas wanted me on the frontlines of the war alongside him, Larry Kramer, and the hundreds of other brave souls. Sadly, that was something I just wasn't ready for, not yet at least.

Not surprisingly, Lucas and I drifted farther and farther away from each other. Ironically, we became lousy partners but ideal roommates. Although we shared an apartment, we led separate lives, barely seeing each other and never interfering with the other's life. Given the listless state I was in, I probably would've been content to continue living the way we were indefinitely. But Lucas wasn't the type to settle for a life of "quiet desperation," to quote Henry David Thoreau, one of his favorite authors.

When our inevitable breakup finally came, I was anything but surprised. To be honest, I was amazed he'd stuck it out with me for almost two years after Dad's death. Our parting was perhaps one of the most amicable, if painful, breakups ever. Lucas told me I could keep our place and he'd find another apartment somewhere in Chelsea, which would be more convenient for all his ACT UP meetings and events. I supposed our Upper West Side home, which was rightfully his, was his goodbye gift to me for whatever unnecessary guilt he might've felt for pulling the plug on our relationship. In truth, though, the fault was mainly mine for all the different ways, both large and small, I'd sabotaged whatever chance we might've had for a happy life together.

"I'm really sorry things didn't work out, that I was so limited in what I could give you," I told him when he came to pick up the last of his things.

"Don't say that," he said, looking straight into my eyes. "It's not your fault." But we both knew he was lying.

"Why aren't you angry with me?"

Lucas shrugged, and I could tell he was trying to decide just how honest he should be. Finally, he said, "Look, I guess I knew from your father's funeral that a part of you would always be unavailable to me. That's all water under the bridge now." What Lucas was too kind to say was that, when push came to shove, he knew I'd always be the son of my parents, steeped in the traditions of a faraway culture and inextricably bound to my ancestors' way of thinking. And a huge part of that was my ingrained sense of obligation—the heavy duty to my family. From the day I was born, I carried with me the weight of their expectations and obligations. It wasn't until I was in my early teens, when studying U.S. history in school, that I first realized I might also have some individual rights, to counterbalance those familial obligations. These weren't just my Constitutional rights as a U.S. citizen, guaranteeing me religious freedom, the right to free speech, and so on. These individual rights also included the basic promise that I could pursue my personal happiness without being unduly encumbered by the government or society at large. Lucas lived in that world, always fighting for his individual rights as a gay man, his noble activism at the core of who he was. I, in sharp contrast, remained mired in a land of burdensome obligations.

When he left our apartment for the last time and I heard the familiar sound of the front door shutting, the automatic lock clicking into place, I was overcome by unrelenting sadness, with waves of regret pummeling me mercilessly. For the first time in my life, I realized I might always be single, too damaged to maintain a long-term relationship, too limited in the love I could selflessly give to another person. If I couldn't make things work with someone like Lucas, I thought, then what hope did I have of ever finding happiness with another man?

That night I couldn't be alone and yet didn't want to be with friends, so I walked over to the cinema complex near Lincoln Center and bought a ticket for whatever movie was playing. It happened to be "Dead Poets Society," an odd selection for me because I'm one of the few people who doesn't "get" Robin Williams. I'd watched a couple episodes of "Mork & Mindy" and found his brand of humor too manic, too frenzied for my tastes. But there I was, sitting in a sparsely filled theater watching "Dead Poets Society" on the night my ex-boyfriend came to remove the last vestiges of his presence from our apartment. It was the type of film I should've disliked, heavy on saccharine sentimentality and light on gritty realism. My mind wandered as the movie played, only snapping into attention during the inspiring scene when John Keating, the unconventional teacher played by Williams, urges his students to carpe diem and "make your lives extraordinary." I was now fully engaged in the lives of Keating's students, especially Neil, who yearned to be an actor. Unfortunately for Neil, played by Robert Sean Leonard, that dream ran counter to the unyielding demands of his stern father, who insisted his son go to Harvard and become a doctor. In a harrowing, haunting sequence late at night, Neil dons the crown he wore earlier playing Puck in a local production of "A Midsummer Night's Dream." He then retrieves his father's gun from a locked drawer and shoots himself. His suicide was a gut punch, leaving me in a daze until the final inspiring "Captain, oh captain" scene. As the film credits rolled, an elderly man sitting behind me tapped me on the shoulder and asked if I was okay. Only then did I realize I'd been sniffling, although I had no idea for how long.

To be honest, when Lucas severed our relationship, I was secretly relieved. I knew I just didn't have the energy to be a committed, equal partner, and I constantly felt guilty for my inadequacies. At the time, I needed my life to be as simple and uncomplicated as possible. Having a boyfriend then was too messy, too unpredictable, too draining on the little emotional resources I felt I had.

The problem, though, was that I chose not to look inward for ways to improve and attain the life I desired. Instead, it was so much easier and more convenient to look outward and blame my parents for all their past shortcomings, especially Mom—not just her failure to welcome Lucas into our family but her fundamental inability to accept that I'm gay. Watching

"Dead Poets Society" only hardened my feelings toward her. Weeks later, when I told her over the phone that Lucas and I had broken up, I imagined—in the ensuing silence—that she was trying to suppress her joy before finally responding with a terse, "Oh."

Soon, my irregular phone calls with Mom became all the more infrequent, and the obligatory cards I sent annually for her birthday, Mother's Day, Thanksgiving, and Christmas became increasingly curt, just a couple sentences to wish her well. Our relationship had broken down, and I had neither the desire nor energy to fix it.

PART III

The Present:
New York City and Washington D.C.
(Autumn 2000)

CHAPTER SEVENTEEN

Last night, after Mom's emotional breakdown at the Statue of Liberty, we talked late into the early morning. Up until then, I'd known only bits and pieces of what had happened to her during the war, because she was always reluctant to talk about the past. It was only in high school that I learned about her family being sent to Arkansas. The blockbuster TV miniseries "Roots" was airing around that time, and my social-studies teacher assigned us a project to trace our own ancestral roots. Dad's half of the family tree was simple enough as he had already told me the story of his parents' immigration when I was a young kid, but Mom's side of the family was a different matter. At first, she was hesitant to contribute any information. When I told her my grade for the class would depend heavily on my roots project, she finally relented. Even so, she provided only the barest of details. Thankfully, Aunt June helped fill in some of the crucial information.

Yet it wasn't until last night that I learned all the missing details of exactly what had happened during World War II, not just Mom's incarceration in Arkansas but her subsequent deportation to Japan. As she told me that long, painful story, we must've gone through a half-dozen pots of tea. And even as I noticed the sun beginning to rise, I still found myself with so many more questions I wanted to ask. But Mom was exhausted, from both the late hour and from having to relive so many harrowing memories as she told me the stories of her childhood and teenage years. When she finally retired to the bedroom to sleep, she said, "I'm so, so tired. Please let's not talk about the past anymore. Too much pain."

Today, it's a little past noon when she wakes up. She has no appetite and seems to have withdrawn within herself. All she wants to do is to sit on the living-room sofa and watch TV, although I know she's not really paying attention to any of the shows; she's just mindlessly staring at the screen. Then, around mid-afternoon, she suddenly decides to go for a walk. I tell her that I'll take her to Riverside Park, which is just a block away, where we can walk along the Hudson River with a view of New Jersey across the water. But she says she really wants to be by herself. "I just want to get a little fresh air to clear my mind," she says.

"Well, then, why don't I walk with you to Riverside Park. I can wait on a bench while you take one of the paths?"

"Don't be silly."

"I'm not being silly. I could use some fresh air too."

"No, you stay here. I don't need a chaperone."

I'm taken aback by Mom's curt tone as well as her insistence to be alone. And I'm also reluctant for her to be off by herself in New York City.

"I'll be back before you know it," she reassures me. "No longer than a half hour."

She's now been gone for much longer than that, and I'm beginning to worry because the sun will soon be setting. My neighborhood is relatively safe, but the thought of her out alone on the streets of Manhattan at dusk unleashes the worst of my imagination. What if she wanders too far uptown and ends up in Harlem? And what if she's mugged by some teenagers who prey on the elderly? Would she quickly relinquish her purse, or would she defiantly resist them? Would they then shove her to the ground, breaking her hip?

As the minutes tick on, I realize I should've loaned her my cell phone. That way I could have at least called her to see if she's okay. I'm tempted to go out looking for her, but where should I go? When I gave her directions to Riverside Park, she didn't appear particularly interested in heading that way. Would she have instead followed Broadway, but then would she have walked uptown or toward Midtown?

I stare out my window, looking up and down the street for any sign of her, my fingers nervously tapping the wooden sill. Growing up in Hawaii I always thought of my mother as such a strong, indomitable woman with a backbone forged from tempered steel. But now, here in New York City, I see her for exactly who she is: a delicate, vulnerable woman at the cusp of beginning the last stage of her life as an elderly person. A frightening thought dawns on me. What if my mother, who suffered so much throughout her young life—a concentration camp in the South, deportation to a foreign country, and the horrific atomic bombing of Hiroshima—would have arrived in Manhattan only to meet an untimely death as the victim of a random mugging, becoming merely another statistic in the city's never-ending cycle of crime? Just as my anxieties get the better of me and I'm putting on a jacket to head out, I hear my front door open. "I'm sorry I took so long," Mom says, "but I lost track of the time."

A wave of relief washes over me, and I quickly forget that I should be upset at her for being gone for more than two hours. "You must be tired from all the walking," I tell her. "Let me order some food for dinner."

"No, let's eat out," she says.

"Are you sure?"

"Yes, very sure."

I look at Mom and can't help but notice how refreshed she is from the walk, energized and cheerful. It's as if she's shed a decade off her age. And she looks almost triumphant, like she just finished a particularly difficult book of sudoku she's been struggling with for months and is now eager to tackle a new challenge. I try to remember the last time Mom looked so invigorated and youthful, but my memory fails me. And then it dawns on me that I'm only now, slowly, beginning to see her in an entirely new light, as the person she was before she became a wife and mother.

"Just one thing," she adds, "I don't want you to take me to a restaurant only because you think I'll enjoy it."

"So, you'd rather I take you to a restaurant I think you won't like?"

"No," she laughs, "you know what I mean. Take me to a restaurant you really want to go to. Don't worry about me."

"Well, there's a good Thai restaurant right around the corner..."

"No," Mom interrupts me. "It doesn't have to be Oriental food. I don't need to eat rice tonight. Really, don't worry about me. Where do you want to go?"

I pause to decipher what she's really trying to say. She knows I would never bring her to a restaurant I wasn't sure she'd like because that just wouldn't be right. A dutiful Asian son is supposed to put his parents first and sublimate his own desires. I'm trying to figure out exactly what she wants me to do when, growing impatient with my hesitation, she says, "If it were just you and Dad, where would you take him?"

Her words sting me. It's a question I never would have expected from her. But she's right. If it were just Dad and me, I wouldn't be struggling, trying to figure out where to have dinner. Things with him were usually so much easier, and he was always eager to try new things. "Well," I say, "I was going to suggest Casa Mexico. It's my favorite neighborhood restaurant. But I wasn't sure if you'd like Mexican food."

Before I can even describe the restaurant and food to her, she says, "Okay, let's go there."

·   ·   ·   ·   ·

As soon as we enter the restaurant on Broadway and 94th Street, Carlos, the owner, rushes over and gives me a warm hug.

"Just the two of you tonight?" he asks, and when I tell him yes, he says, "Oh, okay, but I had a big table all ready for you."

We both laugh, and I introduce him to Mom. Carlos remarks at how young she looks, and then asks her a round of questions: How was her flight from Hawaii; has the weather in New York City been too chilly for her; what does she think about the crowded streets of Manhattan?

After we're seated, Carlos brings us a pitcher of margaritas and says it's on the house. Mom looks at me, surprised. "You must come here a lot," she says.

I laugh and tell her that, when the restaurant first opened, Lucas and I were among the first customers. We loved the food and returned at least every other week. We also often brought friends, who then became regulars themselves.

"Maybe Carlos should give you a commission for all the business you've brought," Mom jokes.

"Oh, he pays his commissions in alcohol," I tell her.

"Well, then," she says, "we better not let this pitcher go to waste."

I'm surprised, because Mom rarely imbibes. She might have a glass of wine for her birthday or sake for a special toast, but otherwise she rarely has a drink. After just a half glass of the margarita, Mom becomes chatty and more animated, and I realize I've never, ever seen her even slightly inebriated. Dad and I, on the other hand, shared many a drink together and I'd seen him more than a bit tipsy on several occasions. I recall one of my favorite memories of the two of us, when we were in Japan for Grandpa's funeral. While Mom was busy with her relatives taking care of all the last-minute details of her father's service, Dad and I walked into town one evening and ended up at an izakaya. As soon as we sat down at the bar, Dad asked the waiter for a bottle of their best sake, along with two cups. I was in high school then, and even though the drinking age in Hawaii was only eighteen at the time, I was still more than a year shy of that milestone. But Dad was so nonchalant about asking for sake for the both of us that the waiter didn't hesitate in fulfilling the order.

When the sake arrived, Dad and I toasted each other—"kampai!"—and drank one cup after another as we gorged on a half-dozen skewers of yakitori, a serving of Japanese dumplings, and small plates of pickled vegetables. When we were done, I stumbled as I tried to get up from the tatami-covered floor and Dad had to catch me. "Yikes, I'm not used to sitting on the floor," I said. Dad laughed, because I'm sure he knew I was drunk.

When we returned to Mom's cousin's house, everyone was thankfully fast asleep, and I somehow made it to my futon in the living room without waking anyone. The next morning I awoke with quite a hangover—my first—but I had to smile at myself, thinking, "gee, I never knew Dad could be so much fun." In retrospect, I believe my father likely woke up that morning thinking the same thing about me.

Now, with Mom at Casa Mexico, I feel like I'm in the reverse situation: a child with a parent who's becoming inebriated, possibly for the first time. I want to ask her if she's ever been drunk before but stop myself, not wanting to make her self-conscious when she's clearly enjoying herself. We devour an order of guacamole—"I had no idea avocados could be this tasty," she remarks—and then she asks me what the restaurant's best dish is. I tell her Casa Mexico is known for its sea bass with a chipotle sauce and black-bean puree, and she tells me to order that for her.

I'm secretly thrilled. It's not just that Mom is so eager to try something she's never had before. It's also that she refrained from automatically ordering the chicken enchilada or another inexpensive dish. At restaurants, Dad and I would always encourage her to have what she really wanted versus reflexively settling for one of the cheapest items on the menu. It was a constant battle, and we rarely won, even on her birthday or some other occasion in her honor. "But I like chicken," was her usual, unconvincing claim.

While I'm savoring this small victory—Mom ordering an expensive house specialty—a sour thought dampens my joy: What if she ends up hating the dish? Mom loves all kinds of fish, but might the sea bass be too spicy for her with that chipotle sauce? Thinking about that possibility, I order the seafood paella for myself, a dish I'm pretty confident she'd like. That way we can easily switch plates if the sea bass isn't to her liking. But after our food arrives and she starts eating her meal, she proclaims it one of the most delicious things she's ever had. Moreover, she especially seems to like the chipotle sauce. I'm pleasantly surprised, although I have to wonder whether the margaritas we've been drinking would have made even a lackluster taco from a street vendor taste like a culinary masterpiece. But, hell, I'm just loving that she's enjoying herself so much.

At one point, Mom looks around the small restaurant and notices there are only parties of two, three, and four seated at the individual square tables scattered around the floor. "What did Carlos mean when he said, 'big table'?" she asks. "Is there another dining room?"

I'd almost forgotten Carlos's offhand remark, and I'm surprised Mom remembered it. It's an inside joke, and I'm not sure whether to tell her the whole story. But we're having such a good time that I decide to roll the dice.

About a year ago, I had come to Casa Mexico with a bunch of friends, maybe eight of us. We'd just caught a performance at the Symphony Space on Broadway and 95th. It was a Saturday night, and we didn't have a reservation, but I suggested Casa Mexico in hopes we might luck out. When we arrived, though, there was a long line outside the restaurant, so we stood there trying to figure out where else we might try. We were just about to head to a Vietnamese place around the corner when Carlos saw me through the large glass windows and came outside to tell us he'd make space for us. He then escorted us, his hand on my left elbow, guiding our group toward the entrance ahead of everyone else waiting in line.

Inside the restaurant, he directed the waiters to quickly rearrange the tables, moving many of the seated customers—some of them in the middle of their meals—just so he could pull together three tables in the center of the floor for our large party. We ended up tightly packed in the small restaurant, which was made all the more cramped because a mariachi trio was playing that night and the musicians were constantly weaving their way among the diners. It was a festive evening, fueled by several pitchers of margaritas. To top things off, Carlos brought around a bottle of top-shelf tequila, offering it to all my friends. But he didn't bring any shot glasses. Instead, he asked us to open our mouths so he could pour the tequila directly from the bottle. We must have been quite a sight, like little hatchlings with our mouths wide open, waiting for Carlos, the momma bird, to feed us. Soon, we joined the mariachi musicians in a congo line around the restaurant.

At the end of the night, remembering all the free tequila we'd had, I wanted to make sure we left a tip sufficient for the extraordinary service we'd received. When the check arrived, I tried, in my drunken state, to divide the total bill roughly by three and leave that amount as the tip, thinking a thirty-three percent tip would be appropriate. I did the math twice in my head, and then signed the credit-card slip. As we all stumbled out of the restaurant, I happened to see our waitress as she opened the black guest-check holder. She looked at my credit-card receipt and almost dropped the holder. She then motioned for the other servers to come look at it. This puzzled me at the time. Why was she so surprised by a healthy, but not outrageous, tip? But then I thought nothing more about it.

Only later that week, when I was doing my laundry and found the credit-card receipt in my pair of jeans, did I learn my tip was far more extravagant than I'd planned. Because we were a large party, Casa Mexico had automatically added a seventeen percent tip, which I'd failed to notice. And then, on top of that, I somehow grossly overestimated the thirty-three percent tip I'd intended to leave. As it turned out, I left a tip almost equal to the original bill, which in my inebriated state I'd failed to notice.

"You sure made that waitress happy that night," Mom says, laughing, as I finish my story.

"Here's the problem, though," I tell her. "Since that night, I've received even better service here. It's like I'm royalty."

"So, that's good, right?"

"But now I feel obligated to always leave an enormous tip. I mean, I love the food here, but this is supposed to be an affordable neighborhood restaurant. I don't wanna go broke eating here!"

We both laugh, and I try to remember the last time I had a conversation like this with her. Ordinarily, I would have resisted telling her the story about that drunken night, afraid she wouldn't find it humorous at all. I'd be wary that she would chastise me for getting so inebriated in public. She might have even scolded me for being careless with my finances: "Do you think money grows on trees?" But now, instead, she's laughing with me over my memory of a wild night when the tequila was flowing all too freely.

Near the end of our meal, Carlos brings two individual flans with their tops perfectly caramelized. "This is on me," he says, and, after he leaves, Mom and I both break out into laughter again. Mom's never had flan before. As she enjoys the rich creaminess of the dessert, I realize something. For the first time since she arrived, I'm wholeheartedly enjoying her presence, something I'd only recently not thought possible. In fact, just days ago, a large part of me had dreaded her visit. Now, here I am, hoping to savor every moment of our time together, all of which makes me think of something.

"Hey, Mom. Instead of rushing off to D.C., why don't we just stay here in New York? That way I can show you a lot more of the city."

Mom looks at me quizzically, as if she's trying to decipher the hidden subtext of what I've just suggested. Then she looks down at her half-eaten flan and says, dejectedly, "I thought you wanted to go to Washington too, but I guess I could always go by myself."

"Oh no, that's not what I meant. It's just that there's so much more to see and do right here in New York."

"Well, to tell you the truth, I've already had my fill of sightseeing here for now. What I really want is to go to D.C. to see the new Japanese American Memorial and to visit Senator Inouye's office."

So, it hadn't been a ruse after all. She really does want to go to D.C., and she's serious about seeing Hawaii's long-time senator there. "I'm sorry," I tell her, "It's just that your time here is so short. I didn't realize you wanted to go to Washington that badly. Of course, we'll go together."

Mom looks relieved, as if she really thought I would let her make the trip to D.C. alone. "I have a favor to ask," she says. "Could you take me to a department store tomorrow? I need something really nice to wear for when I meet Senator Inouye, and I couldn't find anything in Hawaii."

"Sure thing," I tell her, "whatever you'd like to do."

After we're done eating, Mom quickly snatches the check before I can reach for it. "Don't worry," she tells me. "I won't be chintzy with the tip."

"Well, just make sure I can show my face back here again."

We both laugh and later, when we're walking back to my apartment, Mom stops suddenly on the sidewalk and says, "Oh no, did I leave a thirty-three percent tip or just three percent?" She smiles mischievously then, her beautiful face framed so perfectly by the brownstone buildings lining 91st Street.

"Well," I tell her. "I guess I'll find out the next time I'm there."

"Yes, if the next time that pitcher only has water, then you'll know," Mom laughs and playfully slaps me on the shoulder as we continue walking, the moon a shimmering sliver in the distance.

CHAPTER EIGHTEEN

The next morning, we're on a mission to find a dress for Mom. We start off at Macy's, head to Saks Fifth Avenue, and then try Lord & Taylor, without success. When I was a kid, I used to think Mom was the pickiest of shoppers. In Honolulu, we'd spend a half day at the Ala Moana Shopping Center, the largest open-air mall in the world, and she wouldn't find a single item of clothing she liked. We'd wander from one shop to another, eventually making our way from Sears, at one end of the long mall, to Liberty House, at the other end, and she'd still return home empty-handed. Those excursions in futility were frustrating, but now I understand her problem. She's petite—just a little over five feet tall and maybe not even a hundred pounds—and she's now at the tail end of middle-aged. All the dresses either don't fit or she thinks they're too young for her. To me, she still cuts an elegant figure and could stand to be more stylish. On the other hand, no one could ever accuse Mom of dressing in a manner that isn't "age appropriate."

By the time we get to Bloomingdale's in Midtown, it's around noon and I suggest we have lunch there. She's amused we can actually dine in the department store and is game for the experience. Over lunch, though, her mind is distracted, and I know she's worried about not finding just the right dress for D.C.

"Don't worry about what to wear," I try to reassure her. "I'm sure Senator Inouye will just appreciate that you've come all the way from Hawaii." But I know she'll continue to be anxious until we find something to her liking. Mom may be in her mid-sixties, but she still wants to look attractive for her age, and I can empathize with her. As a single gay man in my early forties in New York City, I've found myself becoming increasingly invisible, especially whenever I enter a bar or restaurant that caters to a younger crowd. I hate that feeling, yet it's difficult to strike the right balance—dressing like you haven't given up on life but without looking like you're foolishly clinging to your bygone youth.

If Mom can't find a suitable outfit, I'm afraid it will detract from her enjoyment of the trip to D.C., so I rack my brain trying to think of other stores we might try. Part of the problem, though, is that I'm not really sure what kind of dress she's looking for. And I don't think that she, herself, really knows. In the past, I'd have been irritated at her for taking so much time shopping, but today I feel nothing but sympathy for her quest to find just the right outfit.

After lunch, we make our way to the women's department. A salesperson there takes one look at Mom and recommends we try the juniors' section, where she assures us we'll be more likely to find something that fits. Mom is irritated as she quickly heads toward the escalator. "Honestly," she sighs. "That's what they always tell me: 'try the juniors' dresses.' But all that clothing is way too young for me. I don't want to look ridiculous."

Mom is frustrated and can't leave Bloomingdale's fast enough, but I need to stall her because I'm not sure where we should go next. "Look," I tell her, "we're here anyway. Why don't we just take a quick look at the juniors' section?"

"Well, I guess," she says, willing to humor me.

As we head there, I try to be optimistic, but I'm beginning to have my doubts whether she'll find something before tomorrow, when we leave for Washington. If anything, her odds would've been much better in Hawaii, where the stores cater to Asian customers with typically smaller, slighter bodies. But, of course, I don't mention that to Mom; it's the last thing she needs to hear right now. And, although I know she can be exceedingly particular about what she wears, I'll be the first to admit she has great taste in clothes. When I was in high school and would wear an aloha shirt I received from her for Christmas or my birthday, friends always complimented me, something they never did when I wore clothes that I, myself, had selected. Even when Mom was a teenager, she had quite the sense of style. There's a photo of her and Aunt June taken in post-war Japan with both of them wearing exquisite silk kimonos, complete with traditional brocade obis. When I asked her about that photo, Mom told me she and Aunt June were heading to the movie theater in town that afternoon. They must've been quite the sight, dressed in such elegance just to catch a matinee.

When we get to the juniors' clothing section, we're greeted by a Chinese American saleswoman who's in her early forties. I can see Mom visibly relax as she explains herself to someone who'll be able to relate.

"Don't worry," the saleswoman says. "I know exactly what you mean." She then motions us to follow her and suggests that, instead of a dress, how about a skirt, blouse, and blazer?

Mom takes to the idea and finds a tan skirt and blazer, and then the saleswoman suggests a dark-brown blouse with a geometric pattern—tiny stars within circles —reminiscent of a Japanese fabric. Mom beams as she remarks, "And I have just the shoes to match."

· · · · ·

As we take the subway back to my apartment, I can't help but think of how, in so many ways, Dad and Mom were complete opposites. Dad really didn't care what he wore. In fact, Mom often scolded him for not dressing nicely enough for a wedding or some other special event. When he was shopping for clothes, he'd need no more than fifteen minutes at Macy's and he'd be done. Part of that striking difference was due to their disparate backgrounds. Mom came from money, whereas Dad didn't. Growing up, she was accustomed to some of the finer things in life—and developed a discerning eye for them—although her family later struggled greatly during and after the war.

Yet on a deeper, fundamental level, Dad and Mom were very alike. Both born in Honolulu, they took their U.S. citizenship seriously. The one time Dad didn't need to be reminded to dress well was whenever he went to vote. He'd wear a new aloha shirt, a pair of dress slacks, and polished shoes, while Mom would don one of her finer muumuus. They would look like they were going out for an expensive evening in Waikiki rather than for a short drive up the street to the polling site at my grade school.

Moreover, it now dawns on me that both my parents suffered discrimination, albeit in markedly different ways. When Mom was deported to Japan during World War II, she suffered the small-town prejudice of those in her village. People were suspicious of her and her family because they'd arrived from an enemy country, her classmates shunning her for being too Western. Dad, who was a kibei, was also discriminated against when he returned to Hawaii after having been raised in Japan. He was teased mercilessly for his accented English and called bobora, a derisive word for Japanese immigrants, even though he was, by birth, a U.S. citizen. The discrimination only got worse for Dad in Hawaii after Japan attacked Pearl Harbor (as if that were his fault), just as it got worse for Mom in Japan after the U.S. dropped two atomic bombs there (as if that were her fault). So, while her classmates in Japan ostracized Mom for being too American, the teenage kids in Hawaii taunted Dad for being too Japanese. They were like two sides of the same coin, and perhaps that's what helped reinforce their bond, strengthening their marriage over the years. Ironically, for their wedding photo, it was Mom who wore a resplendent kimono while Dad dressed in a dapper Western suit. It was almost like my mother was proclaiming her Japanese roots as my father asserted his U.S. birth rights.

CHAPTER NINETEEN

At Penn Station the next morning, Mom wants to splurge and buy first-class tickets for the Metroliner to D.C. Initially I try to discourage her, telling her the seats in coach will be more than fine, then I tell myself to relax because she deserves to travel in comfort. But she won't let me pay for the tickets. We struggle with each other at the ticket counter—she's reaching for her credit card with one hand while trying to prevent me from reaching for mine with her other hand, just as I'm trying to do the exact same thing to her. The clerk looks at us in amusement, as if he's watching a well-orchestrated vaudeville act. Then Mom puts her foot down. "Listen, I'm going to be really upset with you. Just let me pay for this," she insists, her firm tone closing the door to any future discussion.

After we've boarded the train and are ensconced in the plush, roomy seats, Mom tells me she'll also be paying for the hotel in Washington. Before I can protest, she hands me an envelope. The letter is from the White House and dated September 16, 1996. Written on cream-colored heavyweight stationery, it states, "On behalf of your fellow Americans, I offer my sincere apologies for the actions that unfairly denied Japanese Americans and their families fundamental liberties during World War II. In passing the Civil Liberties Act of 1988, we acknowledged the wrongs of the past and offered redress to those who endured such grave injustice.... We must learn from the past and dedicate ourselves as a nation to renewing the spirit of equality and our love of freedom." The letter is signed by President Bill Clinton, or at least by his authorized automated letter signer.

I look at Mom and she's smiling. "I finally received the reparation," she says. "That's why this trip is on me."

"I can't believe you got the twenty thousand dollars!"

"Well, yes, finally," she beams, her face breaking into a soft smile.

The Civil Liberties Act of 1988, signed into law by President Ronald Reagan, called for a reparation of twenty thousand dollars for each of the ethnic Japanese who had been unjustly incarcerated during World War II. Ironically, at first Mom had no interest in applying for the redress. I was incredulous, because the money was a miniscule fraction of everything her family had lost. But when I repeatedly urged her to apply, her response was always, "It's all in the past," or, "That was such a long time ago," or, "I don't really need the money." Anytime I brought up the topic, she always ended the discussion with some variation of shikata ga nai, as if the wartime racial hysteria was an inevitable act of god, like an earthquake or a hurricane. Eventually, I stopped nagging her about it, thinking she really just wanted to leave the past behind. What I didn't realize then was, I hadn't been the only one who had urged her to take action.

After Mom and Aunt June had moved back to Hawaii, Grandpa asked them to see if they could get his property back. Aunt June made some preliminary inquiries but soon gave up, while Mom had little desire to reopen the past. Grandpa, though, insisted they pursue the matter, and he kept sending all his important papers, including his property deeds and any ancillary supporting documents. Aunt June was too busy with her career to investigate things properly, while Mom made only cursory attempts, just enough for her to report back to Grandpa that she'd indeed tried but failed.

Once, out of curiosity, I drove Mom to her old neighborhood near downtown Honolulu and asked her where her family's house had been. We circled around and around but couldn't find the location. She said she was lost, because the streets had all changed and the only thing familiar to her was the stream flowing at the edge of Chinatown. "I really don't recognize anything, but our house must have been somewhere there," she said, pointing toward a large complex of drab, three-story concrete apartment buildings that must have covered several acres.

"I wonder who found all the jewelry you buried."

"Well, somebody must have been really happy," she said, her face impassive, as if she had neatly buried her bitter memories of the war along with those valuables.

It's possible that our drive that day stirred something deep inside my mother, or maybe it was the latent guilt she felt for never having followed up on any of Grandpa's past pleadings. Whatever the case, Mom finally relented and applied for the reparation.

I could only imagine her chagrin when, months later, she received a letter denying her application. After the initial shock of that rejection wore off, she must have been furious. And the more she thought about it, the more she likely seethed. How dare the U.S. government offer an apology and then rescind it? When she looked into the matter, she discovered the reason for her rejection, which probably only added fuel to her growing outrage. The federal government claimed she wasn't eligible for the reparation because she'd relocated to an enemy country (that is, Japan) during the war.

Mom was incensed. "I did not relocate," she told me, her voice so adamant. "I was deported." I had to admit I found all that rather amusing because, at first, she didn't even want the reparation money. Then, when the U.S. government refused to give it to her, she became hell-bent on receiving it. So, she appealed the rejection of her reparation application, filing one document after the other, and eventually hired an attorney to plead her case.

Now, as our Metroliner train makes its way from Manhattan to D.C., Mom fills me in on all the details of how she eventually prevailed. As she recounts what happened, I slowly realize the story is more involved than I ever could have imagined.

To be sure, it wasn't going to be easy to make the case that Mom's family didn't voluntarily relocate to Japan but was, for all intents and purposes, deported. Several federal departments and agencies were involved in her family's deportation—the U.S. State Department, the Department of Defense, the FBI, and the War Relocation Authority, among others—and it wasn't clear how the final decision was actually made. Also, Mom couldn't say for sure whether her father eventually agreed to be sent back to Japan and, if so, what coercive tactics might have been applied to sway him to "voluntarily" repatriate.

The more Mom's attorney dug into the matter, the more confusing it became. Initially, the State Department pushed hard to deport Mom's family because it was eager to repatriate U.S. citizens who were stuck in

Japan and other parts of occupied Asia. Rumors circulated that those civilians were being treated harshly in Japanese detainment camps, and the State Department was under increasing pressure to get them back home. But the Department of Defense objected to people from Hawaii being a part of any civilian exchange. The agency was afraid those individuals might have information that would be useful to the Japanese military, such as knowledge of Hawaii's coastlines or updates on the buildup of the military presence on the islands since the bombing of Pearl Harbor. The FBI had similar concerns, fearful that, if Grandpa were sent back to Japan, he'd somehow be able to help that country's efforts in the war.

Throughout the various memos exchanged between the different federal departments and agencies involved, the terminology shifted uneasily to describe the proposed relocation of families like the Minatoyas. At first, the word "repatriation" was used, then "involuntary relocation," and finally "deportation." Interestingly, a number of memos did raise the legality and constitutionality of forcibly sending U.S. civilians to an enemy country during a time of war. But that was as far as Mom's attorney got. He used one Freedom of Information Act request after another, and then the trail went cold. Apparently, some documents were still classified, and an entire FBI file on Grandpa was evidently destroyed in 1979, for whatever inexplicable reason.

Then Mom's lawyer realized he could skin the proverbial cat in a different way. From his research on Mom and her family, he'd learned about her earlier immigration problem, that she was initially denied her U.S. citizenship when she returned to Hawaii after the war. He now seized on that information to make his case. He shrewdly argued that, when Mom was detained at Sand Island years ago, the U.S. government admitted its error in denying her the right of her citizenship because, as was ruled at the time, she was just a minor when her family was shipped to Japan. The salient point was that, whether Grandpa had voluntarily agreed to be sent to Japan or was forcibly deported wasn't relevant. The simple fact was, Mom was still a minor at the time, so she had no say in the matter, and to rule differently now would be inconsistent with the earlier decision to reinstate her U.S. citizenship.

Thanks to that ironclad reasoning, along with a closer scrutiny of the actual language of the Civil Liberties Act, Mom finally received a letter from President Clinton, along with a check for twenty thousand dollars. And by that same foolproof argument, Aunt June, whose application had also been denied, was able to receive the reparation too.

"Wow," I say to Mom, "why didn't you ever tell me any of this before?"

"Well, I'm telling you now."

"I'm not talking just about the reparation money," my voice betraying more resentment and hurt than I intended. "I mean about everything: about Grandpa being imprisoned in Santa Fe, the family being deported, all your suffering in Japan. Everything."

"The past is the past," she says to me. "Shikata ga nai."

"But why not tell me? Were you ashamed of what happened? Because you have nothing to be ashamed for. It's the United States that should be ashamed."

"I'm not ashamed."

"Well, what then?"

Mom looks out the window and, after a long pause, slowly says, "I wanted to bury the past, not because I'm ashamed of anything but because I didn't want any of my pain and bitterness to weigh your life down. It's my burden, not yours."

As I grasp the full meaning of what she's said, I have to turn away from her or else I won't be able to hold back my tears. Without looking at her, my right hand gently clutches her wrist. We sit like this in silence until we hear the announcement that we're almost in D.C. As Mom straightens her body in her seat and adjusts her clothes, I feel such a surge of love and compassion for her. And there's something else. I'm flush with pride for the woman whom I'm blessed to have as my mother.

"Not many people can take on the federal government and win," I tell her, "not once but twice."

She looks at me and smiles. "I bet you didn't know how tough I could be."

"Actually, that's one thing I never doubted."

We look at each and chuckle, softly at first then more heartily. Soon we are laughing loudly, as if we've just heard the funniest joke, and she slaps my thigh to try to get me, as well as herself, to stop. Then, almost as an afterthought, she adds, "Senator Inouye's office did help a lot in getting my reparation finally approved. I need to thank him."

As our train pulls into Union Station, I look at Mom and am reminded of something I've always known: She has a moral compass that's never wavered from true North, even after all she's been through.

.   .   .   .   .

After checking into our hotel, the first thing Mom wants to do is visit the recently opened Japanese American Memorial. The site is near the hotel, so we decide to walk. It's a chilly, gray day in D.C., but thankfully there's no rain in the forecast. All the trees have lost their leaves and, in spite of the hustle and bustle of the street traffic, there's a calmness to the air, especially when compared with New York City.

"It must be so pretty here in the spring, with all the cherry blossoms," Mom says.

She has a map showing the location of the memorial, but we have trouble finding the site. According to the map, it's supposed to be at one corner of a park that's just to the north of the Capitol building, but we can't find where it is, and none of the pedestrians we stop to ask for assistance can help us, even with the aid of Mom's map. Finally, we somehow stumble upon the memorial, which is tucked away from the street, hidden from view.

The memorial is essentially a small austere plaza bordered by a semi-circular granite wall. That wall has inscriptions in bold letters on separate rectangular panels, one for each of the ten different concentration camps: Poston, Heart Mountain, Topaz, Manzanar, Rohwer, Tule Lake, Minidoka, Gila River, Amache, and Jerome. As Mom and I stand in front of the granite panel for Jerome, we both look at the large number inscribed there— 8,497— denoting the total number of people incarcerated at the camp.

"Can you believe," she says, "I was one of those eight thousand four hundred and ninety-seven people?"

At the center of the memorial sits a vertical sculpture. It's a square bronze column with two cranes perched on the top. The cranes, with their bodies pressed against each other, are ensnarled in barbed wire, struggling to take flight.

"My wedding kimono has white cranes embroidered on black silk," Mom tells me. "But on my kimono, the cranes are flying free and can go anywhere they want."

"I don't think I've actually ever seen your wedding kimono, just a photo of it."

"What, you mean I've never showed it to you?" Mom says, somewhat in disbelief. "Well, the next time you're home you have to see it. The entire kimono is hand-stitched, and the obi is thick silk brocade embroidered with gold chrysanthemums. I keep everything stored with mothballs in a locker in my closet. I can't believe I've never showed it to you."

Mom then finds a panel with a list of all the Japanese Americans who died fighting for the United States in World War II. She quickly locates Uncle Richard's name and rubs her finger gingerly across it. "I wish you could have met your uncle," she says. "I think you and he would have gotten along really well."

"What makes you say that?"

"Well, because Richard was always so studious and quiet, just like you. And because he was such a good son... just like you."

She says those words so offhandedly, as if they are well-known truths, like stating autumn will soon give way to winter. I swallow hard, staring at Uncle Richard's name. I don't know what to say, so I redirect the conversation. "Do you think Dad and Uncle Richard would have gotten along?" I ask.

Mom pauses for a while, trying to imagine something she's never considered before. "Yes," she eventually says. "I think they would have. They both were certainly quite fanatic about baseball."

Just as we're about to leave the memorial, we notice several other wall panels with inscriptions of various quotes. One is from President Harry Truman: "You fought not only the enemy but you fought prejudice—and you have won. Keep up that fight, and we will continue to win—to make this great Republic stand for just what the Constitution says it stands for: the welfare of all the people all the time."

As Mom stands there, reading and rereading that quote from President Truman, I tell her, "I wonder if he fully grasped all the ironies of that war. After all, he was the one who made the decision to drop the atomic bomb."

"Shhh," she scolds me. "Don't be disrespectful."

"But you could've easily been killed, if not from the blast then from radiation poisoning."

Mom ignores my remark and begins reading aloud the inscription of a quote from Senator Inouye: "The lessons learned must serve as a grave reminder of what we must not allow to happen again to any group."

Before we leave, Mom asks me to take a photo of her in front of that panel. As I do, I notice she's completely lost in thought, and I wonder if her mind is in Honolulu before the attack on Pearl Harbor, in Arkansas during the war, or in Japan after the atomic bomb was detonated over Hiroshima.

•   •   •   •   •

The next morning, it's barely six o'clock when I hear a faint knocking on the inner door that connects Mom's room with mine. When I get out of bed to open my side of the passage, I see her standing there, fully dressed in the outfit she bought at Bloomingdale's.

"Oh," she says, "were you still sleeping?"

Mom looks so sharp, like she's ready for a job interview at a prestigious law office. But I can't even think of how to compliment her because my mind is still trying to wake up. "Give me fifteen minutes to shower and change," I tell her. "Then we can get breakfast somewhere."

After we finish eating downstairs at the hotel's coffee shop, Mom asks if I can help her carry a bag from her room.

"What bag?"

"Oh, just some omiyage for Senator Inouye and his staff."

When we get to her room, I see it's actually two shopping bags filled with boxes of macadamia-nut chocolates, cans of salted macadamia nuts, and packages of Kona coffee. I now realize that's why she wanted to bring her large suitcase with her, half of which must have been filled with omiyage.

"Why did you bring so much stuff?" I ask.

"I had to. His staff really helped me with the reparation."

It's not even eight o'clock, and I ask her what time Senator Inouye's office expects her. She tells me there's no set time; someone on his staff simply told her to stop by if she was going to be in Washington. As I try to get more details from her, I slowly realize there's no appointment. Senator

Inouye's office was just being kind enough to tell her to stop by, so Mom might very well not get to see him at all. I feel so badly that she's misread their politeness, but I don't say anything. In no way do I want to burst her bubble. I do, though, suggest we wait before going there, thinking our chances of catching him might be better around ten o'clock or so.

To kill some time, we take a cab to drive by several of the major tourist highlights: the National Mall, the White House, and the memorials to Presidents Washington, Lincoln, and Jefferson. "I wish we had more time here," I tell her. "There's so much to see."

"That's okay," she says. "The main thing is that yesterday I got to visit the Japanese American Memorial and today I'll get to see Senator Inouye in his office."

When we arrive there, the day is already in full swing for his staff. Several assistants are either talking on the phone, busily typing on their desktop computers, or rushing in and out of the office. We interrupt one aide who looks the least busy—a young woman who might be just out of college—and Mom explains she's visiting from Hawaii and wants to thank Senator Inouye personally for all his past help. Mom then says she brought some small gifts for everyone on the staff.

The young woman looks unsure of what to do with the two shopping bags of omiyage but, before she can say anything, Mom explains they're just small tokens of appreciation: chocolates and coffee from Hawaii. This seems to put the woman at ease, and she thanks us for bringing the gifts all the way from the islands. Mom then says she'll always be grateful to Senator Inouye for helping pass the Civil Liberties Act of 1988, legislation that included a provision for reparations to Japanese Americans. Mom describes how she was initially denied the reparation, but Senator Inouye interceded to help her eventually receive it.

"That's so kind of you to stop by and also to bring these treats from Hawaii," the young staffer says. "Unfortunately, the Senate is in session today and I believe the Senator has a number of committee meetings."

Mom reaches into one of the bags and unfurls a beautiful lei she made from colorful origami paper. The young staffer's eyes widen as she looks at the three strands of folded cranes, each tiny paper bird nestled into the one before it.

"I made this lei for him," Mom explains, her face gleaming with pride. "In Hawaii, we give leis as a sign of love and appreciation. Although leis are usually made from flowers, I sewed this one from origami cranes. For good luck, people will fold a thousand cranes, but for this lei I used exactly four hundred forty-two, because Senator Inouye was in the 442nd Regiment during the war."

The young woman can't take her eyes off the lei as she admires how delicately the cranes were folded and sewn together. "This is breathtaking," she says. "And you handmade this all by yourself?"

"Yes, because I really wanted to show my appreciation to Senator Inouye, to thank him for all the work he did in getting the reparation for me and everyone else who was interned in the war. Do you think he might have just a few free seconds today, just so I could give him the lei in person?"

"I'll see what I can do," the assistant leaves her work area to confer with another staffer. In a few minutes, she returns to tell us Senator Inouye is on the Senate floor now but will probably be back in the office in around an hour, before heading off to a committee meeting. Perhaps at that time he could meet briefly with Mom. Until then, she asks if Mom and I would like to join a small group on a guided tour of the Capitol. "I think you'll enjoy it," the assistant says, "and we've already reserved a spot for you two."

The tour starts off at the visitor center with a short film about the beginnings of democracy in the United States, and then gives an overview of the Capitol building itself. After the film, we're led on a walking tour of some of the main rooms and spots of interest: the Hall of Columns, the Crypt, the Rotunda, the National Statuary Hall. During the tour, I notice that Mom isn't really paying attention. Her mind is elsewhere, preoccupied with meeting Senator Inouye later, I'm sure. "I can't believe you made that lei," I tell her. "It must have taken you forever with all those tiny origami cranes."

"It wasn't too bad," she says. "It gave me something to do whenever I was watching TV."

"You really are addicted to those Korean soap operas," I laugh.

"If you think I'm bad, you should see your Aunt June."

I chuckle, thinking of the two sisters. Not that long ago, they wouldn't have considered watching anything Korean. Then the Japanese-language programming in Honolulu got worse and worse, with constant repeats of the same shows. Now, Mom and Aunt June are hooked on several Korean soap operas, and everyone knows better than to phone either of them during the early evening, when they're more than likely watching one of their favorite, must-see series.

As our tour exits the Small House Rotunda, Mom and I are approached by the young staffer from Senator Inouye's office. "I'm sorry to interrupt," she says, "but I wanted to grab you now, because if we hurry you might be able to catch the Senator in his office."

· · · · ·

For as long as I can remember, Senator Inouye has represented the people of Hawaii in Congress. I've seen him on TV dozens of times, attending one ceremony or another, meeting foreign dignitaries in Honolulu, and participating in marches and rallies. And I had watched him with great pride during the televised Watergate hearings, his dignity, poise, and integrity so reassuring during such a tumultuous time.

Even so, now, when I meet him in person for the first time, I'm still taken aback by the sheer presence of the man. He's not tall; he's roughly about my height. But he has a distinguished air and gravitas that can't help but be intimidating.

Mom, though, is surprisingly at ease meeting him. She gives him the origami lei and explains about the four hundred forty-two cranes. He seems so genuinely touched by her thoughtfulness and meticulous labor. She tells him her brother also served in the U.S. Army for the 100th Battalion, but that he unfortunately died in combat.

"Did your brother also train at Camp Shelby?" Senator Inouye asks.

"Yes and, like you, he also went to McKinley High School. But I think he was a couple years younger."

The senator invites us into his inner office and asks an assistant to bring us coffee.

"Now, what part of Honolulu is your family from?"

"Our house was two blocks from Aala Park."

"That area has certainly changed over the years," says Senator Inouye, his attention focused intently on Mom.

"I really don't recognize it anymore, but I haven't lived there since I was a child."

"Yes, Honolulu has certainly undergone a tremendous amount of change since the war. Now, my staff tells me you had trouble receiving your reparation."

Mom gives him a brief summary of the difficulties she had, and then she thanks him for his staff's help. Senator Inouye admits he doesn't really remember her case, but he's glad his office could be of some assistance. Just then, a staffer taps on the door and enters. Before she can say anything, Senator Inouye rises to his feet.

"I'm very sorry," he says, "but I have to be at an important committee meeting. How long will you be in D.C.?"

Mom tells him that, unfortunately, we're headed back to New York City tonight and she's flying back to Hawaii a couple days after that.

"Well, please have a safe journey back to New York, and then to Hawaii," Senator Inouye tells her. He then turns to me, shakes my hand firmly, and says, "You have a most remarkable mother."

·   ·   ·   ·   ·

On the Metroliner back to New York City, Mom and I sit in the sparsely filled middle section of the first-class passenger car. A white couple sits a few rows in front of us, and a black family is right behind us. This seating arrangement triggers a vivid memory from Mom's past.

"After a few months in Arkansas," she tells me, "we could apply for a day pass to go into town to shop, so Grandma took Aunt June and me with her on the town bus. At the front of the bus, a huge sign said, 'Colored go to back of bus.' We'd never seen a sign like that. I wasn't even sure what 'colored' meant."

"What did you think it meant?" I ask.

"I really don't know what I thought," Mom responds. "But I remember being so confused, and Grandma didn't know what to do. I guess she thought the safest thing would be to sit in the back."

"That's what I'd have done."

"Well," Mom says, "the driver didn't like that. He stopped the bus and told us, 'You Ornamentals aren't allowed to sit there.' And then he motioned for us to sit in the middle, between the white and black sections."

"He called you 'Ornamentals'?"

"Yes, I'll never forget that. He said 'Ornamentals.'"

"Was he trying to make fun of you?"

"No, I don't think so. He was serious. Aunt June and I wanted to laugh, but we knew better."

I look at Mom and can't quite fully process just how much life she's lived. She was in Honolulu when Pearl Harbor was attacked, she was imprisoned in a U.S. concentration camp during World War II, and she was in Iwakuni when the atomic bomb was dropped on neighboring Hiroshima. And, to top it off, she was also a first-hand witness to Jim Crow segregation in the South before the civil rights movement. Of course, she's my mother and I'll always think of her that way, but now it dawns on me she's also something else: She is living history.

CHAPTER TWENTY

Back in New York City, I awake the next morning refreshed and relaxed. Mom sleeps in. She usually rises with the sun, but not today. I figure the trip to D.C. must have really taken it out of her, maybe not so much physically but emotionally.

As I sit on my sofa, watching the morning news with an oversized mug of coffee, I think about the reparation Mom received, how it's so much more than just the money itself. And it's even more than the apology she received from President Clinton on behalf of the U.S. government. To me, the reparation signifies something much larger.

The way I see it, that money isn't just a token compensation for all her family lost during the war; it also rewards her strength and determination in standing up for what she believed was right. At Sand Island decades ago, Mom could have acquiesced to entering Hawaii as a legal alien, and then later applied for U.S. citizenship based on her marriage to Dad. But she refused to do that. She wanted to correct the past injustice of having been stripped of her citizenship for no good reason. As Mom spent days detained following her return to the U.S.—literally a young woman without a country—she had the wherewithal to fight for what was rightfully hers. She refused to take the easy way out, instead choosing the more difficult path. Now, decades later, her courageous resolve was rewarded after she fought for her proper share of the U.S. redress money.

As my mind swirls with those heavy thoughts, I hear some rustling from my bedroom. Mom comes into the living room, "Ohayou gozaimasu."

"Did you sleep okay last night?" I ask.

"Yes, but I'm still a bit tired. I don't know why."

"Well, the trip to D.C. must have worn you out a bit."

"I know it's my last full day here," she tells me, "but is it okay if I go back to bed? I want to make sure I'm not tired for your performance tonight."

"Sure, I have a few errands anyway, and I definitely wanna practice before my show. I gotta get back in shape."

"Okay, perfect then."

"But I don't want to disturb you with my practicing."

"Oh no," Mom says. "I miss the sound of your playing."

Her words surprise me, but I don't say anything as she returns to my bedroom to catch up on her sleep. At best, I thought Mom was indifferent to my oboe playing. At worst, I thought she'd grown to dislike it because of how it inadvertently drove us apart.

When I practice that morning, I play slow, long scales, caressing each note for several seconds to get my embouchure back into shape. As I hold each sustained tone, my mind starts to empty itself. It's almost better than yoga, bringing a calm, relaxed sense of self.

That afternoon I head out to get some omiyage for Mom to bring back with her. She's already gotten souvenir items from the tourist attractions we've visited: keychains, refrigerator magnets, shot glasses, snow globes, and tea towels imprinted with the Empire State Building, the Statue of Liberty, the U.S. Capitol. But I want to get other items that she can give to friends and relatives, especially Aunt June, and this sends me on a sequence of stops.

First, I go to a bakery in Little Italy to pick up several boxes of Italian cookies and pastries, and then I take the subway to a stationery store on the Upper East Side to purchase some handbound leather writing journals. Finally, I make a stop at a spa back in my neighborhood that sells scented soaps and bath salts.

When I return home, Mom is up and watching "The Oprah Winfrey Show." I apologize for leaving her alone—the errands took longer than I expected—but she says the timing was perfect because she really needed the rest. Then she notices all my shopping bags, and I tell her it's omiyage for her return trip.

"Waaah," she exclaims. "How am I going to carry all that?"

"Don't worry. It'll all fit in your second suitcase. And anyway, I'll be there to help you carry your luggage tomorrow."

"But why did you buy so many things?"

I laugh and tell her it's actually much less than the omiyage she brought with her. "Besides," I tell her, "what would people think if you went home empty-handed?"

She gently slaps my shoulder and shakes her head. I tell her I can start packing the omiyage into her suitcase while she eats some takeout Thai food I brought back with me. "This way, you won't have to worry about packing before your flight tomorrow."

"But when are you going to eat?" she asks.

I explain I purposely had a late lunch in Little Italy so I wouldn't be hungry until much later tonight, because I really don't want to eat before the performance. "I can't play on a full stomach," I tell her.

She looks at me quizzically, and I'm not sure what she's thinking. Then she says, "I don't have to go to the performance. It's all right, really."

Now it's my turn to be confused. Months ago, when Mom was planning her trip, she told me she really wanted to hear me play and asked if I could get her a ticket for any performance of mine. After explaining that the only opportunity for her to see me in anything would be "Beauty and the Beast" on Broadway, I made sure to plan my vacation schedule to return to the musical on the night before she left. Then I got her a ticket so she could attend that particular show.

Mom notices my confused expression and tells me, "I don't want to make you nervous. So, it's okay if I don't go."

Now I finally understand what she's getting at. When I was a kid performing in the Honolulu Youth Symphony, I'd always ask her and Dad to sit way in the back of the auditorium. I thought I'd get too nervous if I saw them peering at me from somewhere in the front few rows.

"Oh no, that's not what I mean," I tell her. "I really want you to come to the performance. It's just that I can't eat now because then I'd have trouble playing on a full stomach."

Mom looks relieved but still concerned. "But you're okay, right? You're not sick, are you?"

I have to laugh. "Mom, ever since I was a kid I could never play on a full stomach."

"Funny," she says, "I don't recall that at all."

. . . . .

At the theater, as I begin warming up my oboe and English horn, I realize just how good it feels to be back in the orchestra pit. I am safely cocooned, surrounded by my fellow musicians, each of us getting ready to perform, listening to one other, making adjustments here and there to ensure the proper balance and intonation of the ensemble. When I take a short break, I try to spot Mom in the balcony, where I purposely got her ticket so she could see me down inside the orchestra pit. As I search for her, I see someone waving. It's her. I wave back and point to Dad's prized Vacheron Constantin watch, its gold-rimmed face just visible on my wrist above the cuff of my dress-shirt sleeve. Tonight, I have both my parents with me.

A few minutes later, the concertmaster signals for me to give the orchestra a tuning "A," and all the other musicians check their instruments for pitch against my note. I look up at Mom right before the lights in the orchestra pit dim. The conductor raises his baton and we begin playing the energetic, light-hearted tunes of the overture. Immediately, I focus on the music, my mind shutting out everything else.

The performance goes well, with just a few minor glitches here and there—a missed cue by the cellist, the actors singing slightly ahead of the orchestra in one of the numbers, the brass players going a tad sharp in the finale—but nothing noticeable by the general audience. We receive a standing ovation, and I look up into the balcony to see Mom, as she alternates between clapping at the performance and waving to me.

After the actors take their final bows and the applause dies down, everyone in the orchestra pit begins packing their instruments and clearing out. Another night, another performance. But tonight feels so special to me, and I'm touched when the conductor says, "Nice to have you back."

I tell him it feels so good to be playing again and ask if he wouldn't mind waiting just a few minutes because I'd really like for him to meet my mother. Just then, from the corner of my eye, I see her approach the orchestra pit and I introduce them.

"Thank you for taking care of my son," Mom says, as she gives him a small bag of omiyage. "Just some treats from Hawaii."

The conductor thanks her for the gifts and asks about her trip, what sights she's seen, whether the weather has been too cold for her, if the crowds on Manhattan are overwhelming. At the end of the conversation he says, "We're very lucky to have your son playing with us. He's a very talented musician."

"I'm glad he hasn't been too much trouble for you," she counters, with typical Japanese American self-effacement.

"Hardly," the conductor laughs, as he thanks Mom again for the omiyage, wishes her a safe journey back to Hawaii, and then makes his way out of the orchestra pit, weaving through the clutter of empty chairs and music stands.

After a performance, I'm usually famished, and tonight is no exception. It's not just because I always refrain from eating anything before a show but also because of the adrenaline of playing for an audience, which seems to burn more calories than an intense workout on a treadmill. I figure we can just get some takeout food from the hot salad bar at a Korean bodega, but Mom insists on going to a restaurant to have a sit-down meal. It's already ten-thirty, though, so we catch a cab to a late-night diner on Broadway, just a few blocks from my apartment. There, Mom flips through the thick menu, page by page, and says she can't believe the cooks can prepare all these dishes on demand, especially at this time of night. Then she adds that, unfortunately, the one thing she really wants isn't on the menu.

"What's that?" I ask.

"They don't have margaritas here."

I want to laugh, remembering the fun time we had at Casa Mexico, but Mom looks genuinely disappointed. Instead, I suggest she have a glass of wine while I order a beer. After the waiter arrives with our drinks, she raises her glass for a toast.

"To my son, such a talented musician," she beams.

"Well, thanks, but it's not like I made it to the New York Philharmonic," I tell her, taking a big gulp of my cold beer.

"Don't put yourself down," Mom scolds me. "Being on a Broadway hit show is nothing to sneeze at. When I'm back in Hawaii, I'll have to tell everyone about the show."

I'm caught off-guard by her sudden surge of pride—and by her effusive words. Flattery isn't one of her strong suits, and I begin to suspect she might have had a margarita during the show's intermission.

When our waiter returns with our food, Mom shows him the Playbill for "Beauty and the Beast" and tells him that I play in the orchestra and that we've just come from a show tonight. The waiter, who's probably been in a few Broadway productions himself, is decidedly unimpressed but smiles politely and says how nice it must have been for her to see me in performance.

I'm now feeling embarrassed but, even after the waiter leaves, Mom continues. "I'm so proud of you," she says. I sit silently, chewing my turkey-club sandwich. My face must betray signs of consternation, because she repeats herself. "Really, I'm so proud of you."

I'm not sure what comes over me next, but before I can stop, I hear myself shooting back to her, "Well, I just wish you'd had a little more faith in me when I was a kid."

I know I should have just accepted her praise gracefully, but I couldn't restrain myself. I don't know why I said what I just did; it's definitely not one of my finer moments. I suppose I wanted to hurt her for thwarting my earlier dreams. An ugly, petty part of me wants to let her know I succeeded in spite of her, not because of her. But, immediately, a wave of regret overwhelms me, followed by a flood of guilt, and I dearly wish I could take back those words.

But instead of being hurt, Mom looks at me like I've completely lost my mind. "Ken-chan, what in the world are you talking about?" her face a display of genuine confusion. "I never doubted for a second you would be successful at whatever you set your mind to."

I'm incredulous, as Mom and I stare at each other across the Formica-topped table. My initial impulse is to accuse her of revisionist history, to condemn her for conveniently forgetting how she put the kibosh on my musical aspirations when I was in high school. And I also want to blame her for making me lose my confidence, leading to pernicious doubts over whether I had the talent to succeed as a professional oboist. Lastly, I want to tell her that, as my parent, she should've supported me and not undermined my most cherished dream. But thankfully I'm able to refrain from saying any of those things.

•   •   •   •   •

Later, back at my apartment, as I lie awake on my sofa, my mind keeps returning to that earlier conversation at the diner. I fidget restlessly, replaying her words and thinking about her honest confusion after I criticized her for not being a supportive parent.

From somewhere deep in the recesses of my memory, I think of something Aunt June told me ages ago. She was reminiscing about Uncle Richard and told me she always felt badly that Grandpa was so hard on him, especially when it came to schoolwork. Whenever Uncle Richard got anything but the highest marks, Grandpa would berate him. "In America," Grandpa would say, his voice so stern, "you have to work twice as hard as the haoles and you have to be twice as good as them. Otherwise, you will be nothing." That mentality must've been a driving force behind the 100th Battalion and 442nd Regiment during World War II—those Nisei men hell-bent on proving they were just as good if not better than their white countrymen. And that's why more than eight hundred of them became casualties in a desperate suicide mission to save two hundred seventy-five Texans trapped in the Vosge Mountains.

Then it dawns on me.

It's not that Mom lacked faith in my talent to make it as a musician. It's just that she didn't want me to be in a profession that's judged so subjectively. After her incarceration in a concentration camp in World War II, she was always afraid I would suffer discrimination in my own life, including in the workplace. Racism robbed her of her childhood, and she didn't want it to steal any chance I might have to excel in whatever profession I pursued. In other words, she wanted to protect me, so she urged me into a quantitative field like engineering, where my performance would be assessed more objectively. That was her baggage from the hateful racism she endured in the war. In Mom's mind, she's always been supportive of me, especially in her zealous efforts to protect me from the world's ugliness. Until now, I'd been too blind to see that.

CHAPTER TWENTY-ONE

I wake the following morning to Mom's gentle tapping on my shoulder. She's already fully dressed, and I quickly look at the clock on my bookcase to see it's only five o'clock. We have plenty of time before her flight, but I know how she always likes to get to the airport hours before she needs to be there. Otherwise, she'll get too nervous, thinking she'll miss her flight. As I head to the bathroom to take a quick shower, I'm amazed she's already fully packed.

"Don't rush," she tells me, and I notice her looking at Dad's photo on my bookcase, her mind only partially present. It really doesn't seem like she arrived just ten days ago. In some ways, it seems like a lifetime ago.

After I shower and change, Mom is still looking at my bookcase, but now she's staring at the maneki ceramic cat she gave me and Lucas years ago. I wonder what she's thinking until, finally, she says, "I really should have gotten this maneki-neko to you sooner, but I had such trouble finding an authentic hand-painted one made in Japan."

"You didn't have to go through such trouble," I tell her. "Any neko would've been fine. It was the thought that counted most."

"Oh no, I couldn't send you a cheap knockoff made in China. I had to get the real thing for you and Lucas."

I look at Mom standing there and, after all these years, I realize something. She honestly did consider my relationship with Lucas to be the real thing, worthy of an authentic maneki-neko. "Funny, but I thought you never liked him."

"Why would you say that?"

I have no idea how to respond. Part of me wants to bring up everything that happened at Dad's funeral, but I wisely hold myself back. I'm still regretful over what I told her at the diner last night, and I don't want to hurl yet another ugly accusation. Besides, it's become increasingly clear to me that her recollection of the past is vastly different from mine, each of our views colored—and reframed—by our own limitations. "That's okay, Mom," I tell her, "maybe it's best to just let the past be the past."

"Yes, shikata ga nai."

•   •   •   •   •

Surprisingly, we encounter very little traffic on the cab ride to Newark airport, arriving there almost three hours early. Mom is traveling in first class on Continental and the receptionist at the airline's VIP club is kind enough to let me accompany her into the premium lounge.

"Look at all the food," Mom says, as we make our way past a variety of breakfast items, all neatly presented, as if we're the first to arrive. There's a large steam table with trays of scrambled eggs, bacon, Canadian ham, and pork sausages. And then I notice another long buffet with different types of cereals, a large bowl of assorted fresh fruit, and a large basket filled with muffins of various flavors.

The plush, spacious lounge is almost empty, with just a handful of people dressed in business attire, so Mom and I are able to have an entire sofa and circular coffee table to ourselves. This is the first time I've been in any airline's lounge, and I'm totally enjoying the experience.

"I'm so glad you flew first class," I tell her.

"Well, I had the reparation money, and it's such a long flight. I thought I'd treat myself."

"Good for you. Dad would have wanted you to fly in comfort."

Mom smiles at me, but then her expression gradually turns pensive. After taking a few small nibbles at the edge of her blueberry muffin, gently peeling away the fluted paper liner, she tells me it's been so terribly lonely without Dad. She says that, even though she always thought she might outlive him, she never really allowed herself to consider the possibility he would die so relatively young, leaving her with years and years to go on without him. "I went from my father's home to my husband's home, and so I've never had to live by myself and, even now, I'm not sure if I know how to do that," she tells me in Japanese, as if the bluntness of English would make it too awkward for her to confide in her son an intimacy of such vulnerability.

She then puts down her muffin, looks me directly in the eye, and says, "Ken-chan, why don't you move back home to Hawaii?"

I'm caught completely off-guard, and I don't know how to respond. I've never actually considered the possibility of moving back to Honolulu. I can't even envision myself living back there now, having been away for so long. What would life there be like as an adult gay man? Mom just used the word "home" to refer to Hawaii but, for me, I've now been away from the islands longer than I lived there. At this point, "home" is New York City. Of course, Hawaii will always have a special place in my heart; I was born and raised there. But when I look back at the boy I was growing up in Honolulu, he seems only vaguely familiar and yet oddly remote from the man I am today.

Mom looks at me, almost pleadingly. I've never quite seen her like this, and I'm worried she doesn't understand why I've ended up living so far away from her. I try to explain that Honolulu just doesn't have the opportunities for musicians that New York City does, and that maybe I could move back to Hawaii after I've become more established as a professional musician.

"Okay, maybe not Hawaii now," she says, "but what about Los Angeles? Lots of opportunities there for you, and I thought you liked living in California. That way you'd be so much closer to Hawaii."

Again, I'm caught off-guard. When I left L.A., I closed any possibility of ever returning. In my mind, I ended that chapter in my life and moved on. But I realize I never really explained to her the full story of why I moved to New York City. From the little we communicated during those strained years she likely assumed I moved solely because of Lucas. So, from her perspective, why wouldn't I want to move back to L.A. now that Lucas and I are no longer together? The last thing I want is for Mom to think she's the reason why I now live on the other edge of the U.S., almost as far from Hawaii as I could possibly be without leaving the country. So, I explain to her exactly what happened years ago with Project Music for Kids, hoping she will understand why I can't return to L.A., because I'm likely still blacklisted there. But as I'm recounting everything about the PMK scandal,

I realize I'm rambling, sometimes recalling details out of chronological order, and Mom looks confused.

"I'm sorry, I'm not explaining this well," I tell her. "But all this happened so long ago, and I guess, although I was disappointed and angry at the time, I've put it all away in my mind and moved on."

Mom nods at me, knowingly. And I can tell she's trying to absorb and understand everything I've just told her. Then she says, "You left L.A. not because you did anything bad. Other people did bad things, and you couldn't look the other way because you had to support a friend."

I'm taken aback at how succinctly she has summarized what I've incoherently babbled about for the past fifteen minutes. Even though my meandering explanation of that unsavory saga was likely impossible to follow, she implicitly trusted in my judgment and ability to separate right from wrong.

"Mom, I can't believe you could follow all that."

"But what I don't understand," she says, "is how you were able to stand up for what you believed was right, even though you knew you were going to have to pay for it. Weren't you scared?"

It takes me a few seconds to process Mom's comments. At first, I think her question is merely rhetorical, but she's looking at me like she's actually expecting an answer. Unsure of what to say, I tell her, "Well, I guess the apple didn't fall far from the tree."

Mom stares at me with a puzzled expression, and I realize she has no idea what I'm referring to, so I add, "You're one to talk. After all, I wasn't the one who took on the U.S. government, not just once for my citizenship but a second time for the World War II reparation."

Mom still looks so confused, as if I'm talking in non sequiturs. And then, all of a sudden, she makes the connection. Her mouth breaks into a wry smile, she laughs and kicks my leg playfully. "What are you saying?" she asks. "I'm just a simple housewife who didn't even attend college."

"Hardly," I tell her, emphasizing the word, and we both smile knowingly at each other.

Sitting there in the comfortable lounge, we watch a Continental 747 as it leaves the gate, its massive body being towed by an improbably small tug.

"I guess we're just two nails, you and I," Mom says, as the airplane makes its way toward the runway, where it will accelerate down the asphalt, its jet engines whirling, heat waves distorting the nearby air.

I know immediately what she's referring to. "Deru kugi wa utareru," I say, as we both continue watching the 747, afraid to look at each other for fear our emotions will get the better of us.

"Ken-chan, you have to understand. I never wanted your life to be difficult. Really, so much easier not to be a nail. But sometimes, I guess we can't help being who we are."

I tell her the only thing I can: "Shikata ga nai." After a long pause, we both smile wistfully as the airplane finally takes flight.

•   •   •   •   •

We still have more than an hour before Mom's flight, so I figure we're better off hanging out in the lounge for a few more minutes before heading into the mad crush of people at the gate. I get up to use the restroom and, when I return, I see that Mom has fallen asleep, her body comfortably settled into the plush sofa. Not wanting to disturb her, I slip quietly into the adjacent armchair. She has enough time for a quick nap before she needs to be at the gate, and a little rest might do her good, considering how early she woke this morning.

As she sleeps, I stare at her intently, noting everything. The deep lines in her forehead, the liver spots on her hands, her heavy breathing. She looks so peaceful, serene even, as if her conscience is floating unencumbered somewhere oceans away. I want so much for this perfect instant of time to continue forever. I want to burn it deep into my memory, not just so that I never forget it but so I'll always be able to retrieve it, at a moment's notice, to cherish whenever I desire. I want to remember the clothes she's wearing, her brown leather handbag resting on her lap, the delicate way her head is cradled on the soft, cushy sofa.

Thinking of our earlier conversation, I laugh to myself at how she claims she's "just a simple housewife." In actuality, she is anything but that. To me, she's beautiful and graceful beyond words, and her mind is as sharp as a samurai's katana. With her abundant intelligence, she could easily have been anything she wanted, yet what she wanted most was to start a family and have a child. Still, beneath that soft, elegant exterior lies the courage and strength of a dozen tigers.

Mom's eyes open suddenly, and she quickly glances at her watch. "How long was I asleep?" she asks, startled.

"Mom, I love you."

She looks at me, completely baffled by my sudden burst of sentiment. Then her expression turns to sheepish embarrassment.

"Maybe we should go to the gate," she says.

·   ·   ·   ·   ·

As the airplane that Mom just boarded taxis toward the runway, I struggle with conflicting emotions. Half of me wants to reach out and pull the aircraft back, and the other half is comforted knowing she's returning to Hawaii, her home.

As I watch, the DC-10 lifts into the bright, blue sky, headed to an island in the middle of the Pacific Ocean, so far away physically and yet so close emotionally to my heart. The airplane grows smaller and smaller in the sky, and I imagine Mom settling back into her comfortable first-class seat. I think of her opening a magazine, flipping through it, and maybe finding an article that piques her interest.

When the plane hits cruising altitude, I can picture the seatbelt sign turning off and a flight attendant walking down the aisle, offering the first-class passengers complimentary champagne. Mom likely can't remember the last time she had the bubbly wine, but she would know for sure she's never in the past allowed herself a drink before lunchtime. And yet, today, on this long flight back to Honolulu, she'll somehow feel it's the most natural thing to do. As she sips the champagne and looks out the small oval window at the ground thousands of feet below, her body will relax, absorbed by the cushiony seat, her mind so impossibly light and free.

AUTHOR'S NOTE

Although *Two Nails, One Love* is a work of fiction, it is based on real-life events. Much of this history is well known, such as the attack of Pearl Harbor; the mass incarceration of 120,000 people of Japanese descent, the majority of whom were U.S. citizens; and the atomic bombing of Hiroshima. But some of the events described are less familiar, specifically, the deportations of U.S. citizens of Japanese ancestry during World War II. Even many historians may not be aware of this shameful event, but the deportations are detailed in *Quiet Passages: The Exchange of Civilians Between the United States and Japan During World War II*, by Scott Corbett (Ph.D. dissertation, U. of Kansas, 1983); *Mercy Ships*, by David Miller (London: Continuum UK, 2008); and the Densho website (www.densho.org).

Another historic event discussed in *Two Nails, One Love* is the signing of the Civil Liberties Act of 1988, which provided for financial reparations for the survivors of the U.S. concentration camps. That landmark legislation was spearheaded by a number of legislators, including Representatives Barney Frank, Norman Mineta, and Bob Matsui, and Senators Spark Matsunaga and Daniel Inouye. The narrator of *Two Nails, One Love* is a fictional character, as is his mother, so their meeting in the novel with Senator Inouye did not occur, but I've included a description of that imaginary encounter to convey the gratitude that many Japanese Americans feel toward the late Senator.

Aside from Senator Inouye and other well-known public figures, the names of other characters and organizations are fictitious, as are the personal events described. No identification with actual persons, places, or organizations is intended or should be inferred.

Like the narrator's mother, my own mother was among the 8,497 people incarcerated at the Jerome Relocation Center in Arkansas and she, too, was deported to Japan during World War II. Unfortunately, my mother rarely ever talked about that time in her life, and so I had to rely on a variety of sources to ensure the accuracy of many of the historical details of the places and incidents described. These included the *Jerome Relocation Center* memory book (Editor Patricia [Kirita] Nomura), especially the articles "I Was a Person Without a Country" by Annabel Takeko Nekomoto Yamane, "Excerpts from George Hoshida's Autobiography," and "Eleanor T. (Aoki) Kirito's Diary"; various issues of "Communique: Official Bulletin of Jerome Relocation Center, Denson, Arkansas"; CSPAN video interviews of Grace Sugita Hawley; *Midnight in Broad Daylight: A Japanese American Family Caught Between Two Worlds*, by Pamela Rotner Sakamoto; the play "Hold These Truths," by Jeanne Sakata; *A Captive Audience: Voices of Japanese American Youth in World War II Arkansas*, editor Ali Welky; the Densho website (www.densho.org); the PBS documentary "Time of Fear"; the World War II Japanese American Internment Museum in McGehee, Arkansas; and the Japanese American Memorial Pilgrimages (JAMP).

ACKNOWLEDGMENTS

I have a vague memory of my parents going to an exhibit about the World War II internment of Japanese Americans. This was way back when I was a young kid growing up in Honolulu, and the only thing I really remember with any clarity about that event was that, after they returned from the exhibit, my mother told me that she had been sent to a relocation camp when she was a teenager. But she said it so offhandedly, as if it had been such a trivial part of her young life, that I thought little of her remark. It was only years later that I would realize the enormity of what she had actually told me. This epiphany came to me in my high school social-studies class, when our teacher—Barbara Kakuda—kicked away the rock that had been hiding an ugly truth: that virulent racism had led to the mass incarceration of 120,000 people of Japanese descent, including many U.S. citizens like my mother, during WWII. Since that awakening, I have known that I needed to write something about those terrible events, but what I wanted to write kept changing, assuming different forms over the ensuing years. At times it seemed like I had already written a book inside my head, but actually getting the words down on paper was an entirely different matter. The journey has been long, difficult, and often dispiriting, but I've been incredibly fortunate to have had tremendous help and support along the way.

I am grateful to the friends who encouraged me to write and publish *Two Nails, One Love,* even when I felt like giving up. Among the many cheerleaders who continually told me that this story had to be told were Eileen Roche Ahuja, Joseph D'Adamo, Lilith Fondulas, Fred Hill, Alice Iaquinta, Iris and Carey Inouye, Jay Lordan, Madhusree Mukerjee, Elaine Odell, the late Patrick Rand, Costas Rodopoulos, Lawrence Tom, Bob Young, and my dear cousins Frances Yamada and Lee Watanabe. I also thank Curt Schade for telling me about the "Then They Came for Me" exhibit in Chicago, Gary Rozeboom for taking me to the Japanese American Memorial to Patriotism During World War II in D.C., and Kimiko Marr, founder/CEO of Japanese American Memorial Pilgrimages (JAMP), through which I was able to visit the site of the Jerome Relocation Center in Arkansas, where my mother and her family had been incarcerated.

If it takes a village to raise a child, then it often takes a community to nurture a novel. For me, that community has been "You Know You're Japanese American When...," a Facebook group that is deftly moderated by Corinne Westphal, Becky Pittman, and Hiroshi Omori. I have learned so much from the group's many members, especially Susan Hayase, Ayano Ichida, Gerry Iguchi, Misa Joo, Judy Kamibayashi Louff, Karen Kiyo Lowhurst, Linda Harms Okazaki, Luriko Ozeki, Mitch Sako, Ginny Yamamoto Syphax, and Michael Yamasaki. Doumo arigatou gozaimasu!

I am also greatly indebted to the early readers of my manuscript: Neil Horikoshi, Noreen McLaughlin, Michael O'Halloran, and Costas Rodopoulos. In particular, Costas read some of the earliest, rawest pages and offered numerous suggestions for substantial improvements. He has been a huge supporter of my novel, helping me to weather the disappointment of dozens of agents rejecting it. After several rewrites, my manuscript still needed considerable fine-tuning, and the editor who helped me make that final push was Alice Shimmin. I'm also grateful to Steve Moyer, for his assistance in proofreading the text, and for his invaluable feedback.

Capturing the essence of a book in a single visual image is no easy feat, and I thank Jana Brenning for her compelling cover design. She was able to beautifully convey the mood and meaning of my novel, using photographs of fabrics from my mother's kimono and obi in such a creative and thoughtful way.

Last, but certainly not least, I thank my dear husband, Gerry Flood, who stood by me with continual encouragement and unwavering belief, even as I struggled through the difficult process of writing, rewriting, and editing. He has been a never-ending source of support and love, even as I became increasingly despondent that my manuscript would never see the light of day. My debt to him is enormous.

ABOUT THE AUTHOR

Alden M. Hayashi has been an editor and writer at *Scientific American*, the *Harvard Business Review*, and the *MIT Sloan Management Review*. After more than thirty years covering science, technology, and business, he has recently delved into writing fiction. *Two Nails, One Love* is his first novel. For more information, please visit www.aldenmhayashi.com.

NOTE FROM THE AUTHOR

Word-of-mouth is crucial for any author to succeed. If you enjoyed *Two Nails, One Love*, please leave a review online—anywhere you are able. Even if it's just a sentence or two. It would make all the difference and would be very much appreciated.

Thanks!
Alden M. Hayashi

Thank you so much for reading one of our **LGBTQ** novels. If you enjoyed the experience, please check out our recommended title for your next great read!

Past Grief by Edward J. Leahy

"This important, nail-biting crime thriller about MS-13 sets the bar very high. One of the year's best thrillers."

-BEST THRILLERS

View other Black Rose Writing titles at www.blackrosewriting.com/books and use promo code **PRINT** to receive a **20% discount** when purchasing.

CPSIA information can be obtained
at www.ICGtesting.com
Printed in the USA
BVHW082334070921
616209BV00008B/178